GORDON'S
GAME:
LION'S
ROAR

GORDON'S GAME: LIONS ROAR

Gordon D'Arcy
and Paul Howard

Illustrated by Alan Nolan

PENGUIN BOOKS

PENGUIN BOOKS

UK | USA | Canada | Ireland | Australia
India | New Zealand | South Africa

Penguin Books is part of the Penguin Random House group of companies
whose addresses can be found at global.penguinrandomhouse.com.

Penguin
Random House
UK

First published by Sandycove 2021
Published in Penguin Books 2022
001

Typeset by Jouve (UK), Milton Keynes
Printed and bound in Great Britain by Clays Ltd, Elcograf S.p.A.

The authorized representative in the EEA is Penguin Random House Ireland,
Morrison Chambers, 32 Nassau Street, Dublin D02 YH68

A CIP catalogue record for this book is available from the British Library

ISBN: 978–1–844–88530–5

www.greenpenguin.co.uk

I was in the back garden, kicking a rugby ball backwards and forwards over the washing line, pretending it was the last minute of the third Test against South Africa and I was attempting a drop at goal.

In my head, I was saying, 'The entire series rests on young D'Arcy putting this ball over the washing line!'

But it couldn't just go OVER the washing line. No, that would be WAY too easy. It had to clear the washing line between Dad's crisp, white work shirt and the yellow dress that my little sister Megan was planning to wear to a birthday party later that day.

'D'Arcy!' my inner voice said. 'We know he has the ability – but does he have the nerve?'

As I prepared to launch another drop-kick into the air, I heard Dad shout from the house:

'GORDON ... D'ARCY!!!'

It was possible that Dad was providing a co-commentary on my latest effort to be the hero for the British & Irish Lions. But it was equally possible that he'd noticed the rugby-ball-shaped patches of mud all over Mum's freshly laundered bedsheets.

I decided that I should disappear for a few hours, just in case. But, as I was about to make myself scarce, Dad shouted:

'GORDON D'ARCY, COME IN HERE! YOU'RE NOT GOING TO BELIEVE WHAT I JUST FOUND IN THE ATTIC!'

I had to admit, I was curious. Which was why – rugby ball in hand – I made my way towards the back door. Dad was standing on the doorstep, holding what, from a distance, looked like a book.

'What is it?' I asked.

'It's a video cassette,' he replied, then he handed me what turned out to be a small, plastic case.

On the front, there was a giant crest and it was split into four quarters. One contained the same shamrock that was on my Ireland jersey, one the English rose, one the Scottish thistle and one the Prince of Wales feathers that the Welsh players wore on their chests.

Above it, it said, 'Pride of Lions' and then underneath, 'The Official History of the British & Irish Lions'.

'What's a video cassette?' I asked.

'This is how we watched things,' Dad said, 'before there was downloads and streaming and so many remote controls on the coffee table that I don't even know how to switch the TV on any more.'

I popped open the little case and inside was a black, rectangular block of plastic. On the underside, there were two white holes, two or three inches apart.

I held it up to my face and looked through the

two holes – like it was the viewfinder that my older sister Shona had brought back from her school trip to Paris.

'I can't see a thing,' I told him.

He burst out laughing.

'You don't watch it like that!' he said. 'You have to put it into a video recorder! Come on, I've rigged it up in the living room.'

I followed him inside. Under the TV sat a large, silver box that I'd never seen before. Dad took the video cassette from me and slipped it into what looked like a letterbox in the front of this strange contraption.

'I thought it would be good for you to watch this,' he said. 'I know your heart is set on playing for the Lions next summer. It might be good for you to know a little bit about why it's such a special honour.'

He was down on his hands and knees now, pressing the buttons on the front of the thing.

'Doesn't it come with a remote control?' I asked, sitting down on the sofa.

'No,' he replied, 'in the old days we used to have to stand up and walk across the room to change the TV channel!'

People in the old days seemed VERY strange to me.

'Here we go!' he said, sitting down next to me and rubbing his hands together.

A picture appeared on the screen and then flickered into life. I was suddenly watching a montage of players from all different eras – even from the olden days, when the footage was in black and white and the players wore three-quarter-length shorts and had long, droopy moustaches.

'*The British & Irish Lions is the most elite rugby team of them all,*' the presenter said. '*It is unique in that, once every four years, it brings together the very best players from England, Ireland, Scotland and Wales to take on one of the three powerhouses of Southern Hemisphere rugby – New Zealand, Australia or South Africa.*'

'You'll be part of a great tradition,' Dad said, 'as you're about to find out.'

A giant of a man appeared on the screen then.

'*Being selected,*' the man said, '*meant that you were one of the best fifty players in Britain and Ireland – and also one of the best players in your position in the world!*'

'Who's that?' I asked.

'That,' Dad announced, 'is Willie John McBride – the greatest Lion of them all! He's from Toomebridge in County Antrim. He was a second-row and he holds the record for the most Test appearances for the Lions. He played seventeen matches across five tours!'

'Five tours? Wow!'

'Including 1974, when he captained the team against South Africa and they didn't lose a single match! And will I tell you something else about him? When he delivered his pre-match team talk, he was smoking a pipe!'

'A pipe? What, in the dressing room?'

'Yes, IN the dressing room! And, before you ask, Gordon, no, you can't have a pipe for Christmas!'

'What if I promise that I won't put tobacco in it?'

'Gordon, you're not having a pipe!'

'The 1950s was the romantic era of the Lions, when some of the greatest personalities in the game wrote their names in rugby folklore.'

'That's Tony O'Reilly!' Dad shouted, pointing at the screen. 'He was one of Ireland's greatest ever wingers. He scored thirty-eight tries for the Lions, a record that still stands to this day!'

'But it was in the 1970s that the idea of a Lions series really started to capture the public's imagination. In 1971, the great Welsh fly-half Barry John helped inspire them to a 2–1 series win against the All Blacks.'

'Barry John!' Dad said. 'Now there was a player! He could make the ball do anything he wanted with his boot. They used to call him The King.'

Of all the eras covered in the programme, this

was my favourite. The team seemed to be full of Welshmen with long, wavy hair and thick sideburns. There was Barry John and Gareth Edwards and Gerald Davies and J. P. R. Williams, and they played the kind of exciting, running rugby that made me fall in love with the game in the first place.

'These guys are amazing!' I said. 'Look how COOL they are!'

'You should let your hair grow for the tour,' Dad said, 'and get yourself some stick-on sideburns!'

I laughed.

We watched the Lions beat the soon-to-be world champions Australia in 1989 after the legendary David Campese accidentally handed the ball to the Welsh winger Ieuan Evans right on the try line.

We watched Jeremy Guscott kick a last-minute drop goal to beat world champions South Africa in 1997.

And we watched a young Brian O'Driscoll, tearing through FIVE Australian players to score a try at the end of a sixty-metre run in 2001.

'That's BOD!' I shouted.

It was one of those tries you could watch all day long. The crowd sang 'Waltzing Matilda' – except they changed the words to 'Waltzing O'Driscoll'.

I suddenly realized that I had butterflies in my stomach.

'Well?' Dad said. 'Do you know what it means to play for the Lions now?'

I did – and I knew something else as well . . .

I wanted to be a Lion more than anything else in the world!

1 *Stripy Paint*

'Hey, Gordon,' Conor called out to me, 'would you pop downstairs to Maintenance and get me a tin of stripy paint?'

'Stripy paint,' I repeated, not really thinking about the words. 'Yeah, no problem.'

'Purple-and-gold stripes,' he added.

Conor, Peter and I were really going up in the world that summer. We'd left our jobs in McWonderburger, Wexford, and now we were working in the Ferrycarrig Hotel, four miles outside the town where we lived, right on the River Slaney.

I was a porter's assistant and my main job was to help load and unload luggage from the coaches that pulled up in front of the hotel. It involved a lot of heavy lifting, which I enjoyed because it helped me stay strong. There was also a lot of waiting around, which allowed me, time to monitor the growth of my biceps – and think about rugby!

Conor was working as a desk assistant and was far busier than me. Occasionally, he would ask me to run errands for him.

'Stripy paint,' I muttered to myself as I made my way downstairs to the boiler room. 'Purple and gold. Stripy paint. Purple and gold. Stripy paint . . .'

Purple and gold were the colours of the Wexford hurling team, who had just won the Leinster Championship – and were now only two matches away from winning the All-Ireland!

Liam Griffin, the coach of the team, also happened to be the owner of the hotel. Perhaps he was planning to repaint the lobby in the team's honour, I thought.

The head of Maintenance was an old, silver-haired man named Mark Browne. He dressed in a blue boiler-suit and had a great, hacking laugh that always ended in a fit of coughing that turned his face fire-engine red.

'Stripy paint?' he asked.

'Yeah,' I told him. 'Purple and gold, if you have it.'

'Stripy?' he repeated. 'Paint?'

Then it started: 'HA! HA! HA! HA! HA! HA! HA! Stripy! HA! HA! HA! HA! HA! HA! HA!

Paint! HA-HA-HA! HUH-HUH-HUH! HUH! HUH! HACK! HACK! HACK! BLEUGH! BLEUGH! HACK! BLEUGH!'

'Are you alright, Mark?' I asked.

The poor man was doubled over.

'Just give me . . . a moment,' he managed to say. 'I'll be alright in –' but then he was suddenly off again.

'HA-HA-HA! HUH-HUH-HUH! HUH! HUH!
HACK! HACK! HACK! BLEUGH! BLEUGH!
BLEUGH! BLEUGH!'

After a few minutes, the laughter finally stopped
and Mark wiped his eyes with the back of his hand,
then removed a handkerchief from the pocket of
his boiler-suit and mopped the sweat from his brow.

'Conor sent you, did he?' he asked.

'Yeah,' I told him. 'What's so funny?'

'Think about it, Gordon! Stripy paint? Paint's not
stripy, is it?'

The penny finally dropped. It was another one of
Conor's practical jokes.

'He belongs on a stage, that kid,' Mark said. 'How
do you keep falling for it?'

That was a VERY good question!

Over the course of that summer, Conor had sent
me to various parts of the hotel to get him:

• A roll-on air freshener.
• A rung-less ladder.
• A bucket of electricity.
• A roof-rack for a motorbike.
• A glass hammer.
• A can of steam.
• Bird-feed for the cuckoo clock.

- A length of wireless cable.
- A leg of salmon.
- A carton of ants' milk.
- A banana straightener.
- A box of rubber nails.
- A tin of elbow grease.
- Some sparks for the fire.
- A paper-stretching machine.
- A bottle of dry water.
- Some colourless ink for the printer.
- A left-handed screwdriver.
- An ejector seat for a helicopter.

I apologized to Mark for having wasted his time.

'Not at all,' he said. 'That's made my day. I can't wait to tell the wife. Stripy paint!' And then the laugher started again. 'HA! HA! HA! HA! HA! HA! HA!'

I decided to leave him before he did himself an injury and I made my way back upstairs.

Conor was rolling around the floor of the lobby laughing his head off, and I couldn't help but laugh as well.

'That's the last time you're EVER going to catch me out!' I vowed.

But it wouldn't be. He knew it and I knew it.

I returned to the porter's desk at the front of the hotel.

I spotted Peter then. He was outside, picking up litter from the gravel. He was working as the groundskeeper's assistant and his job was to ensure that the grounds of the hotel were immaculately clean at all times.

'Hi, Gordon,' he greeted me. 'Why is Conor rolling around the floor in there?'

'He sent me on another fool's errand,' I explained.

'What was it this time?' he asked.

'A tin of stripy paint,' I told him. 'Purple and gold.'

'Didn't he ask you last week to get him a chocolate teapot?'

'Yes, he did,' I said.

I forgot to put a chocolate teapot on the list.

'How do you keep falling for it?' he wanted to know.

'Mark asked me the exact same thing,' I said. 'I think my mind is somewhere else.'

'I know exactly where your mind is – it's in South Africa!'

He was right. It was six weeks since Clive Woodward, the Head Coach of the Lions, had phoned the office of McWonderburger, Wexford, to ask me if I was interested in playing for –

'What's wrong?' Peter asked. 'Gordon, you've suddenly gone very pale.'

'You don't . . . think . . . it was Conor, do you,' I stuttered, 'PRETENDING to be Clive Woodward?'

As well as being a very good practical joker, Conor was the best mimic I had ever heard. He could do literally ANYONE'S voice.

'No,' Peter tried to assure me, 'Conor was there when you got the call.'

'Was he?' I asked.

The day was such a blur, I honestly couldn't remember.

'Now that you say it,' Peter said, 'I'm not one hundred per cent sure.'

'Perhaps he was in the next room,' I suggested, 'on his mobile phone?'

I turned around and looked at Conor. He was picking himself up off the floor of the lobby, clutching his sides, which were clearly sore from laughing.

'He wouldn't do that,' Peter told me, pushing his glasses up his nose with his finger. 'Conor's jokes are funny. They're not cruel.'

'It's just when I think about it,' I said, 'I mean, Clive Woodward? He coached the England team that won the World Cup! And he rang me in

McWonderburger, Wexford, to ask me if I was interested in playing for the Lions? Does that not seem a bit –'

'A bit what?' Peter asked.

'Well, a bit far-fetched,' I said.

'No more far-fetched than Warren Gatland asking you to play for Ireland. Or Joe Schmidt asking you to play for Leinster.'

'The other thing is, when I spoke to him, I could have sworn he said they were playing Australia.'

'But the Lions *aren't* playing Australia.'

'I know.'

'They're playing South Africa.'

'So why would he have said Australia?'

'It might have been a slip of the tongue.'

'Or perhaps,' I said, 'there's another explanation. Perhaps he said Australia because it wasn't Clive Woodward at all.'

We stared into the hotel at Conor.

'He wouldn't have kept the joke up for this long,' Peter said. 'Would he?'

It was at that exact moment that we heard what sounded, to our ears, like a helicopter approaching. Peter and I turned around and looked up into the sky. It was a bright summer's day and we had to shield our eyes to see it. At first, it was just a far-distant speck. But we watched it grow bigger and bigger, while the noise of the engine grew louder and louder, like a lion's roar, until we could see it almost directly over our heads.

It was a bright red helicopter – and it was about to land in front of the hotel!

We ran for cover as it touched down. As it did so, the wind from the rotor blades blew the freshly cut grass across Peter's freshly raked gravel!

'It took me two hours to get that clean!' Peter complained.

We watched the rotor blades slow down until they eventually stopped. Then the engine died and the door was thrown open.

A man stepped out onto the gravel. His head was bald and perfectly round in shape and he had a sort of lopsided grin on his face. And I felt instantly bad for believing the worst of Conor. Because I recognized the man immediately.

It was Clive Woodward!

2 Preparation, Preparation and Preparation

'Meeting with Gordon D'Arcy. Second of August. Fourteen hundred hours.'

He was speaking into a headset microphone – to whom, I had absolutely no idea.

'Present at meeting,' he said, 'Sir Clive Woodward, Head Coach of the British & Irish Lions, and Gordon D'Arcy, of Clongowes Wood College, Leinster and Ireland.'

'And Wexford Wanderers,' I added.

'And Wexford Wanderers,' Clive confirmed. 'Purpose of meeting, to discuss Lions Tour to South Africa. Departure date – three-hundred days and counting.'

Conor and Peter were watching from the opposite side of the hotel lobby.

'Gordon,' Clive said, 'can you tell me what, in your view, are the three most important things in the life of a rugby player?'

'Errr,' I said, racking my brains for the answer.

He decided not to wait. 'Preparation, preparation and preparation,' he said. 'Can you repeat that back to me?'

'Preparation, preparation and preparation,' I replied.

'I heard you the first time,' Clive said, his mouth twisting into another of his lopsided grins. 'Joke to break the ice. Subject seems suitably amused. Meeting proceeds.'

I was already learning that he was a very different kind of coach from Vinnie Murray, Warren Gatland or Joe Schmidt.

'Should we, em, maybe sit down?' I suggested.

'One thing you'll learn about me, Gordon, is that I never sit down,' he said. 'I do all of my best thinking on my feet. Now, let's talk about your diet.'

'My diet?'

'Starting with breakfast. What do you eat first thing in the morning?'

'Er, well, cereal mostly – either Sugar Crispies or Choco Choco Choco Puffs.'

He stared at me like I'd said earwigs and earthworms.

'Sugar Crispies?' he said – sounding aghast at even the name.

'Yeah,' I told him, 'they're puffs of toasted rice coated in sugar.'

'And Choco Choco Choco Puffs?'

'They're puffs of toasted rice coated in –'

'Yes, I think I can guess what they're coated in, Gordon. And let me tell you, sugar is only good for short-term energy gains. Do you think Lions eat Choco Choco Choco Puffs?'

'Well,' I told him truthfully, 'there *is* a lion on the

box. Larry the Lion. You must know the TV ad? *So, so chocolatey! They feel yummy in my tummy!*' I sang.

He stared at me blankly.

'This Larry the Lion wouldn't last ten minutes in a Test rugby environment against South Africa,' he said, 'especially with a diet based on empty calories and quick-releasing carbs. You need food that's high in nutrients. Mashed avocado on whole wheat toast with a poached egg on top. Chia seed pudding with dried apricots and goji berries –'

'I should be writing this down.'

'Everything that I say to you today will be typed up and a copy couriered to your home within one hour of this meeting.'

At that stage, I didn't know much about his approach to coaching, but I could see he brought organization to a whole new level.

'Other suggestions for breakfast,' he said. 'Porridge with peanut butter and bananas. Soft fruits with Greek yoghurt, chopped nuts and a drizzle of honey. And eggs, eggs and more eggs. Hard-boiled or soft-boiled. Sunny side up, over easy or over hard. Poached, baked, basted or shirred. Hard-scrambled or soft-scrambled. Have an omelette. Have a frittata. Knock 'em back raw like boxers do.'

'Euuuggghhh!!!'

'Hey, that's how I like 'em! What do you have for lunch?'

I didn't want to tell him that I usually had a second bowl of Choco Choco Choco Puffs. Luckily, he had no time to wait for my answer.

'For lunch,' he said, 'you should be eating a salad made up of vegetables of SEVEN different colours.'

'Seven? Right.'

'And lean meat with it – maybe some chicken. Then, for dinner, lean steak or fish, with potatoes and vegetables of FIVE different colours.'

'Five – got it.'

'Or even some fish with rice. Now, can I ask you about training? Do you have a daily workout routine?'

'Yes,' I said, 'I get up at eight o'clock in the morning and I do fifty chin-ups, fifty press-ups and fifty sit-ups while listening to a Garth Brooks cassette on my mum's Walkman.'

'Yes, I too enjoy the music of Garth Brooks. But eight o'clock is VERY late to be getting out of bed.'

'Is it?'

'Of course. Half the day is already gone. Do you know what time lions get up in the wild?'

'I'm going to take a guess and say half seven or a quarter to eight?'

'They get up when it's still dark, Gordon. Because that's when their senses are at their most heightened. Tomorrow, I want you out of bed at oh six hundred hours.'

'Is that, em, six o'clock in the morning by any chance?'

'Yes, it is. All timings will be military timings. And tomorrow I want you to do two hundred chin-ups, two hundred press-ups and two hundred sit-ups.'

'Two hundred? Of each?'

'Yes, of each. And I want you to do a ten-kilometre run – preferably through a muddy field.'

'I'll be exhausted by the time I get to work!'

'If you want to play for the Lions, this is what you must do. And, by the way, trust me on the raw eggs!'

'I, er, think I'll pass on that.'

'Meeting concludes, fourteen hundred hours and twenty-two minutes. Two minutes behind schedule. That's annoying. I think it was all that talk about Lenny the Lion.'

'Larry the Lion,' I corrected him.

'Whatever,' he said. 'I hate to be knocked off schedule. I'll make sure to mention that in the minutes of our meeting, which you should receive within the hour.'

He turned his back and started to make his way out of the hotel towards the helicopter. That's when I decided to ask the question that had been on the tip of my tongue ever since I'd watched the Lions video with Dad.

'So when do I get my jersey?' I asked.

Clive stopped walking. He turned around and fixed me with a look. 'Your jersey?' he said, sounding confused.

'Yeah, my Lions jersey,' I reminded him. 'Hey, I'm not saying I'm going to wear it in bed, but it would be nice to have it, just to show to my family and friends.'

Clive smiled his lopsided smile at me.

'Gordon,' he said, 'only those who make the *final* squad get a jersey.'

Now, it was my turn to be confused. 'But I thought I *had* made the final squad,' I said.

'No,' he told me, 'you've made the *preliminary* squad – a group of a hundred players, from which I will choose the fifty who will travel to South Africa.'

'So you're saying half of the players in the preliminary squad . . . won't even make the trip?'

'That's right. I'll be choosing the *final* squad next

March and it'll be based on form. So stay fit – and try not to get injured in the meantime!'

He started walking again.

'I definitely won't get injured!' I said, following behind him. 'I want to play for the Lions too much!'

'Many do,' he said to me over his shoulder. 'I'll be in touch.'

I looked around for a pilot and discovered that there wasn't one.

'Wait a minute,' I called after him, 'do *you* fly that helicopter?'

'Of course, I do,' he replied. 'You didn't think it flew itself, did you? Return to helicopter, fourteen hundred hours and twenty-three minutes. Next item on itinerary – meeting with Paul O'Connell, sixteen hundred hours, Limerick.'

And with that, the engine started up – again, roaring like a lion – and the rotor blades began to turn, blowing my hair back. The helicopter lifted off the ground, tail-first, nose-down, then righted itself and took off in the direction of Limerick.

Peter and Conor came and stood beside me.

'So what was he like?' Conor asked.

I was telling the truth when I replied, 'Like no one I've ever met before.'

3 *The Time I Did Something Very, Very, VERY Stupid*

It was one of the greatest days in the history of Wexford. The county's hurlers had beaten Limerick to win the All-Ireland championship for the first time in twenty-eight years – and they were coming back to the Ferrycarrig Hotel for the celebratory banquet!

It felt like Christmas Eve. The hotel was full of people. Half of Wexford had turned up to welcome the players home. Conor, Peter and I helped to build the giant bonfire in the grounds of the hotel that was to be lit just before the fireworks display started at midnight.

It was just after nine o'clock when the team bus appeared, slowly making its way up the driveway, through the throngs of people. The players waved through the windows and they showed the crowd the famous Liam MacCarthy Cup. The people cheered and chanted:

'*Wex! Ford! Wex Ford! Wex! Ford! Wex! Ford!*'

The bus eventually came to a stop outside the hotel and the players clambered off, looking tired but smiling with elation.

That was when *the* most unbelievable thing happened. Liam Griffin walked up to me and said, 'It's Gordon, isn't it?'

I was speechless. Though I'd seen him around the hotel during the two months I'd worked there, I'd never exchanged a single word with him. He always seemed so busy. But I was in complete awe of him. I thought he was the best hurling coach in Ireland.

That was one of the things I loved about sport. I had won the Six Nations and the Grand Slam with Ireland and the European Cup with Leinster. I had played with, and against, some of the best rugby players in the world. And yet I still had heroes in other sports – and when I happened to meet them, I stared at them, as open-mouthed as any other fan.

'G . . . G . . . G . . . Gordon,' I stuttered. 'That's right, Mr Griffin.'

'Call me Liam,' he said. 'Here, take this, will you?'

He pushed something into my hands. I looked down. It was the Liam MacCarthy Cup. It was a silver trophy, with sort of squarish edges and four giant jug handles around the sides.

'Would you give that a bit of a clean and maybe throw a lick of polish on it?' he asked. 'It's looking a bit grubby from the lads handing it around on the bus. The Lord Mayor of Wexford is on his way and I want him to be able to see his face in it!'

'Leave it with me, Mr . . . I mean, Liam.'

I took the trophy to the front desk and I asked Alma Galvin, the Senior Receptionist, where I might find some silver polish and a cloth.

'The very man!' she said. 'Mr Rossiter is looking for you!'

Mr Rossiter was the Head Porter and also my boss.

'Why is he looking for me?' I asked.

'Our lovely Japanese guests are about to leave,' she explained. 'They need their bags put on the bus.'

'But I'm supposed to be polishing the Liam Mac-Carthy Cup,' I told her.

'You can polish that after,' she insisted. 'They've got a ferry to catch. They're booked on the night sailing to France.'

The ferry went from Rosslare in Wexford to Cherbourg in northern France. Apparently, Paris was the next stop on their European tour.

'Fine,' I said. 'I'll load the bags quickly.'

It turned out, however, that this was easier said than done. It was part of the Japanese custom, when saying hello, or goodbye, or thank you, to join their hands as if in prayer and then bow. As I loaded their luggage into the undercarriage of the coach, each and every guest stopped by to say a personal thank you – and it was only good manners for me to respond in the same way.

So it was:

Bag on the bus . . .
And bow . . .
Bag on the bus . . .
And bow . . .
Bag on the bus . . .
And bow . . .

It took twenty minutes to complete the task. When all of the bags were safely stowed on board, I gave them one final bow and waved them off.

Then I heard my name called.

'Gordon!'

I turned around. It was my friend Aoife. She was wearing a purple-and-gold woollen headband and was carrying a giant 'Go Wexford!' flag. I was so happy to see her.

'Were you at the match?' she asked.

'No,' I said, 'I was working. Were you at it?'

'Yeah, with my dad. We came straight here from Croke Park. How was your summer?'

'Er, good,' I said. 'Clive Woodward showed up a few weeks ago – in his helicopter.'

'What?' she laughed. 'Why?'

'He just wanted to make sure I was eating and training like a Lion!'

'And were you?'

'Er, apparently not.'

'Did you tell him about the Choco Choco Choco Puffs?'

'Yeah, I might have mentioned them.'

'*So, so chocolatey! They feel yummy in my tummy!*' she sang.

We both laughed.

'Well, the good news,' I said, 'is that I've completely changed my training regime and my diet since then. He couriered a food plan to my house –'

'Couriered it?' she asked.

'Yeah,' I told her, 'this Lions set-up is unbelievable, Aoife. It's like being part of an army or something.'

'Did you get your jersey yet? You're probably wearing it in bed, are you?'

'No, it turns out I haven't made the final squad yet.'

'I thought you had.'

'No, I've made the preliminary squad, which is one hundred players. He has to whittle that number down to fifty by next March.'

I saw my dad in the crowd then and I waved to him. He came over to us. He was with my sisters, Shona and Megan, and they too had been at the match.

'Hi, Gordon,' said Dad. 'Hi, Aoife.'

Megan interrupted. 'Gordon, I like hurling better than rugby!' she announced.

I laughed.

'Bear in mind,' I told her, 'Wexford don't win every year. As a matter of fact –'

I suddenly stopped mid-sentence. Aoife could tell instantly that something was wrong.

'Gordon,' she said, 'you look like you've seen a ghost.'

'Aoife,' I said, 'I think I've just done something very, very, VERY stupid!'

'What?'

'I was loading all the luggage onto the Japanese tour bus. I must have been distracted.'

'Gordon, what did you do?'

'I think I put the Liam MacCarthy Cup on the bus!'

4 A High-Speed Chase

'Doesn't this car go any faster?' I asked.

'I'm not James Bond!' Dad snapped. 'I'm already right on the speed limit here.'

'Well, do you think you could maybe BREAK the speed limit?' I asked. 'Just this once?'

'I'm not getting penalty points,' he said, 'just because you were stupid enough to put the Liam MacCarthy Cup on a bus that's about to board a ferry to France.'

'You've done some pretty dumb things in your time,' Aoife added, 'but this is definitely the worst, Gordon! What were you thinking?'

'I don't know,' I said. 'It was all the bowing. And the bending down to pick up the cases. I think the air must have gone to my head.'

Dad pressed down on the brake and brought the car to a halt.

'What are you doing?' I asked. 'Why are you stopping?'

'Because we're approaching a set of traffic lights,' he answered, 'and they happen to be red.'

'Oh,' I said, 'so you're going to stop every single time we come to a red light? You're being ridiculous now!'

'Why don't you just let your dad drive?' Aoife suggested. 'Try the Ferrycarrig again!'

I did. But the number just rang and rang and rang. I was about to hang up when a voice came on the line:

'Good evening. The Ferrycarrig Hotel. This is Alma Galvin speaking. How may I direct your call?'

Never in my life was I more relieved to hear another human voice.

'Alma!' I exclaimed. 'It's Gordon! Gordon D'Arcy!'

'Oh, Gordon – where are you?'

'It's a long story. Do you remember that group of Japanese guests? Do you have a phone number for anyone in their party?'

'I probably do somewhere, Gordon, but it's against hotel policy to give out the phone numbers of our guests.'

'This is an emergency, Alma! Please! I'm BEG-GING you!'

'Sorry, Gordon, it'd be more than my job is worth!'

'What about the coach driver? Does he have a mobile phone?'

'Hughie?' she said. 'He's got one, but he never answers it! He's half deaf! By the way, Mr Griffin is looking for you!'

'Liam Griffin?'

'Yes, he said he gave you the Liam MacCarthy Cup to polish and he's wondering where you've gotten to.'

'I'm, I've, nearly finished it.'

'Well, you'd better hurry up because the Lord Mayor of Wexford is just about to arrive.'

'What?'

'His car is at the bottom of the driveway.'

I was in serious, SERIOUS trouble here. I had to think fast.

'Alma, is Peter there?' I wondered.

'Peter with the glasses?' she asked. 'Always has his nose stuck in a book?'

'Yes, that's him.'

'Hold on.'

The line went quiet for a moment. I offered Dad some more helpful driving hints.

'Would you not drive in the other lane?' I asked. 'It's empty.'

'That's for traffic coming in the opposite direction,' Aoife pointed out.

'Fine,' I said. 'I just thought I'd check.'

A second later, I heard Peter's voice.

'Gordon?' he said. 'Mr Griffin is looking everywhere for you.'

'I know you're going to laugh at this,' I said, 'but I accidentally put the Liam MacCarthy Cup on a bus to France!'

He didn't laugh. He was silent for a long time. I suppose it WAS a lot to take in.

'*How* did you accidentally put it on a bus to France?' he wanted to know.

'It's a long story,' I said. 'But right now, you and Conor HAVE to stall everyone.'

'And how do you propose we do that?'

'Well, I was thinking that Conor could keep Mr Griffin and the players entertained with some of his jokes.'

'Okay.'

'And you could maybe offer to show the Lord Mayor of Wexford around the grounds of the hotel – give him a long, boring lecture about the history of the place.'

'Why does Conor get to be the funny one,' he asked, 'while I end up having to be the boring one? I can be pretty funny myself sometimes, Gordon.'

'Can you?'

'Yes, I'm always cracking up the rest of the Maths Club with my jokes at school. Why was six scared of seven? Because seven eight nine! Do you get it? Seven *ate* nine?'

Now, it was my turn to be silent.

'Okay,' he said, giving in. 'I'll be the boring one.'

'THERE'S THE BUS!' I shouted as I hung up the phone.

We were on the motorway now and I could see it just ahead of us on the road.

'*Now* I can pull into the other lane!' Dad said.

He pressed his foot to the accelerator and soon the car pulled level with the bus. I started waving frantically through the window, trying to catch the attention of any of the Japanese tourists on board.

Finally, one of them spotted me, but he mistook my waving for a gesture of friendliness and started waving back.

Then the others started waving back as well.

'I don't think they're getting the message,' I said.

'I've a better idea,' Shona said, opening the

sunroof. 'Stick your body up through that. Me, Aoife and Megan will hold onto your legs.'

I didn't have a better idea – so that's what we did. I stood up in the back of the car and Aoife, Shona and Megan all wrapped their arms around my legs like they were rugby-tackling me. With my upper body sticking out through the open sunroof, I started waving my two arms like I was drowning.

But still they failed to understand me. Several of those on board took out their cameras and started taking photographs of this seemingly crazy boy who had his head and shoulders sticking out of the top of a moving car.

And that's when we heard the sound of a siren behind us:

NEE-NAW!
NEE-NAW!
NEE-NAW!

'Oh, no,' Dad said, 'it's the Gardaí!'

'Keep driving!' I heard Aoife tell him. 'Try to out-run them.'

I think she'd really gotten into the excitement of the chase.

'Are you mad?' Dad asked her. 'It won't only be penalty points I'll be facing – it'll be time in prison for resisting arrest!'

'Dad,' Shona chimed in, 'if they knew what was going on, they would totally understand. It's just, we don't have time to stop and explain it to them! By the time we did, the bus would be on the boat to France!'

So Dad kept his foot on the accelerator, while I continued to wave my arms, and the Gardaí continued their pursuit . . .

NEE-NAW!
NEE-NAW!
NEE-NAW!

. . . except now they were talking to us through a speaker, barking orders at us:

'PULL OVER THAT VE-HICKLE THIS INSTANT!'

But Dad kept going and we soon drew level with the front of the bus. I kept waving my arms, trying to catch the eye of Hughie, the driver. But he didn't see me.

And he didn't hear me shouting . . .

'STOP! PLEASE! STOP!'

. . . what with him being half deaf and everything.

And then the Gardaí were right on our rear bumper and one of them was leaning out of the front passenger window, shouting at me:

'TELL THE DRIVER TO STOP THAT VE-HICKLE!'

'I CAN'T!' I roared back.

'WHAT DO YOU MEAN, YOU CAN'T?

AND WHAT KIND OF A GOBALOON ARE YOU, STICKING YOUR HEAD UP THROUGH THE SUNROOF LIKE THAT? YOU'LL GO UNDER A LOW BRIDGE AND IT'LL BE NO HEAD AT ALL YOU'LL BE LEFT WITH!'

'I'LL JUST HAVE TO TAKE THAT CHANCE! I HAVE TO STOP THIS BUS!'

'WHY?'

'BECAUSE I ACCIDENTALLY PUT THE LIAM MACCARTHY CUP IN THE LUG-GAGE HOLD!'

Those words changed everything. I could see the two Gardaí in the car staring at each other in open-mouthed disbelief that ANYONE could be so stupid.

But they believed me, because suddenly they were ordering us to overtake the bus, which Dad did.

'I'm driving twenty kilometres per hour OVER the speed limit!' he said, like it was the most exciting thing he had ever done. 'And I have full permission from the Gardaí to do it!'

Once we overtook the bus, the Gardaí did the same thing, then they pulled into the lane in front of it. Hughie soon got the message that he was being instructed to pull into the hard shoulder.

We all came to a stop. I stepped out into the hard shoulder.

'What in the name of all the saints is going on?' one of the Gardaí asked as he got out of the car. He was a tall, stringy man with red hair. Then the other Garda, who was short and plump, got out of the car as well.

'I accidentally put the Liam MacCarthy Cup on the bus,' I told them.

'I thought that was what you said,' the one with the red hair said. 'Except Fintan here didn't believe me. He said no one in this world could be so stupid as to do the like of that!'

'Gordon would!' Aoife shouted from the car. 'I can vouch for him!'

'Thanks a bunch, Aoife,' I said.

The Gardaí walked with me to the bus. Hughie got out.

'What seems to be the problem?' he asked. 'I was well within the speed limit!'

'This young lad here,' the short, plump Garda told him, 'says he accidentally put something on the bus that shouldn't be on it.'

'What is it?' Hughie asked.

'I don't really want to go into specifics,' I said.

'But do you think you could let me have a look in the luggage hold?'

'You'll have to be quick,' he said. 'We've got a ferry to catch.'

He stuck a key in the little lock and the spring-loaded door opened upwards. I climbed into the luggage hold, crawling over bags and cases until I finally spotted it, towards the front end.

Moments later, I emerged from the belly of the bus, clutching what I'd been searching for to my chest. I could see Hughie looking at me with his mouth hanging open.

'Is that . . . what I think it is?' he asked.

'No,' I assured him, 'it, er, just looks like it.'

I was about to run back to the car, but the Garda with the red hair said, 'You're not going anywhere, young man –'

'Please,' I begged him, 'you don't understand! I have to get this back to the Ferrycarrig Hotel before it's missed!'

'Let me finish,' he continued. 'I was going to say you're not going anywhere, young man . . . without a Garda escort!'

And so, with its siren blaring, the Garda car cleared a path in front of us. Dad took the next ramp off the motorway, then we made our way back to Wexford again.

'A car chase!' Megan said. 'That was even more exciting than Wexford winning the All-Ireland!'

When we arrived back at the Ferrycarrig, I waved thanks to the Gardaí. Peter was outside with the Lord Mayor, explaining to him how many different types of birds he'd seen in the grounds of the hotel.

'Seen a cormorant. Seen a Bewick's swan. Seen a Great Crested Grebe. Seen a Greenland white-fronted goose. Seen a red-breasted merganser . . .'

The Lord Mayor, I couldn't help but notice, was fast asleep – while standing up!

Yes, Peter had done a real job on him.

'You took your time,' Peter hissed at me.

'Sorry,' I said.

'They're in the banquet hall,' he told me. 'Hi, Aoife.'

'Hi, Peter,' she said. 'Do you want me to give you a hand waking up the Lord Mayor?'

'That would be great,' he said.

I ran into the hotel and asked Alma, for the second time that evening, where I might find some silver polish.

'Here you go,' she said, handing me a spray can and a cloth.

I sprayed the trophy with the polish and rubbed it with the cloth as I ran to the banquet hall. I could hear the laughter long before I reached the room. Conor was killing them in there.

'Moooooore!' the players shouted. 'Moooooore! Moooooore!'

Conor spotted me as I ran into the room.

'I don't think we've time for any more of my stories,' he said, 'because the Liam MacCarthy Cup is here – and the Lord Mayor of Wexford as well, I think I'm right in saying, am I, Gordon?'

'Yes,' I said, 'he's right behind me!'

I found Liam Griffin's table and I handed him the trophy.

'Look at the shine on it!' he said. 'You must have put some work into that!'

'You wouldn't believe me if I told you,' I said.

'Here,' he laughed, 'you should have heard some of Conor's stories about this friend of his – he sent him out for a bucket of purple-and-gold-stripy paint! And the fella actually went for it! Have you ever heard the likes of it?'

5 Think Like a Lion – and Act Like a Lion!

Conor and Peter were doubled over. It was the following day, and it was apparently STILL funny.

'It took . . . Wexford . . . twenty-eight years to win it,' Peter said, laughing so hard that his glasses were fogged up, 'and Gordon D'Arcy . . . five minutes . . . to lose it!'

'All I know,' I said, 'is that if it hadn't been for you two, and Aoife and my dad, and Shona and Megan, and those two Gardaí, I would be a national laughing-stock right now! I wouldn't be the boy who won the Grand Slam for Ireland, or the boy who won the European Cup for Leinster – I'd be the boy who lost the All-Ireland for Wexford!'

Which was the cue for another bout of hooting laughter.

We were back in our old dormitory in Clongowes Wood College and it was the night before school started. There was a real buzz about the place as friends who hadn't seen each other for months caught up with one another again.

'You know, I'm tired of being the brainy one,' Peter said suddenly. He was lying back on his bed with his hands behind his head. 'I want to do something different this year.'

'What,' Conor asked, 'other than getting A's in all of your exams?'

Peter sat up, leaning on his elbow.

'Exactly,' he said. 'I'm sick of everyone thinking that I'm just this boring brainiac.'

'You're not boring,' I assured him.

'Gordon, I made the Lord Mayor of Wexford fall asleep – standing up!'

'Yeah,' Conor said, 'but you did that deliberately, though.'

'Well, I want to be known for something different this year,' Peter told us. 'Maybe it'll be rugby.'

Peter had been an excellent rugby player back in our Wexford Wanderers days. He still enjoyed throwing the ball around with me and Conor and Aoife, but he'd been more focused on his schoolwork since we'd started in Clongowes.

'Peter,' I said, 'that's a great idea. You're an amazing player.'

'I think you're good enough to make the school team,' Conor agreed.

Then I had an idea. 'Why don't you train with me?' I suggested.

'With you?' he said. 'Would that be okay?'

'Of course!' I told him. 'You as well, Conor.'

I reached into my bag and I pulled out the Training and Diet Plan that Clive Woodward had couriered to my mum and dad's house. I handed it to Peter.

'*To be a Lion*,' he read, '*you need to think like a lion – and act like a lion!*'

'Apparently that means you've got to get up at six o'clock in the morning,' I said.

'*Two hundred chin-ups!*' Peter exclaimed. '*Two hundred sit-ups! Two hundred press-ups! Followed by a ten-kilometre run!* Have you been doing this every day, Gordon?'

'Most days, yeah,' I said. 'There's a Diet Plan on the next page.'

Peter turned to it.

'Please tell me you don't eat raw eggs,' he said.

'No,' I laughed. 'There are lots of things I *am* prepared to do to be a Lion – but that is NOT one of them!'

He handed the document back to me.

'Okay, I'm doing it,' he said. 'I want to train like a Lion. I'll get up at six tomorrow.'

'I'll do it as well,' Conor said. 'The more, the merrier!'

Suddenly, from outside the dorm, a voice said, 'Knock, knock!'

We all froze!

Because we knew only one person who entered a room by saying, 'Knock, knock!' instead of actually knocking.

He stuck his head around the door and our worst fears were confirmed . . .

It was Flash Barry!

'Hey, Dudes!' he said, far happier to see us than we were to see him. 'How the hell are you?'

We didn't answer him. Flash Barry had acted as my agent when I first broke into the Ireland squad – and he had brought a whole world of trouble down on my head.

'Darce,' he said – he still had the habit of pointing his fingers at you like they were guns, I noticed – 'you look seriously ripped there! You must tell me your secret! Conor, loved that show you wrote last year – cracked everyone up! And what about you, Peter – still a total brainiac, are you?'

'I'm not *just* a brainiac!' Peter pointed out.

'Sure you're not,' Barry replied. 'Anyway, guys, I can't help but notice that there's a free bed in here.'

'It's not free,' Conor blurted out. 'It's, em, taken.'

'Oh,' Barry said, sounding disappointed. 'Who's sleeping in it – do you mind me asking?'

'It's, em, Bob,' I told him.

'Bob?' Barry repeated. 'I didn't know there was a Bob in this school.'

'Yeah, Bob Bobson,' Conor said, thinking on his feet. 'He's from, er, Bobblestown.'

'Bob Bobson from Bobblestown? Why haven't I heard of this dude before?'

'He's new to the school,' Peter said. 'It's his first day tomorrow. We said we'd look after him.'

'That's a real pity,' Barry said, sadness in his eyes, 'because, well, the four of us had some laughs when we shared this room, didn't we?'

Conor couldn't listen to any more of this.

'NO,' he yelled, 'WE DIDN'T HAVE LAUGHS IN THIS ROOM! YOU RUINED EVERY-THING!'

Barry put on a shocked face. '*Ruined* everything?' he said, then he turned to look at me. 'Darce, what's this dude talking about?'

'You told me to stop training!' I reminded him. 'And to stop eating healthily! And to embrace the celebrity lifestyle! I got thrown off the Ireland team because of you!'

'Yeah,' he said, 'but you got back on the team again, didn't you? And, when you think about it, that was down to me.'

I couldn't believe what I was hearing.

'Down to *you*?' I repeated. 'How do you figure that out?'

'Well, if I hadn't got you kicked off the team in the first place,' he explained, 'then you might never have found the strength of character to come back and win the Grand Slam.'

'That's a bit of a stretch,' Peter told him. 'And, far from having laughs in this room, you threw me and Conor out! You told Gordon you could get him some better friends than us now that he was in the big league.'

Barry listened to what Peter had to say with a deepening look of sorrow on his face.

'Okay, I'm going to level with you,' he said, looking at each of us in turn with his big, puppy-dog eyes, 'I don't have anywhere else to go. No one wants to share with me. No one in this school likes me any more.'

'I'm sure that's not true,' I told him, even though I suspected it was COMPLETELY true!

'Name someone, then,' he challenged me. 'Name one single person who likes me.'

'You're sort of putting me on the spot here,' I said.

'You see? You can't. No, I've burned all my bridges – like a complete and utter idiot. Now, when people see me coming, they turn their heads and look the other way. And just when I'd turned over a new leaf as well.'

'A new leaf?' I asked.

'Yeah,' he said, 'I've changed my ways, Darce. I used to be Flash Barry. Now, I'm just Barry. You see, I want people to like me the same way they like you guys. But they don't. People look at me and they go, "Oh, no, look who's coming! It's Flash Barry! Let's get out of here!"'

'Barry —' I tried to say.

'Hey, it's cool,' he said, cutting me off. I could hear a sort of quiver in his voice, like he was on the verge of tears. 'You guys are right. I *would* ruin everything — like I always do. Hey, don't worry about me, guys. I've got a sleeping bag here. I can make a bed for myself around the back of the school where the bins are stored. Yeah, it'll be cold at night, and there's rats out there, but that's all I deserve. Hey, maybe one of *them* might want to be my friend!'

Barry left the room and Conor, Peter and I looked at each other. I could tell we were all thinking the same thing.

'BARRY!' I called out.

'Yeah?' he said, instantly poking his head around the door again. It was almost as if he was standing outside, waiting for us to change our minds.

'Why don't you sleep in here with us?' I asked.

Barry smiled.

'Really?' he said.

'Yes, really,' Conor told him. 'But no more of your stupid schemes, okay?'

'Like I told you, Conor, that's not me any more! Flash Barry is dead and gone! I'm just Barry now!'

'That's good to hear,' I said. 'I really hope it's true.'

Barry stretched himself out on the bed beneath Peter's bunk and put his hands behind his head.

'So,' he said, 'which one of us is going to break the bad news to Bob Bobson from Bobblestown?'

6 *No Such Thing as a Friendly*

It was great to be back playing rugby with my friends again. That was the thing I most missed about Clongowes during the summer. While we'd spent many of our days off work throwing the ball around, what I really craved was the high-intensity, heavy-tackling, competitive part of the game.

So I was counting the hours until Mr Murray, the Head Coach, took us for rugby on our second day back at school. Divided by our choice of bibs into teams of orange and yellow, we played fifteen against fifteen for half an hour each side and I threw myself into tackles as if the World Cup was on the line.

That was until Mr Murray pulled me to one side.

'Gordon,' he said, 'maybe don't put so much weight into those tackles. It's only a friendly game.'

'There's no such thing as a friendly in rugby,' I told him, remembering something I'd heard Paul O'Connell say when I'd played for Ireland. 'That's why even the friendlies are called Tests.'

'Well, that may or may not be true,' Mr Murray replied, 'but no one else here is at your level and we don't want to turn them off the game, do we?'

'No, Mr Murray.'

He did something then that he often did if a match was too one-sided. At half-time, he chose two players from the team that was winning – Conor and Peter, as it happened – and told them to switch sides. We were leading by 20–0 at that point, but suddenly the other team had the numerical advantage of seventeen playing against thirteen.

'Mr Murray!' my teammates complained.

'You're twenty points ahead,' he pointed out. 'You've already won the match. The challenge now is to see can you ensure that it *stays* won!'

Having four fewer players meant we were forced to defend what we had. We didn't cross the opposition twenty-two even once in the second half. The only time we got the ball into the opposition half, in fact, was when we were kicking off at the restarts.

The rest of the time we spent running around

frantically, trying to hold back wave after wave of attacks.

Peter pulled back one try, then Conor a second – I was delighted for them – and, with both tries converted, the deficit was 20–14, which meant it was a one-score match with only a minute to go.

'Okay,' I told my teammates during a break in play, 'it's all hands on deck now. The next time the ball goes dead, it's over.'

Conor received the ball and set off on one of the mazy runs that he was famous for before he broke his leg attempting to jump the Gollymochy, the river that runs through the grounds of the school.

Despite the injury, I was happy to see that he hadn't lost any of his pace – or, more importantly, any of his fearlessness. He rode one tackle, then another, before offloading the ball to Barry, who carried it for about thirty metres before I tackled him to the ground. When the ball was pulled from the ruck, it found its way into Peter's hands – twenty metres from our try line.

I could see in his eyes what he was planning to do. He was going to go for the five points himself. I happened to be standing between him and his moment of certain glory. Friend or not, I knew I had to stop him from scoring. But, remembering what Mr Murray had said about this being a friendly match, I decided to go easy on Peter. Instead of tackling him hard, I thought I'd just run him into touch.

What a mistake that proved to be!

As I moved slowly towards him, Peter suddenly found a new gear, changed the direction of his run and left me grasping at thin air. When I turned around, he was placing the ball right under the posts, to make the conversion impossible to miss.

'Okay,' I said to Peter, 'WHERE did you learn how to do that?'

He laughed.

'I was expecting you to tackle me,' he said. 'What happened?'

Mr Murray blew the final whistle. It was over and we had lost.

'Good effort, Gordon,' he told me.

'Thanks,' I said. 'Although I'm exhausted after that.'

'How was your summer?' he asked, while I tried to catch my breath. 'I heard Clive Woodward was in touch.'

'Yeah,' I said, 'he's asked me to join the Lions preliminary squad.'

'It must be exciting to know that you're one of the players he's considering taking to South Africa.'

'It is.'

'The Lions is a really special thing, Gordon. You're talking about players from four different rugby cultures, each with their distinctive style of playing the game.'

'I really want to play for them, Mr Murray.'

'Then you know what you have to do, don't you?'

'Stay fit and avoid injury.'

Mr Murray chuckled. 'There are more important

things than avoiding injury,' he said. 'The easiest way to avoid injury would be not to play at all, wouldn't it? You could stay in your bedroom, playing rugby on your Xbox.'

'I suppose,' I said.

'If you start thinking about avoiding injury all the time, then you're not going to be committing yourself to tackles. The most important thing is to keep playing and keep improving. Clive Woodward will bring you to South Africa if you're playing well. He won't bring you just because you're uninjured. Do you understand?'

I told him I did.

Mr Murray gathered us all into a circle then. 'Well done, everyone,' he said. 'I was very impressed by quite a few of you today.' I noticed that he looked at Peter as he said it! 'Over the next few weeks, I'm going to be choosing the squad for the Leinster Schools Senior Cup. That's why I've arranged a match for us against Wesley College this Friday. I'll be posting the team on the noticeboard tomorrow evening. I want to see how you do in a real match situation, even if it's a friendly.'

I opened my mouth to speak.

'Yes, I know, Gordon,' Mr Murray laughed, 'before you say it – there's no such thing as a friendly!'

7 Do You Know about Nelson Mandela?

I had started to think about South Africa a lot. Even though I didn't know if I'd be going there yet, I found myself constantly daydreaming about this exotic, faraway country, about which I knew almost nothing.

The furthest I'd ever travelled at that point in my life was Paris. And, while it was very nice, it was less than two hours away by airplane – and they didn't have lions and elephants and crocodiles just wandering around the place like I'd heard they did in South Africa.

In my Computer Science class, I typed the words 'South Africa' into a search engine and here were some of the things I learned:

- South Africa is the southernmost country on the continent of Africa and has a population of 59 million people.
- South Africa is teeming with wildlife, including the black rhino, the cheetah and the famous springbok, a horned antelope with very powerful back legs that allow it to leap great heights and distances. The springbok is the symbol of the South African rugby team.
- South Africa has three capital cities: Pretoria, Bloemfontein and Cape Town, although the largest city in the country is Johannesburg.
- South Africa has eleven official languages – English, Zulu, Xhosa, Afrikaans, Sepedi, Setswana, Sesotho, Xitsonga, Swazi, Tshivenda and Ndebele.

I had butterflies in my stomach just reading the names!

I told Peter about the facts I'd learned while we were having lunch in the cafeteria.

'Hey, do you know what you should do this afternoon?' he said. 'Talk to Mr Stuyvesant about it!'

Mr Stuyvesant was the only South African I knew. He was a short, mostly bald man, who tried to disguise his shortness by wearing shoes with soles that were three inches thick, and his mostly-baldness by growing his hair long at the sides and then combing it sideways across his mostly-hairless head.

He taught us Physics, which I thought was *the* most BORING subject in the world. But Peter said he had spoken to him once about the country where he was born and he made it sound like the most fascinating place in the world.

'You should definitely ask him about it,' Peter said.

That afternoon, we were sitting in Physics class.

'Newton's laws of motion,' Mr Stuyvesant was saying, in a slow, drawling voice, 'are three laws that describe the relationship between the motion of an object and the forces acting on it.'

He spotted a piece of chalk on the floor. He bent down to pick it up and his hair fell forward. We all tried to stifle our laughter as he straightened up again and his hair hung down on one side of his head. Conor sometimes put pieces of chalk on the floor so that this would happen. Mr Stuyvesant smoothed it back across his bald patch with his fingers.

'Sir,' I suddenly blurted out, 'what's South Africa like?'

He immediately brightened up. 'South Africa?' he said. 'Why are you asking me about South Africa?'

'Because I'm hoping to go there next summer,' I told him, 'with the British & Irish Lions.'

'Ah, yes, you're the famous rugby player! So, what do you know about it?'

'I know that it's the twenty-fifth-biggest country in the world. And I know about all the animals. And I know it has three capital cities and eleven official languages.'

He nodded.

'And do you know about Nelson Mandela?' he asked.

I'd heard his name before, but I didn't know who he was, or why he was important.

'Not really, Sir,' I told him.

'Well, even if you never end up going to South Africa,' he said, 'everyone in the world should know about Nelson Mandela. All of you, close your books.'

I could hear the excitement rippling through the classroom. No boring Physics this afternoon!

'South Africa is known as the Rainbow Nation,' Mr Stuyvesant said, 'because of its cultural diversity. But for many, many years, long before all of you were born, it was infamous around the world for a system called Apartheid. Now, does anyone know what that word means?'

Peter's hand shot up. 'It means *apart-hood*,' he said, 'meaning the state of keeping things separated.'

'Very good,' said Mr Stuyvesant. 'And in South Africa, what was kept separated were people of different races. About eighty per cent of South Africans are black, but for many years they were treated as third-class citizens by the country's white rulers. Not only were they not allowed to vote, their land was taken from them and they were forced to live in the most appalling slums called townships.

'An organization called the African National

Congress was set up to fight this injustice and its leader was Nelson Mandela, although his tribal name was Madiba. He led many protests against the government on behalf of his people. He was arrested, put on trial for treason and sentenced to life imprisonment. Most of the twenty-seven years that followed he spent on Robben Island, living in a cold, dark cell, which he was only permitted to leave to go to work, breaking rocks in a quarry.

'But soon, people all over the world began to hear the story of Nelson Mandela – and, through him, of the terrible injustice of Apartheid. Political leaders from all over the world began to put pressure on the South African government, which eventually realized that the days of white-only rule were numbered.

'In 1989, the South African government gave in to the pressure and began to dismantle the Apartheid system, giving equal rights to everyone, regardless of their skin colour. And in February 1990, hundreds of millions of people around the world watched as Nelson Mandela was released from prison.'

I looked around the classroom. Everyone was hanging on his every word – and that never happened in Mr Stuyvesant's class.

'Now, Conor, you've just spent twenty-seven

years of your life in prison, where you're barely given enough food to survive on and you're only allowed out of your cell to carry out hard labour. How angry would you be?'

'Very!' Conor replied.

'Well,' Mr Stuyvesant said, 'Nelson Mandela wasn't angry. Or, if he was, he didn't show it. Instead, he spoke about peace, forgiveness and reconciliation. People wondered how a man who had suffered so much could have so little hatred or desire for revenge in his heart?

'In 1994, South Africa held its first elections in which people of every race could vote. And Nelson Mandela was elected as the President of this new Rainbow Nation, represented by a brand-new, multicoloured flag of black, gold, green, red, white and blue.

'Now, Gordon, this part of the story will really interest you. The following year, South Africa was due to host the Rugby World Cup. And Nelson Mandela was a huge rugby fan. As a matter of fact, when the Lions toured South Africa in 1955, Mandela went to see one of the Tests. And he cheered for the Lions!'

I remembered that one from Dad's video cassette. Tony O'Reilly was the star of the tour in 1955.

'Why did he cheer for the Lions?' I asked.

'Because to him, the South African rugby team didn't represent the country that he lived in,' he replied. 'Black players weren't allowed to play for the national team and black fans had to sit in a special section behind one of the goals.'

'Probably the worst seats in the ground,' I said.

'They sat there. And, like Nelson Mandela, they booed the South African team and hoped they'd lose. But, with Apartheid gone, Mandela knew that the 1995 Rugby World Cup was an opportunity to unite this new country behind a single cause. This meant persuading the black population to get behind this team that had always been a symbol of white domination. So, one day, while the South African team was training, President Mandela arrived in a helicopter.'

'Did he fly it himself,' I wondered, 'like Clive Woodward?'

Mr Stuyvesant laughed.

'No, I'm pretty sure he had a pilot,' he said. 'He got out of the helicopter and apologized for the interruption. He said he wanted to meet all of the players and shake their hands. And that moment played a huge part in convincing black South Africans to get behind the team – that and the fact that the team had its first non-white player, a brilliant black winger named Chester Williams. When South Africa played their opening match against Australia in Cape Town, I was lucky enough to be there!'

'Wow!' we all said in a single voice.

'Nelson Mandela waved to the crowd and tens of thousands of white people, who once saw him as the enemy, chanted his name: "Nel-son! Nel-son! Nel-son!" That was the love that people had for him. Francois Pienaar, the South African captain, had to bite his lip to stop himself from crying during the national anthem – he bit it so hard that it bled for the entire match.'

'Who won?' Barry asked.

'We did,' Mr Stuyvesant replied. 'South Africa beat Australia. And the following day, the South African players got on a boat together and they sailed to Robben Island to visit the prison cell where Mandela had spent so much of his adult life. And what they couldn't understand was how a man who was treated so cruelly could have so much generosity in his heart.

'It turned out that President Mandela was right. Rugby really could bring people together. The entire country began to unite behind the team as the World Cup went on. We beat Western Samoa in the quarter-final – Chester Williams scored four tries! – and France in the semi-final. Then, in the final, we beat the All Blacks, with their legendary winger, Jonah Lomu.'

'Whoa!' we all exclaimed. Everyone had heard of the great Jonah Lomu.

'Five years after he was released from prison,' Mr Stuyvesant said, 'it was Nelson Mandela who presented the World Cup trophy to Francois Pienaar. Mandela said to him, "I want to thank you for what you did for South Africa," and Francois Pienaar replied, "You've got it wrong, Madiba – thank *you* for what *you* did for South Africa."

'And that night, the country celebrated as one. People of all races danced in the streets, celebrating a rugby victory for a Springbok team, waving the flag of this new country that was not a black country or a white country any more, but a country for all South Africans.'

At that exact moment, the bell sounded to end the class, but no one moved. We didn't want to leave. Mr Stuyvesant laughed.

'Usually,' he said, 'you're all out that door before the bell has stopped ringing. Go on, away with you all. The story's over. Tomorrow, we're going back to Newton's laws.'

As I was leaving the room, Mr Stuyvesant called me back.

'If you go to South Africa, Gordon,' he said, 'and if you get an opportunity to meet Nelson Mandela, don't miss it. It'll be one of the proudest moments of your life to say you shook the hand of one of the greatest men who has ever lived.'

8 *Guess Who's Back!*

That night, I was in the cafeteria, eating my dinner, when I suddenly noticed that Peter was standing over me with a big grin on his face.

'I know!' I said. 'Spaghetti Bolognese, huh?'

'I'm not smiling because it's spaghetti Bolognese for dinner,' he said. 'Mr Murray has picked the team – for the match against Wesley!'

I'd forgotten he said that he was going to post it on the noticeboard.

'And?' I asked.

'I made it!' Peter said.

I punched the air.

'Yes!' I exclaimed.

'You're playing too,' he added. 'Of course, you are – you're Gordon D'Arcy! But Conor got picked as well!'

For some reason, though, I was more excited for Peter than I was for any of us.

'What position are you playing?' I asked.

'He's put me in at number eight,' he said. 'He told me he hasn't made his mind up yet whether I'm a forward or a back.'

Peter used to be tall for his age, but he'd stopped growing when we were still in primary school, giving the rest of us a chance to catch up!

'I'm delighted for you,' I said. 'Although I'm not surprised after the way you played yesterday.'

'Well, I'm not getting carried away with myself,' he insisted. 'It's just a trial. I'm sure there'll be quite a few other players he'll want to take a look at as well. But at least I've been given a shot.'

It was at that exact moment that Conor arrived, looking far less happy than Peter did. I thought to myself, he clearly hasn't heard the news yet.

'Mr Murray put the team up on the noticeboard!' Peter told him. 'You're starting at full-back, Conor!'

'Yeah, I saw that,' he replied, unsmilingly. 'Gordon, there's something you need to see.'

'What?' I asked.

'It's Flash Barry.'

'I thought he was just Barry now.'

'No, he's back to being Flash Barry again – trust me.'

'Oh, no,' said Peter, 'what's he done?'

'Come with me,' Conor said.

I left my spaghetti Bolognese and we all headed for the dormitory building. Nothing could have prepared me for what I saw.

There was a queue of about a hundred boys leading all the way to the door of our room. Barry had moved his study desk over to the door and was sitting behind it. In front of him was a cashbox stuffed with fifty-euro notes and also a copybook, into which he was scribbling each boy's name.

'Two hundred and fifty euros,' he was saying. 'That includes all flights, accommodation, transfers and tickets to see the great Gordon D'Arcy star for the mighty Lions!'

'What in the name of God are you doing?' I asked – even though the answer was perfectly clear.

There was a poster on the wall that said: 'Flash Travel!' Beneath a huge photograph of me, it said, 'Lions Tour to South Africa! Book Now!'

Barry looked up at me.

'Ah, the dude himself!' he chirped.

'Barry,' I said, 'I asked you a question.'

He flicked his thumb at the poster. 'I've set myself up as a tour operator,' he said. 'Two hundred and fifty yoyos to see all three Tests. I know what

you're thinking – how can this dude afford to do it so cheaply?'

'That's not what I was thinking,' I told him. 'But now that you mention it – how *can* you afford to do it so cheaply?'

'By keeping my overheads low,' he said vaguely.

'You're just using Gordon's name to rip people off!' Peter told him.

Barry had the nerve to act offended. 'How DARE you!' he said. 'How DARE you suggest that I would exploit Gordon's status as a world-class rugby player for my own personal gain!'

'You did do that before,' I reminded him, 'when you were my agent.'

'Yes, I did. But that was the *old* Barry. If you must know, I'm not making a single cent out of this thing.'

'Then why are you doing it?' Conor asked.

'Because Gordon happens to be a friend of mine,' he said.

'I would have said roommate more than friend,' I pointed out.

'My only motivation,' he insisted, placing his hand over his heart, 'is to give everyone the opportunity to see the great Gordon D'Arcy in action in beautiful, beautiful South Africa!'

'But I don't even know if I'm GOING to South Africa yet!' I tried to tell him.

He shushed me.

'Keep that to yourself,' he said. 'You'll scare away the customers.'

'Barry, you can't use my face to sell tickets for a Lions tour when I won't know if I've made the final squad until next March!'

'You'll make the final squad, Darce.'

'How do you know?'

'Because I have every faith in you!' he said.

I noticed that Peter was shaking his head. 'Two hundred and fifty euros seems impossibly cheap for a month-long trip to South Africa,' he pointed out. 'Are you absolutely sure you can do it for that price, Barry?'

'Of course,' Barry insisted. 'I've done my research, Dude – right down to the last detail. Speaking of which, Peter, you might know the answer to this question – where exactly *is* South Africa?'

'It's in Africa,' Peter told him.

'Right,' said Barry. 'I thought it might be. It has that kind of ring to it alright.'

'It's down in the southern part of Africa,' Peter added. 'You could actually describe it as the South of Africa.'

'Good to know,' Barry said, pointing the finger guns at him. 'Good to know.'

9 *Disaster!*

I had the ball in my hands and I went to play a pass to Gus Rainey, who was next to me at outside-centre. But Gus had mistimed his run – he'd moved ahead of me, so that if I made the pass to him, it would be forward. I looked around for another Clongowes shirt. And then . . .

Oooooommmmppphhh!!!

I was tackled hard around the waist and dumped onto the flat of my back. I didn't know what had happened to the ball, just that I didn't have it any more. It had spilled out of my hands. I sat up, badly winded, and saw that Wesley's number eight had it – but, by the time I got to my feet, Peter had taken him down and now *we* had it again.

Trials matches were always like this – and by *this*, I mean chaos!

Everyone was trying to catch the eye of the coach by doing something spectacular. And, because you had no idea when you might be substituted, it made everyone a bit too desperate for things to happen quickly.

Antoine Drion, the Wesley out-half, was enjoying the game of his life. He was small for his age, with a low centre of gravity, which meant he was difficult to knock over, and he moved faster than any player I had ever seen.

As well as that, he was totally unpredictable. When you expected him to run one line, he ran another. When you thought he was going to pass to a team-mate, he'd sell you a dummy. When you thought he was going to go around you, there was a flash of hands and he'd play a quick reverse pass to one of his teammates. He had us all completely flummoxed!

Some of our players were a little bit rusty after the summer holidays. Our timing was off. Passes were being misplaced. Balls were being dropped. Tackles were being missed. We just weren't clicking as a team. A lot of our players were trying to perform some piece of individual magic that might impress Mr Murray.

Like Gus, for instance, who was having a bit of a nightmare. To try to compensate, he threw a long, loping pass to Peter, who was in acres of space. But Antoine Drion anticipated what Gus was going to do. He took a step forward, intercepted the ball and set off for what looked like a certain try.

Antoine was fast, but, luckily for Gus, Conor was faster. He took off after him and took him down with a beautiful ankle-tap just as he crossed our 22-metre line.

We were losing 10–0 as half-time approached. I was telling my teammates to relax and try to do the simple things well, instead of trying to make an impression on Mr Murray.

But then, minutes later, came the moment that changed everything.

Antoine had the ball in his hands and he was running towards me. I prepared to throw myself into the tackle, determined not to make the same mistake I'd made against Peter.

But I made a different mistake – and it meant disaster for me.

One of the first things you learn when you start playing rugby is how to tackle a player safely. You don't throw yourself in with your arms outstretched – you lead with your shoulder, then, once the contact has been made, you wrap your arms around the player with the ball.

But just as I prepared to tackle him head-on, Antoine stepped off his left foot to cut outside me. Instinct took over – my absolute need to stop him from going past me. I stretched out my left arm to try to grab him around the waist – but, as he sped past me, the point of his elbow struck my forearm hard.

I heard two things in quick succession. The first was a loud crack. The second was a piercing scream, like an animal roaring:

'RRRRRRAAAAAAGGGHHH!!!'

I didn't realize it at the time – but the scream had come from me!

The pain in my arm was like nothing I had ever felt before. I realized that I was lying on the ground, which came as a surprise to me because I didn't remember falling. My eyes were shut tightly and my teeth were clenched and I was still making that noise, except over and over again now:

'RRRRRRAAAAAAGGGHHH!!!'

I became aware of the other players gathering around me. I could hear voices, filled with concern,

asking me what happened and then, a second or two later, the same voices exclaiming, 'Oh my God!' in horror.

Peter's voice was the first I recognized.

'His arm is broken,' he said.

I opened my eyes and attempted to sit up.

'Don't look at it, Gordon,' I heard Mr Murray say and I felt my head being gently turned away to the right. 'Don't let him see it.'

I could hear someone being sick. Was that in response to the sight of my arm, I wondered?

'How bad is it?' I asked through my clenched teeth.

'Try to stay calm,' Mr Murray said. 'The ambulance is on its way.'

'Ambulance?' I asked. 'I want know how –'

I tried to move my arm and a savage pain ripped through my entire upper body.

And that was when I lost consciousness.

10 *The Worst News Ever*

I could hear a persistent beeping sound in my ears.
It sounded like a heart monitor: BOOP! BOOP!
BOOP! BOOP!

Wait a minute, I thought – it *is* a heart monitor.
Then I remembered the accident. And the talk of an
ambulance.

And then . . .

'He's waking up!' I heard a woman say. 'He's waking up!'

Her voice sounded familiar.

Wasn't that . . .

'Mum?' I said. My lips were stuck together and
my voice came out in a sort of low mumble, so that
it sounded like:

'Hmum?'

'He's awake!' she said. 'Get the doctor! Get the doctor!'

I managed to wrench my eyes open. The brightness hurt my eyes, so I quickly closed them again.

Then I could hear other voices.

'You're alright, Gordon,' a girl's voice said, 'you're just a little bit groggy from the anaesthetic, that's all.'

Was that . . . Aoife?

'Where am I?' I asked.

It was a man's voice I heard this time.

'You're in St Vincent's Hospital,' he said.

'Ian?' I mumbled.

'Shona's here as well,' he said, 'and Megan.'

'Hi, Gordon!' Megan said.

'How are you feeling?' Shona asked.

'I'm a bit, I don't know, confused,' I told them.

I attempted to open my eyes again – this time with more success. There were a lot of people in the room. I spotted Aoife, standing next to Conor and Peter at the foot of the bed. Conor and Peter were still wearing their rugby gear.

'Who won?' I asked.

'No one,' Peter said, like it was a dumb question. 'It was abandoned.'

'Abandoned? Why?'

'Er, because you broke your arm!' Conor said.

I looked down at it for the first time. It was encased in plaster from the elbow to the wrist and lying uselessly beside me on the bed.

'Did I faint or something?' I asked.

'You passed out,' Peter said, 'from the shock and the pain. Then the ambulance arrived and they gave you nitrous oxide.'

'I remember having a fit of giggles – although that feels like it was a dream.'

'That's why they call it laughing gas. You were absolutely hysterical.'

'Wait a minute,' I said, 'you were in the back of the ambulance with me?'

'Yeah, so was Mr Murray,' Conor said, 'and also –'

'Mr Murray?' I repeated – still feeling a little bit out of it. 'Is *he* here as well?'

'Yes, I'm here,' Mr Murray said from somewhere within the crowd of bodies surrounding the bed.

'Why did you abandon the match?' I asked. 'You shouldn't have abandoned the match.'

'The match wasn't important,' he said. 'Gordon, there's someone here who wants to see you.'

My vision was a bit blurred – I presumed from all the painkillers. But I could just make out this small figure making his way towards the top of the bed.

'I'm so sorry,' a tiny voice said.

It was Antoine Drion.

'Sorry?' I asked. 'What have you got to be sorry for?'

'I broke your arm,' said Antoine – and his voice cracked.

'You didn't break my arm,' I told him. 'It was my stupid fault for trying to tackle you like that. I'm the one who should be apologizing to you.'

'Why?' he asked.

'Because you were having the game of your life,' I told him. 'You were on FIRE, Antoine! And, because of me, the match was abandoned.'

'There'll be other matches,' he said. 'I just hate to think that you might miss out on the Lions tour because of me.'

An awful silence descended on the room – as if Antoine had said out loud what the others had only dared to think.

Now I was thinking about it too.

Just how badly broken was my arm? Was this the end of my dream of playing for the Lions against South Africa?

Suddenly, I heard a loud voice bark: 'There are too many people in here! You'll all have to leave! Gordon needs rest! I only want to see his parents by his bedside!'

Everyone cleared out, except Mum and Dad. The man introduced himself to me.

'Hello,' he said, 'I'm Bill Quinlan. I'm the surgeon who operated on your arm.'

Operated on it?

'How did it go?' Dad asked.

Hang on, I thought, did he say I'd had an operation?

'It was a very complicated procedure,' the man said after a long silence. 'You broke your arm in eight places, Gordon. The radius and ulna, the main bones in your lower arm, were completely shattered. I had to use screws to hold them together.'

'What,' Mum said, 'screws like we have at home in the tool-box?'

'The very same,' he told her.

'So, when will I be able to play rugby again?' I asked.

'Rugby?' he said.

'Yeah, it's just that I'm a member of the preliminary Lions squad – and I'm hoping to be one of the fifty players that Clive Woodward brings to –'

The surgeon took a deep breath.

'This is one of the worst breaks I have ever seen,' he said. 'I don't want to give you false hope, so I'm going to tell you the truth. It's quite possible that you will never, ever regain the strength in your arm that you once had.'

'No!' I cried, not wanting to hear any more. 'I want to play for the Lions! Willie John McBride smoking a pipe! Welshmen with long hair and side-burns!' and then I suddenly burst into song. '*Waltzing O'Driscoll, waltzing O'Driscoll, you'll come a-waltzing O'Driscoll with me.*'

'He's delirious,' I heard Dad say. 'It must be the painkillers.'

'THE ENTIRE SERIES,' I yelled, 'RESTS ON YOUNG D'ARCY PUTTING THIS BALL OVER THE WASHING LINE!'

'You must listen,' the surgeon said in a grave voice. 'Gordon, you have to prepare yourself for the possibility . . . that you might never play rugby again.'

11 *Time Slows Down*

There isn't much to say about the months that followed. The time between me breaking my arm and the Christmas holidays rolled slowly by in an unhappy blur of days.

Clive Woodward phoned me at school a week after the accident. I took the call in Mr Murray's office. He said he'd seen the X-rays of my arm, then he let out a long exhalation.

'What does that mean?' I asked.

'The bones in your arm have been completely shattered,' he said.

'Should I still get up at oh six hundred hours and run ten kilometres in the mud while laying off the Choco Choco Choco Puffs?'

'Look, I hope your arm will have fully healed by the time I pick the final squad for South Africa. But

91

I'm going to be straight with you – I've never seen a player come back from a break as bad as that.'

I was thrown into a state of shock.

'Thanks,' I said – like he'd just paid me a compliment.

'Let's hope for the best,' he said. 'Only time will tell.'

While I wished away the school year, willing my bones to heal, life at Clongowes went on as normal. The match against Wesley was rearranged. Then there were further trials matches against Gonzaga and St Gerard's.

With my arm in a sling, I watched from the side-lines as Conor and Peter played well enough to make the final squad for the Leinster Schools Senior Cup. I was delighted for both of them. Conor had come back from a broken leg, while Peter had worked so hard at his rugby.

They never stopped encouraging me. They made sure I continued to train like a Lion. As the winter drew in and the mornings darkened, they shook me awake just before six o'clock and insisted that I performed the Lions exercise plan with them. I couldn't do the chin-ups or the press-ups, but I could manage the sit-ups and the ten-kilometre run around the school grounds.

On these runs, they would try to get me to stay positive. As our feet splashed through the mud, Conor would tell me that he knew exactly what I was going through. When he broke his leg trying to jump the Gollymochy, he thought it would never be right again. And, while he waited for it to heal, it was as if time slowed down, which is exactly how it felt for me.

Peter talked to me about South Africa, about all the things I was going to see there next summer, to focus my mind on the goal waiting for me at the end of this.

'You have to get better,' he said. 'You're going to get to meet Nelson Mandela, remember?'

I really wanted to meet Nelson Mandela.

Flash Barry was encouraging in his own way. Each morning, when we returned from our morning workout, usually soaked to the bone and shivering cold, he would ask me if my arm felt any better than it did the day before. This, I knew, was less out of concern for me than it was for the future of Flash Travel's €250, all-inclusive Tour of South Africa.

He had taken €50 deposits from almost two hundred students and quite a few had made inquiries about having their money refunded in the event of me not making the tour.

'Better or worse than yesterday?' Barry would ask.

'Probably the same,' I'd tell him.

'The same?' he'd say, failing to hide his disappointment. 'I've got a lot riding on this, Darce!'

Mum and Dad rang the school every second night to check on me and to tell me that half the population of Wexford was saying prayers for Gordon D'Arcy's arm. Mum said her friend Mrs Deasy from Foulksmills Crescent arranged a novena to pray for my arm. Then she rang to say that Mrs Bent from Pomona Road was praying for my arm in Knock. Then Mr Ryan from John F. Kennedy Drive was praying for my arm in Medjugorje. Then Mrs Davaney from O'Hanrahan Way was praying for my arm in Lourdes.

And then came the big one!

Mum rang me one Saturday afternoon in November to say that my Auntie Maura was going to Rome next week and she was going to try to have a word with the Pope himself!

'Sometimes,' she said, 'if you want to get something done, you have to go to the top man!'

Aoife sent me e-mails every single day, featuring stories about all sorts of athletes who'd returned from career-threatening injuries, many of whom were told, like me, that they might never play again. And whenever I happened to see her when she was practising her kicking on the Clongowes pitch, she would produce a black marker and write an inspirational quote on my cast. By Christmas, almost every inch of plaster was covered in her words of wisdom:

'What follows the setback is the comeback!'

And:

'You are mentally stronger than you physically feel!'

And:

'Tough times don't last – tough people do!'

But I went home to Wexford that Christmas feeling a deep sense of sadness at how my life had been changed in an instant by a freak accident. A few months earlier, I was excited about wearing the famous red jersey of the Lions – now, I didn't know if I'd ever play rugby again.

What made the uncertainty worse was that I had no idea whether the bones in my arm were healing underneath the cast.

A few days after Christmas, I was sitting in front of the TV one afternoon, watching Dad's history of the Lions video for probably the twentieth time.

Paul O'Connell was on the screen. He was asked what it meant to be a Lion and he smiled and said, '*When you pull on that red jersey, you can't help but think about all the legends of the game who've worn that number before you. That's why playing for the Lions brings out the best in players – because they know it's a rare privilege that even some of greatest players in the game never get to experience.*'

And that was when the phone rang. It was Dad who answered it.

'Gordon!' he called out. 'It's for you!'

'Me?' I said, stepping out into the hallway.

It was hardly ever for me. Dad covered the mouthpiece with his hand and mouthed the words, 'It's Clive Woodward.'

Then he handed me the phone.

'Hello, Clive,' I said.

'Telephone conversation between Sir Clive Woodward, Head Coach of the British & Irish Lions,' he said, 'and Gordon D'Arcy, of Clongowes Wood College, Leinster and Ireland.'

'And Wexford Wanderers,' I reminded him.

'And Wexford Wanderers,' he confirmed. 'Twenty-ninth of December, fifteen hundred hours. Question to break the ice – how was your Christmas?'

'Er, fine, thank you,' I told him.

'And how's the arm?'

'It feels okay – although I won't know for sure until the cast comes off.'

'When is that happening?'

'The surgeon said the end of February.'

He took a deep breath. I could tell what he was thinking. He was picking the final squad for the tour in the middle of March – which meant he would have, at the very most, two weeks to decide whether he should bring me to South Africa or not.

'It's not a lot of time,' he admitted.

'I know,' I said.

'Anyway, the reason I'm ringing is because we're having our first squad get-together on New Year's Day in the Vale of Glamorgan.'

'Where's that?'

'It's in Wales. It's a two-day, team-building exercise, so all the players can meet up and get to know each other. Injured or not, I'd like you to be there.'

'I will be.'

'We'll do a couple of training sessions over the two days. Obviously, you'll have to sit those out. But it'll be good for you to meet the rest of the group. We'll be doing some team-bonding exercises as well. It'll be a good experience for you, even if –'

He didn't finish his sentence. I did it for him.

'Even if I don't make the tour?' I asked.

'Exactly,' he said. 'Now, a courier should be arriving at your door with your plane tickets . . . any . . . minute . . . now . . .'

DING-DONG!

A few seconds later, I heard the front door being opened and Mum shouted, 'Gordon! Who's sending you packages?'

The guy was good!

'You'll be flying to Cardiff,' he said, 'at oh eight hundred hours, where you'll be collected and driven to the team hotel. The full itinerary is in the envelope. Telephone conversation between Sir Clive Woodward and Gordon D'Arcy terminates, fifteen hundred hours, four minutes and twenty-seven seconds.'

Then he hung up.

12 *Mystic Martha*

'Tell me what he said again,' Ian demanded.

The entire family was sitting around the dinner table, eating a curry that Mum had made from the final leftovers of the Christmas turkey.

'Just that it's going to be tight,' I told him. 'My cast doesn't come off until the end of February and he has to pick the fifty players he's bringing to South Africa two weeks later.'

'Your arm is going to be fine!' Mum said confidently. 'Sure, didn't Auntie Maura have a word with the Pope?'

'Did Auntie Maura meet the Pope?' Megan asked.

'Well, not exactly,' Mum said. 'There were a lot more people at his Mass than she expected. But she shouted to him across St Peter's Square. "Pray for Gordon D'Arcy's arm – it's the left one!" She's almost sure he heard her.'

The doorbell rang.

'That'll be for me,' Shona said. 'I asked someone to come around to have a look at Gordon's arm.'

'Who?' I asked.

'Her name's Martha,' she said. 'Except she calls herself Mystic Martha. She's a sort of faith healer.'

'A faith healer?' Dad laughed.

'Why does he need a faith healer,' Mum wanted to know, 'when we've already got the Pope on the case? He's next in line to God, you know.'

The doorbell rang a second time.

'We should try absolutely everything,' Shona said. 'What do you think, Gordon?'

'Why not?' I shrugged.

I followed Shona out into the hallway. So did everybody else.

'I wouldn't miss this for the world!' Dad said, rubbing his hands together.

'Dad,' said Shona, rebuking him with a look, 'don't you DARE make a joke out of this! You either, Ian!'

'We'll be on our best behaviour!' Ian promised her.

Shona opened the door. Standing on the doorstep was a woman who looked about a hundred years old. She was wearing long, flowy, purple robes, an enormous turban and giant, hoopy earrings. She smiled.

'You must be the D'Arcys!' she said.

'God, she's good!' Dad muttered under his breath.

Ian laughed. I have to admit, I did too.

'Come in,' Shona said.

Martha took one step into the hallway and then stopped. She closed her eyes and tilted her head back. We watched the end of her nose wiggle.

'I'm already getting something!' she announced.

We all looked at each other, eyebrows raised in curiosity.

Martha suddenly opened her eyes.

'Curry!' she said. 'Am I right?'

Mum looked at Shona, then back at Martha.

'Em, yes,' she said. 'It's the last of the Christmas turkey.'

'I'll have a plate of that when I'm finished,' Mystic Martha said. 'It's just I haven't had anything to eat since lunchtime.'

'Er, right,' Mum said. I could see that Dad and Ian were both covering their mouths with their hands to stop themselves from exploding with laughter.

Shona showed Martha into the living room. Everyone followed.

'So,' Martha said, 'which one of you has the broken arm?'

I was thinking, is that not perfectly obvious?

'Er, that'd be me,' I said, raising my plaster cast in the air.

There was more laughter from Dad and Ian.

'Give it to Mystic Martha,' said Martha.

I held my arm out to her and she took hold of my middle finger. She closed her eyes again and started muttering:

'Hooba . . . Hooba . . . Sootan . . . Sooka . . . Hab . . . Hab . . . Hab . . . Babba Don . . . Babba Don Doo . . .'

'She's communing with the spirit world,' Shona whispered to me.

'Oh, right,' I said.

Martha opened her eyes again.

'Well, the good news,' she announced, 'is that it wasn't a bad break you suffered.'

Dad and Ian were doubled over with laughter.

'Er, yes, it was!' I told her. 'The surgeon said it was one of the worst breaks he'd ever seen!'

She closed her eyes again, then quickly reopened them.

'Sorry, the whispers from the spirit world are faint today,' she said. 'Yes, you're right – it *was* a very bad break.'

'Eight places,' I told her.

'Eight,' she repeated. 'Yes, I'm getting that now.'

'So can you help me?' I asked.

'The good news is yes,' she said, letting go of my finger. 'But, first, I'm going to ask you to eat something.'

From somewhere within her robes, she produced a clear, Ziploc bag, stuffed with green leaves.

'What are those?' I asked, as she pressed some of them into the palm of my hand.

'They're strawberry leaves,' she said. 'They have mysterious, healing properties.'

'Riiiggghhhttt!' I said, uncertainty in my voice.

'Pop them in your mouth and chew them,' she instructed me. 'But don't swallow them.'

Dad and Ian were laughing so much now that they had to leave the room. I did as I was told.

'Now,' she said to Shona, 'your brother needs to be lying down with the top of his head pointing in a northerly direction. This sofa is pointing from east to west. Help me turn it around.'

The strawberry leaves tasted DISGUSTING, but I chewed them while Shona and this very strange woman picked up the sofa and turned it ninety degrees.

'Now,' Mystic Martha said, 'you lie down on the sofa there, Graham.'

'Gordon,' I reminded her.

'That's it – with your head this end, pointing north. Okay, tell me, which is your broken arm again?'

'Er, the one in the plaster cast?'

'Well, hold it up in the air. That's it – keep it vertical while I say my incantation.'

'Your what?' I asked.

'It's a sort of magic spell,' Shona said. 'Just go with it, Gordon.'

Martha placed her two hands either side of my arm.

'Can you feel the heat coming from my palms?' she asked.

'Er, no,' I told her.

I honestly couldn't feel a thing.

'Well, don't be afraid of it,' she said. 'It's the heat that's going to heal your bones.'

Then she closed her eyes and started to chant – again, she was using words that I didn't recognize:

'Ongung . . . Ongung . . . Rappa pappa too . . .
Ongung . . . Ongung . . . Rappa pappa too . . .
Sanfin . . . Sanfin . . . Woorg . . . Morcha . . .
Faffa nanna . . . Faffa nanna hi . . . Ongung . . .
Ongung . . . Rappa papa too . . .'

This continued for several minutes. I was staring at Shona, trying to send a message with my eyes. And that message was:

'THIS WOMAN IS A CRAZY PERSON!'

Eventually, very abruptly, the chanting stopped.

'There!' the woman said. 'That should have fixed it! Now, I'll have some of that curry that your mum was offering me a minute ago!'

'Er, yes,' said Shona, 'come through to the kitchen. We can put the sofa back later.'

I felt completely and utterly bewildered by what had just happened. I stood up and spat the strawberry leaves back into my hand. And I would have happily written off the entire experience – except for one final thing that Mystic Martha said to me.

'*Panthera leo!*' she said, smiling at me in a, well, mystic way.

'What?' I asked.

'Did you know that in certain cultures, Graham –'

'Gordon.'

'– it is believed that each of us has a spirit animal that helps guide us? Mine is a hawk. Your sister's – I can tell just from looking at her – is a bear.'

'Er, okay – and, just as a matter of interest, what's mine?'

'I just told you,' said Martha. '*Panthera leo!*'

'I've never heard of it,' I said.

'Your spirit animal,' she said, 'is a lion!'

13 *Teacupping*

'How was your Christmas?' Paul O'Connell asked me.

'Ah, you know,' I said, indicating my plaster cast, and he nodded like he knew only too well.

We were standing in the crowded lobby of the Glamorgan Golf and Country Club.

'I heard it was a bad break,' he said.

'Clive Woodward said it was the kind of injury that usually finishes careers,' I told him.

'You can stop that now.'

'What?'

'Thinking negatively. You have to believe you will come back.'

I liked Paulie a lot. I'd played with him for Ireland and against him when I played for Leinster and he played for Munster. He was a giant of a competitor and he never, ever gave in.

'Let me tell you something,' he said. 'There isn't a bit of my body that hasn't been injured at some point. Knees. Hips. Shoulders. Arms. Groin. Back. Ankles. Neck. I've missed everything from a week to a whole year with injuries. The physical recovery is the easy part – what you go through mentally is a lot harder.'

'What do you mean?' I asked.

'The worst thing about being injured is watching the world go on without you. It's watching your teammates train and feeling like you don't exist for them any more. It's watching your teammates win matches and feeling like they don't need you now. It's a lonely time.'

I was looking around the lobby of the hotel. I spotted lots of players I recognized, some I'd played with or against and some I knew from TV. I saw Owen Farrell, the English out-half, and Liam Williams, the Welsh winger, and Stuart Hogg, the Scottish full-back. I saw Martin Johnson – an absolute mountain of a second-row – laughing with Lawrence Dallaglio, his England teammate with the perfectly hairless, cue-ball head. I saw Johnny Sexton, deep in conversation with Conor Murray.

There was lots of noise and lots of laughter.

A man appeared. I noticed he had the Lions crest on the breast pocket of his blazer.

'Gentlemen,' he shouted, trying to make himself heard above the general commotion of one hundred rugby players catching up with each other. 'Please make your way to the main Conference Suite!'

Paulie and I joined the flow of people. When we reached the Conference Suite, there were two men dressed in lion costumes standing on either side of the door. They were handing out teacups to each and every player. They were small, bone china ones, with pink flowers on them – the kind my mum kept behind glass in the good room, only to be used when we had special guests.

I looked at it and thought, that's weird! Especially when we walked into the room and I noticed that there wasn't a tea or coffee urn anywhere to be seen.

The room was set up as if for a conference, with rows and rows of chairs facing a low stage. We made our way to the third row – near enough to the front to look like we were interested, but not so close as to look like we were desperate.

It was kind of like school really.

Brian O'Driscoll was already sitting there.

'Hey, guys,' he said, 'what's with the cups?'

'Hopefully, BOD, they'll be coming around with tea,' Paulie said. 'I'm parched.'

BOD nodded at my cast. 'How's the arm?' he asked.

'I won't really know,' I told him, 'until the end of February.'

He just nodded. I could tell what he was thinking. It was going to be very tight.

'Stay positive,' he said.

'I'll try,' I told him.

Soon, all of the seats were filled and the air sparked with excited conversation and laughter. I was picking out voices behind me. I didn't know who they belonged to, but I could hear all the different accents. English. Irish. Scottish. Welsh.

Suddenly, the room fell dark and a voice came through the speakers:

'Gentlemen, please put your hands together for the Head Coach of the British & Irish Lions, Sir Clive Woodward!'

Clive stepped out onto the stage, wearing a blazer with the Lions crest on it, a cravat around his neck and the same headset microphone he wore the last time I met him.

Everyone balanced the teacups on their knees so that they could clap. With my left arm in a cast, all I could do was slap my right hand off my thigh, making the teacup rattle and tinkle.

'Good morning, Lions,' he said. 'Happy New Year and welcome to the Vale of Glamorgan for what I hope will be a very useful couple of days of meeting, greeting and bonding. It's fitting that we should have our first get-together today, on the first day of what I hope will be a very special year for some of you. I say *some of you* because there are one hundred and one players in this room – and, as you know, I can only bring fifty of you to South Africa.'

One hundred and one? I thought there were a hundred players in the preliminary squad. I'd read the list of names so many times that I could say it off by heart. Who was the extra player, I wondered?

'Now,' said Clive, 'when you walked into the room this morning, you were each handed a teacup.'

'Aye,' shouted Stuart Hogg, the Scottish number fifteen, 'wheer's the tea, Clive? The tongue is hanging oot ah mah heid here!'

Everyone laughed.

'Those cups aren't meant for tea,' he said. 'Those cups are souvenirs.'

'Souvenirs?' shouted Martin Johnson. 'What's

wrong wiv a stick of rock wiv "Vale of Glamorgan" written froo it?'

There was more laughter.

'I want you to bring those teacups with you everywhere,' Clive said, 'and those of you who are lucky enough to make the final squad, I want you to still have them when we return – triumphant – from South Africa.'

'Why?' Paulie asked. 'What are they for?'

'They're a permanent reminder of something,' Clive explained. 'It will be the principle behind everything we do.'

Suddenly, Clive pressed a clicker in his hand, then on the giant, white screen behind him, four letters appeared, each about six feet in height:

TCUP

'Teacup,' Clive said, 'or TCUP, is going to be our secret weapon!'

'So what does it mean?' asked Adam Jones, a big Welsh prop with a crazy lion's mane of hair.

'It stands for Thinking . . . Calmly . . . Under . . . Pressure,' Clive said, leaving a long pause between each word. 'Thinking . . . Calmly . . . Under . . . Pressure is what leads players to make the right decisions

when the heat comes on. Thinking ... Calmly ...
Under ... Pressure is what separates the great
players from the good players. Gordon D'Arcy,
stand up.'

I stood up.

Clive pressed the clicker with his thumb and a
series of scribbles appeared on the screen behind
him. There were numbers in circles – some red,
some green. Then there were arrows and boxes and
a giant H. At first, it looked like Maths homework.
But then I realized that the giant H was a set of goalposts and what we were looking at was some kind of
tactical plan.

'The Lions are the reds,' he said, 'and the South

Africans are the greens. There's a minute to go in the final Test and we're losing by a point. That's you there, at twelve. You have the ball. You have five seconds to tell me, what's the play?'

'The play?' I repeated, suddenly flustered.

'Four,' he said.

'Errr . . .'

'Three.'

'Hang on.'

'Two.'

'I think I'd probably . . .'

'One. Time's up. What *weren't* you doing there, Gordon?'

'Sorry?'

'You *weren't* Thinking . . . Calmly . . . Under . . . Pressure. Now, those of you who make the final squad of fifty will become used to this. I'm going to throw different scenarios at you at unexpected times and ask you what you would do. And you'll have five seconds to answer. We are going to practise Teacupping so much that it becomes a habit.'

Behind me, there was a sudden smash. It sounded like a cup breaking.

'I might need anuvah one of these,' I heard Lawrence Dallaglio say. 'I've only gone and dropped it!'

'We're going to have a light training session this

afternoon,' Clive said. 'I don't want any of you going mad. Tonight is yours to mingle and get to know each other. Then tomorrow, we've got a very special guest who's coming here to tell you what it means to be a Lion.'

As the meeting broke up, Clive caught my eye and indicated that he wanted to talk to me. I stayed behind after all the others had left.

'Meeting between Sir Clive Woodward, Head Coach of the British & Irish Lions,' he said, 'and Gordon D'Arcy, of Clongowes Wood College, Leinster and Ireland.'

'And Wexford Wanderers,' I reminded him.

'And Wexford Wanderers,' Clive added. 'The first of January, eleven hundred hours and seventeen minutes. Sorry about that earlier, I didn't mean to embarrass you.'

'It's fine.'

'It's just that an ability to think on your feet is a skill you'll need if you want to be a Lion. Anyway, I'm glad you came. Obviously, it's going to be difficult for you sitting out the training session. But I just wanted to make you aware of something. I've called up one more player.'

'Yeah, you said there were one hundred and one of us.'

'Look, I rate you very highly as a player – that's why I included you in the squad. But I also have to prepare for the possibility that your arm might not recover in time. Which is why I've decided to bring in another inside-centre.'

'Who?'

'I've asked Jonathan Davies to join the squad.'

Jonathan Davies was the Welsh number twelve and one of my favourite players in the world. In that moment, I looked up and I saw him standing in the doorway of the Conference Suite, waiting to talk to Clive.

'Right,' I said – in my disappointment, it was the only word I could manage.

'I'm sorry, Gordon,' he told me. 'I hope you understand.'

14 *Food Bill*

WOOMPH!!!
SHMACK!!!
BAMMM!!!

Clive had told the players not to go mad, but they clearly weren't listening. What was supposed to be a light training session had turned into all-out war. The players had been divided into four teams and two matches were going on at the same time on two adjoining pitches.

It reminded me of the trials matches we had at school. Players were throwing themselves into tackles with full intensity. Within fifteen minutes, you could see that many of them were already exhausted and quite a few were limping around the pitch.

It was a bitterly cold afternoon and I stood

watching on the sideline, focused mainly on one player. Jonathan Davies. He was having the game of his life – the best player on either pitch by some distance. He was going on long, mazy runs, beating players and sidestepping tackles. Out of the corner of my eye, I could see that Clive was grinning from ear to ear, clearly impressed with him.

I felt so low in that moment. I remembered what Paulie had said that morning about feeling like you don't exist any more. And that's how I felt in that moment. The laughter of the players seemed to mock me. I thought to myself, I shouldn't be here. I shouldn't have come.

I decided to go for a run around the pitch – to try to get warm, but also to feel like I was doing something, not just standing around like an idiot. I had done one full circuit of the two pitches when I heard a player ask another, 'Here, who's the Food Bill with the cast on his arm?'

'That's Gordon D'Arcy,' came the reply. 'Broke it in eight places. They don't know if he'll ever play rugby again.'

I turned around, but I couldn't see who'd been talking, so I continued running. I did four circuits in all, then Clive blew his whistle and said, 'Training session terminated – seventeen hundred hours.'

I walked back to the bus with the rest of the players. I took a seat next to Martin Johnson, who looked like he'd been in a fight with a bear. He had two black eyes, scratches on his face and his lip was cut.

'Aw, 'at was great fun!' he said.

'Yeah,' I said, 'it certainly looked it.'

'How's your arm doin', mate?'

'I, er, won't know anything until the end of February.'

'Whoa, 'at's going to be tight.'

'Yeah, I know.'

Jonathan Davies stepped onto the bus then and there was a huge cheer. I presumed it was in acknowledgement of how well he'd played.

Soon, the driver started the bus and we were on our way back to the hotel.

'Martin,' I said, 'can I ask you a question?'

'Johnno,' he corrected me. 'Call me Johnno.'

'Okay, Johnno, then. What's a Food Bill?'

'A Food Bill?'

'Yeah, I heard someone call me a Food Bill.'

'Look, injured players are sometimes referred to as Food Bills.'

'Why?'

'Because that's all they are.'

The penny suddenly dropped.

'Because they don't really contribute in any way,' he said, 'except to eat the food.'

'Oh,' I said, instantly hurt.

'You don't wanna take it too seriously,' he said. 'It's just rugby banter, innit? That's what we do! We take the mickey aaht of each uvver.'

'Right.'

'It'd be worse if they were saying nuffink abaaht you at all. Seriously, mate, don't take it to 'art. When your arm's all fixed up, you'll laugh abaaht it.'

That wasn't how I felt, though.

I sat in silence for the rest of the drive back to the hotel. When we got there, I went straight up to my room and got under the bedcovers, feeling completely and utterly miserable.

About twenty minutes later, the phone on my bedside table rang. I answered it. It was Johnny Sexton.

'Darce,' he said, 'what's going on?'

'What do you mean?' I asked.

'We're about to have dinner.'

'I, em, thought I might give the dinner a miss.'

And the breakfast, I thought. And the lunch. I don't want to be looked on as a Food Bill. I had an apple that Mum had put in my bag for me. That would be my dinner.

'Are you alright?' Johnny asked.

'I'm just a bit tired,' I told him. 'I think it might be jetlag.'

'Jetlag?' he said, then he laughed. 'The flight was less than an hour.'

'I know, but I'm still a bit worn out from it. I thought I might just have a nap.'

'Fair enough. Will we see you later on?'

'Later on?'

'We're having a night out – for team-bonding.'

'I don't know. I'll see how I feel when I wake up.'

I hung up the phone. I had absolutely no intention of going out. All I wanted to do was stay locked in my room until it was time to go back to the airport.

I opened my bag and started stuffing all of my clothes inside it.

My phone beeped. I picked it up. It was a text message from Aoife:

'Well, are you having a good time?'

I started to write a reply. I wrote: 'No, I'm utterly miserable here, Aoife. I was mad to think I could still make the tour. I should never have come.'

But then I deleted it and I sent her a message that said: 'Yeah, I'm having the time of my life! I love being a Lion!'

15 *A Very Special Guest*

I didn't come down for breakfast the following morning. I ate a packet of cheese and onion crisps that Mum had also put into the bag, then I headed for the Conference Suite, where Clive Woodward had told us that a very special guest would be coming to talk to us.

'Where were *you* last night?' Martin Johnson asked as he sat down beside me.

'Oh, I was, em, a bit tired, Johnno,' I told him.

'You missed a right good night – that right, Faz?'

Owen Farrell was sitting behind us.

'Yeah,' he said, 'it *were* a right good night. Met a few of the Irish, Scottish and Welsh lads who I'd not really spoken to before. I'm used to thinking of you lot as the enemy, Darce. Weird that we're all on the same side now.'

Adam Jones arrived then and sat down on the other side of me. His shaggy mane of hair was standing proudly on end.

'Good nait last nait, eh, boys?' he said in his Welsh accent.

'I were just saying, it *were* a great night,' said Faz.

Suddenly, I felt an even stronger sense that I didn't belong here, that I was an outsider. It was like joining a new school in the middle of term – I felt like everyone had already bonded in my absence.

'Who's gonna be speaken?' Adam asked as the chairs around us began to fill up. 'Anyone have any idea?'

Everyone shook their heads. Then Clive Woodward stepped onto the stage.

'Good morning,' he said. 'I trust you all had a good, restful evening and were tucked up in bed by ten o'clock.'

There were ironic cheers.

'Okay,' he said, 'the man I'm about to introduce you to is not just a Lion, but a winning Lion. He toured three times, playing against Australia, New Zealand and South Africa, and enjoyed two series wins. In 1997, he was a member of the team that beat South Africa. Not only that, but he scored the winning drop goal that secured the decisive second

Test. Gentlemen, please put your hands together for the great . . . Jeremy Guscott!'

Wow!

The place went absolutely wild as Guscott walked out onto the stage. The man was a living legend. I'd watched him kick that drop goal about a thousand times.

'Thank you,' he said, a big smile on his face. 'It's great to be here today to talk to you about what it means to be a Lion. I was very fortunate to have the career that I had. I won Five and Six Nations Championships. I won a European Cup. I played in three World Cups. But none of that comes anywhere close to the thrill I got playing for the British & Irish Lions.

'For me, it remains the ultimate honour in rugby – bigger than anything else. There's an old saying that what's rare is precious. The Lions only come together once every four years. Only fifteen players can start each Test. To look at the crest on that jersey, and to realize that you are considered the best player in your position in England, Ireland, Scotland and Wales, just fills you with pride.

'And to pull on that famous red jersey, and to think about all the legends of the game who've worn that number before you, will make you feel – honestly – ten feet tall!

'When you set off on a Lions tour, you know that you have an opportunity to make history – as we did when we beat South Africa in 1997.

'We were massive, massive outsiders. They were the world champions and no one really gave us a chance. In the first Test, in Cape Town, we pulled off a shock and beat them. Then we moved on to Durban for the second Test. And everyone said, South Africa won't get caught like that again.

'We braced ourselves for the backlash. And it came. We froze a bit, while they played like men possessed. They scored three tries and we didn't come close to scoring even one. But here was the thing. Their kicker had an absolute nightmare and he missed every single shot at goal, while we had Neil Jenkins –'

There was a loud cheer from all the Welshmen in the room.

'– one of the greatest kickers in the history of the game. And he didn't miss a kick. With two minutes to go, we were level at fifteen points each.'

I could feel the hairs stand up on the back of my neck because I had watched the moment so many times on Dad's Lions video. And here I was, listening to Jeremy Guscott himself describe it in detail.

'We crossed the South African twenty-two and we were attacking their line. And that was when I suddenly found myself in the wrong place at the right time! Gregor Townsend was our fly-half. If anyone was going to attempt a drop at goal, it was going to be him. But he had tried to barge his way over the South African line and he was missing from his position. So, for reasons that I can't explain, I slipped into the pocket.

'Matt Dawson had the ball and he looked for Gregor. And I was standing there instead. I could see it in his eyes. He was thinking, what the hell are you doing there? He threw the ball to me and I caught it. I didn't even think about it. I just kicked it. I struck it pretty well for someone who didn't usually kick drop goals.

'It flew through the air, end to end, and in that moment, something really strange happened. In the five seconds it took for the ball to clear the bar, my entire rugby life flashed before my eyes. I remembered playing as a toddler, as a child, as a teenager – as if my entire life was leading up to that moment when I kicked the goal that won the series.

'People often ask me what was it about that

particular Lions team that led us to upset the odds like we did. The answer is togetherness. And I think this might be the most important lesson that I can pass on to you.

'When you go away with a team – any team – it can be difficult. You get sick and tired of seeing the same ugly faces at breakfast every morning.'

We all laughed.

'Why's he looked at me when he said vat?' asked Johnno.

'As well as that,' Guscott continued, 'players who don't make the Test team can become bitter and resentful.'

Now I felt like he was looking at me.

'It's not a nice feeling,' he said, 'if someone is sniping at you behind your back, or maybe giving you a hard time in training, just because they think you took their place in the team.

'So we decided that wasn't going to happen to us. There was going to be no jealousy and bitterness. We agreed on a code of conduct. If you were in competition with another player for the same place and you lost, you went over and you shook his hand and wished him all the best.'

I looked around for Jonathan Davies. I caught his eye and we gave each other a smile and a nod.

'Playing for the Lions,' Guscott said, 'was the greatest moment of my career. It was like a dream for me. And it's a dream that's going to come true for some of you. Good luck. And thank you.'

The whole room burst into a round of spontaneous applause. If we didn't know before what a special honour it was to be a Lion, no one could be in any doubt now.

But it also reminded me of the incredible experience that I might miss out on. I looked down at my useless left arm, willing it to heal.

'Nath-en evah goes away,' I heard a voice say, 'until it teaches us what we need to know.'

128

It was Adam Jones.

'What?' I asked.

'I'm readen your plastah cast,' he said.

Nothing ever goes away until it teaches us what we need to know.

It was halfway down my forearm.

'Did *you* wrate that, Darce?' he asked.

'No,' I told him, 'it was my friend, Aoife.'

'Well,' he said, 'Aoife sounds like a verray, verray clevah girl to me. Don't give up hope, ked.'

16 *The New Gordon D'Arcy*

'Well?' Conor asked.

'Well what?' I wondered.

'*Well what?* You just spent two days hanging out with the Lions! How was it?'

It was our first day back at school after the Christmas holidays.

'It was fine,' I told him.

'Did you meet Martin Johnson?' Peter asked.

'I did,' I said, 'except everyone calls him Johnno.'

'What's he like?'

'He seems nice.'

'And what about Adam Jones?' Conor said. 'Is that his real hair? Because I've heard it's a wig.'

'No,' I assured him, 'it's definitely his real hair.'

'So what did you do?'

'We learned about teacupping.'

'What's that?' Peter asked.

'Oh,' I said, 'it's Thinking Calmly Under Pressure.'

'Interesting.'

'And then Jeremy Guscott came and talked to us about what it means to be a Lion.'

'Wow!' Conor exclaimed. 'That's like . . . WOW!'

'There was a training session as well. Although obviously I couldn't take part. I just watched.'

'That must have been hard,' Peter said.

'It was, em, fine,' I said, deciding not to tell him about the Food Bill comment I'd overheard. 'You heard about Jonathan Davies, I suppose?'

'He's just called him up as a standby,' Conor pointed out.

'I don't know, Conor. Even if the bones in my arm heal, I won't have the chance to play much rugby before Clive chooses his final fifty.'

I suddenly remembered something. Clongowes were playing Blackrock College in the first round of the Leinster Schools Senior Cup the following week.

'Hey,' I said, 'wasn't Mr Murray announcing the team today?'

Peter was about to say something, but he didn't get the chance, because Flash Barry suddenly stepped into the room.

'Hey, Darce!' he said. 'How's that arm of yours?'

but he didn't wait for my answer. 'I don't want to put pressure on you, but one or two people are still asking me about refunds.'

'Why would that put pressure on Gordon?' Conor asked.

'Hey, don't shoot the messenger, Dude!' Barry said. 'I'm just letting you know, Darce, that this news about Jonathan Davies has made people a little twitchy. A lot of them are going to start coming to us, looking for their money back.'

'*Us?*' I said. 'What do you mean by *us?*'

'Well, one or two people may have got the impression that you were involved in Flash Travel.'

'But I'm not! Flash Travel was your idea!'

'Hey, you shouldn't have allowed your photograph to be used on the poster. You know, you really should protect your image rights better than that, Darce. Did you learn nothing from me when I was your agent?'

'Yes,' I said, 'I learned never to trust you! I can't believe we gave you a second chance!'

'Gordon has nothing to do with Flash Travel!' Peter told him.

'Yeah, that's not *strictly* true?' Barry said. 'I made him a director of the company.'

'What?' I said. 'He can't do that without my permission, Peter — can he?'

'Look,' Barry said, 'hopefully your arm will get better and the refund issue will go away. By the way, guys, I believe congrats are in order!'

He was talking to Conor and Peter.

'Congrats?' I said. 'What for?'

'That's what I was about to tell you,' Peter explained sheepishly. 'Me and Conor are both in the team to play against Blackrock College.'

I felt my mouth twist into a smile. 'That's amazing news!' I said — and I meant it. 'I'm delighted for you!'

'Really?' Conor asked.

'Why wouldn't I be?'

'We didn't want to come across as too happy,' Peter explained, 'in case you thought we were rubbing your nose in it.'

'You *should* be happy!' I told them. 'You've both worked so hard for this! All those early mornings! All those ten-kilometre runs! You deserve it!'

'See?' Flash Barry cut in. 'That's Darce all over. His generosity knows no limits. I've been telling people that when they've asked about getting their money back.'

I decided to ignore Barry.

'So you're happy for us?' Conor said.

'Of course, I'm happy for you!' I insisted.

'What if I told you,' Peter added, 'that Mr Murray has asked me to wear the number twelve jersey?'

'You're playing in *my* old position?' I asked.

Peter nodded, then nervously pushed his glasses up on his nose.

'I'm, em, delighted for you!' I told him.

And I didn't know if he could hear the very, very slight note of reservation in my voice.

17 *Rock and a Hard Place*

There was a buzz about the school that day. There always was when the school team played. But this year the excitement was even more intense than usual. Clongowes versus Blackrock was one of the great rivalries in schools rugby and beating them was an obsession for us.

'How are you feeling?' I asked Peter, just before he climbed onto the coach.

'Nervous,' he told me.

'Nerves are good,' I reminded him. 'Nerves are your body's way of telling you to focus. Remember Jimmy O'Connor used to tell us that at Wexford Wanderers?'

He nodded. 'It's just that I've never played in Donnybrook before,' he said. 'I've never really played in front of a big crowd.'

'If you're listening to the crowd, then you're not concentrating on your job. Just focus on the next tackle, Peter, the next lineout, the next ruck, the next scrum.'

'Thanks, Gordon.'

Conor walked past us, spinning a rugby ball in his hands.

'Come on, Peter!' he said, without even looking at us. 'Let's show these Rock boys how we Wexford lads roll!'

We couldn't help but laugh.

'Nerves don't seem to be an issue with Conor,' I said.

Peter shook his head. 'I honestly don't think he's scared of anything,' he told me.

Conor was going to be playing alongside him at outside-centre.

'Just keep talking to each other,' I reminded him. 'With centres, it's all about communication.'

I watched Peter get on the bus. Then I heard a voice behind me say: 'Are you travelling with us, Gordon?'

I turned around. It was Mr Murray.

'Er, no,' I said, 'I thought I'd travel with the supporters.'

'Are you sure?' he asked. 'You *are* a member of the squad – injured or not.'

But I'd already thought about it. The players were all high on excitement. The last thing they needed was my miserable face and injured arm overshadowing their day.

'It'll be nice to cheer them on from the stands,' I said, 'with the rest of the school.'

I made my way to where the coaches for the supporters were parked and I got on board the first one. Everyone was singing songs and chanting the names of the first XV. No one seemed to notice me slip onto the bus and take my seat at the front.

I daydreamed the entire way to Donnybrook. When the bus eventually pulled up outside the stadium, I jumped off and joined the crowds of people making their way inside.

The Blackrock College supporters took up one entire side and both ends of the ground.

I took my place among our supporters and I joined in the chant:

'Clon! Gowes! Clon! Gowes! Clon! Gowes!'

But we struggled to make ourselves heard over the voices of the Blackrock crowd. There were thousands of them – and they were LOUD!

The game got under way. The first half was a very tight, cagey affair. Blackrock chose to kick the ball rather than run with it, which I took as a compliment to us – they were clearly not taking any risks.

We were catching the ball really well, then attacking off those kicks.

Conor and Peter were playing brilliantly, like two players who were totally in sync with each other. If one missed a tackle, the other made the tackle for him. Then they'd exchange a high-five and get back to work again.

It was great to watch. They were so different as players and as people. Peter was so serious and conscientious, whereas Conor did everything with a big smile on his face – they complemented each other perfectly.

It was 6–6 at half-time. Two penalties each – ours were converted by James McElwee, our full-back.

When the first half ended, I heard my name called and I spotted Aoife in the crowd, waving at me from about fifty metres away. I waved back. She gave me the two thumbs-up, as if to say, 'They're doing great!'

In the second half, Blackrock decided to throw caution to the wind – and it paid off for them immediately. They set off on a sweeping move downfield, full of fast hands and accurate passing. An offload in the five-metre channel put their winger away. He

crashed over to score a try in the corner and Blackrock went into an 11–6 lead.

Their number ten missed the conversion by a matter of inches. But everyone in the crowd expected Blackrock to ease further ahead. Even our supporters went quiet, bracing themselves for a blue-and-white onslaught.

But it never came. And that was mainly down to Conor and Peter. They played some of the best rugby I'd ever seen. Every time they had the ball in their hands, you could see the determination on their faces to make yards – and they did. Slowly, phase by phase, they started to inch their way closer and closer to the Blackrock twenty-two.

There were about five minutes left when Peter and Conor finally opened the opposition up with an amazing switch play. It was a move that Mr Murray got us to practise over and over again. Conor had the ball. Peter ran across his path. As he did so, Conor made a motion like he was tossing the ball into his hands. All of the Blackrock players followed Peter's line – but he didn't have the ball.

Conor had passed it to himself!

He ran for the line – his face smiling like a split orange – and deposited the ball under the posts.

'YEEEEEESSSSSS!!!!!!' I roared. 'WHAT A TRY!'

The Clongowes crowd went wild. And for the first time in the match, the Blackrock supporters were silenced.

James McElwee kicked the points. And then we knew it was a matter of defending stoutly to hold on to what we had.

Peter was unbelievable in those last few minutes. He threw himself into tackles and he ran to the point of exhaustion.

The game seemed to go on forever. The eighty minutes were up. But we had to face a further five minutes of agony while we waited for the ball to go dead.

It was ruck after ruck after ruck. Standing six feet tall, Bob Casey, the Blackrock second-row, was taller than most of our dads – and it took everything we had to stop him bashing his way through our defence. But our players always managed to get their tackles in fast, just as the opposition player was receiving the ball, so that he was off balance.

Then their number eight dropped the ball in his desperation to gain just a couple more inches and Peter swung his boot at it and kicked it into touch.

We had won! We had beaten Blackrock College!

I was so happy for the team, but especially my two friends, who had been the two best players on the pitch.

I had my two arms – the good one and the injured one – in the air and I was shouting, 'YEEESSS!!!'

And that's when I felt a hand on my shoulder. I turned around and it was one of the Sixth Year boys.

'Darce,' he said, 'I'm going to need my money back.'

'Look, Flash Travel has absolutely nothing to do with me,' I told him.

'So why is your face on the poster?'

'Because Barry used it without my permission.'

'Well, somebody's going to have to give me my fifty euros back – especially after what I heard earlier.'

'What do you mean? What did you hear?'

'Clive Woodward was on TV,' he said. 'He said he rated your chances of making the tour as one in five.'

In that moment, I suddenly came crashing to Earth again. I felt a sense of sadness that I could never put into words. And, thinking that no one was looking, I slipped out of the ground.

18 *A True Friend*

PAP!
PAP!
PAP!

'What in the name of God is that?' I wondered.

It was Saturday morning and I had the dorm to myself. Conor and Peter had gone home to Wexford for the weekend, while Flash Barry hadn't been seen for two days, ever since Clive Woodward rated my chances of making the Lions tour at one in five.

I was trying to enjoy a lie-in, but then the noise started again.

PAP!
PAP!
PAP!

It was as if someone was throwing pebbles up at the window.

Hold on – someone *was* throwing pebbles up at the window.

I threw back my duvet and made my way over to the window. I pulled back the curtain and looked down.

PAP!

It was Aoife.

She was dressed in her rugby gear and had a sack of rugby balls slung over her shoulder.

I opened the window.

'Nice pyjamas!' she said.

Fine, I was wearing Spiderman pyjamas – but only because my Leinster rugby ones were being washed.

'Why aren't you training?' she wanted to know.

I showed her my cast.

'What's the point, Aoife?' I asked.

'The point,' she said, 'is that you still have a chance of making the Lions squad!'

'One in five,' I reminded her. 'That's how Clive Woodward rates my chances.'

'Stop feeling sorry for yourself! And, by the way, I saw you leaving the match early!'

'What match?'

'Peter and Conor's match.'

Oh, no, I thought. I didn't think anyone had seen me.

'I stayed until the final whistle,' I told her.

'But you didn't stay for the lap of honour,' she insisted. 'It was Conor and Peter's big moment, Gordon! What were you, jealous?'

'No!'

'The world doesn't revolve around you, Gordon D'Arcy! Conor and Peter have always supported you. Every time you played for Ireland and every time you played for Leinster, they were there – and they were happy for you.'

'I *was* happy for *them*!'

'So why didn't you stay for the lap of honour?'

I didn't have an answer for her. And so, as we often do when we're confronted with truths about ourselves that we'd rather not know, I tried to shut the conversation down.

'I'm going back to bed!' I said, then I pulled the window closed.

'I really thought you were a better friend than that!' I heard her shout through the glass.

I got back into bed and I pulled the covers over my head. But I knew it was going to be impossible to sleep now. Why did I leave the ground before the lap of honour? Was I jealous? Had I really come to believe that the world revolved around me?

After fifteen minutes of torturing myself with these thoughts, I threw back the duvet and got out of bed again. I put on my rugby gear, then I made my way outside.

I could see Aoife, practising her kicking, attempting to put the ball between the posts from close to the sideline.

She didn't even look at me. I knew she was probably still mad at me, so I started running laps of the pitch. I did twenty altogether, while Aoife kept sending balls sailing through the sticks.

I started to get tired then and I stopped at the corner flag at the end that Aoife was kicking into. I was bent over, with my hands on my knees, trying to catch my breath, when I realized that she was standing beside me.

'Here,' she said, offering me a carton of milk. 'It's good for your bones.'

'Thanks,' I said, taking it from her.

There was silence between us.

'Maybe I *was* a bit jealous,' I admitted. 'I don't know what happened. I just suddenly felt –'

'What did you feel?' she asked.

'I felt sad,' I told her. 'Just really, really sad.'

'But it's okay to feel sad, Gordon. Sadness is just another part of life – like happiness. My mum says the important thing to remember is that it doesn't last forever.'

'But what if my arm never heals, Aoife? What if I never play rugby again?'

'You'll get over it. And you'll find other things in your life that will bring you happiness.'

She was the wisest person I knew, and I was so lucky to have her as a friend.

'Thanks,' I told her.

'Is there any room left on that cast of yours?' she asked.

I examined it carefully. There was a little bit of white space left on the inside of my arm, near to the elbow.

'There,' I said.

She had a marker in her hand. She bit off the top. And, with it clamped between her teeth, she wrote one final motivational message on my cast. It said:

'A true friend will say good things behind your back and hard things to your face.'

And then she said, 'Come on – are we training today or not?'

19 *Stepping Up to the Mark*

It was the day of the semi-final of the Leinster Schools Senior Cup. Clongowes were playing Gonzaga and Donnybrook Stadium was full to capacity.

I was sitting with Aoife in the stand, watching the teams warm up, when she suddenly let out an exclamation.

'Oh, no!' she said. 'He's tweaked something!'

My first instinct was to look for Conor and Peter. But they both seemed to be moving fine.

'Who?' I asked.

'Des Dillon,' she said.

Des was the captain of the school team. He played in the second-row and was a really inspirational leader.

'He was doing lineout practice,' Aoife said, 'and

148

he came down badly on his ankle. It looks like he's either broken it or sprained it.'

I watched him hobble about the place, but in the end he gave up and fell down onto his hands and knees. Mr Murray checked on him, a look of deep concern on his face. I watched Des shake his head, as if to say, no, he couldn't play.

A wave of shock and disappointment swept through the Clongowes supporters. We had lost one of our best and most experienced players – but also our captain.

'Who would you give the armband to?' I asked Aoife. 'Seeing as you're a captain yourself.'

'No contest,' she said. 'Peter.'

'Peter?' I said, surprised. 'He and Conor are the youngest players on the team.'

'Being a captain has nothing to do with age,' she said. 'It's about having the courage to lead.'

Des handed the armband to Mr Murray, before being helped off the pitch. Mr Murray looked around until his eyes fixed on Peter. He called him over. We watched them exchange a few words.

When Mr Murray held out the armband, Peter didn't hesitate. He took it from him and pulled it on, then he started clapping his hands together, barking instructions at the other players and making sure their heads didn't drop.

We had the best possible start to the match. Conor scored a brilliant opening try in the corner. Our forwards worked really hard in the scrum, gaining us some vital yards. Then, when the ball popped out, a double miss pass into the wide channel allowed Conor to get over the line.

Then, despite the horrible angle, James McElwee managed to convert it with his awesome left foot.

And while Gonzaga managed to pull the score back to 7–3 with a penalty, two more tries from Conor – one just before half-time and one just after the restart – both of them converted, put us into a commanding 21–3 lead.

Gonzaga came back at us, like we knew they would. They scored two tries in just three minutes. Suddenly, the score was 21–17 – and that was when Peter really proved his worth.

Some of the Clongowes players were beginning to lose their nerve. We watched him pat some players on the back, grab some by the two shoulders and shake them. I guessed he was reminding everyone of their defensive responsibilities.

Aoife turned to me. 'The match is going to be a test of Clongowes' physicality.'

She was right. Gonzaga played a game that was based on attacking narrowly and constantly trying to turn rucks into mauls. But, because Peter had prepared the Clongowes players for it, Gonzaga couldn't make any inroads against us.

The minutes were up. Brian O'Riordan, the Gonzaga second-row, made one last desperate attempt to break our resistance. He stood up from a ruck with the ball in his hands, calling his teammates in for the maul. But at that stage of the game, they were exhausted and they were too slow to reach him. Dara Kelly, the Clongowes flanker, pounced – he spun him around and held him up, managing to win us a scrum. And from that scrum, Conor kicked the ball into touch.

When the match was over, me and Aoife screamed Peter's name at the top of our lungs. But, being naturally short-sighted, he couldn't pick us out until Conor steered his head in our direction.

We waved at him and we shouted at him how proud of him we were. Aoife was right. Peter had proved himself to be a leader – and the most logical choice as captain. And now he would be leading Clongowes into the Leinster Schools Senior Cup final!

20 Cast Off

I was more nervous that I'd ever been in my life. I was sitting in the hospital waiting room, about to hear the results of my X-rays, and all I could think was: what if this is the end? The end of my dream of playing for the Lions? The end of my rugby career?

'It's going to be fine,' Dad said, but I could tell that he was just as worried as me.

'Of course, it will,' Mum added. 'You've had the Pope himself praying for you, Gordon!'

'Yeah, that's if he heard Auntie Maura shouting at him across the square,' Ian pointed out.

'Sure, you'd have to have a good set of ears on you if you wanted to be the Pope,' Mum said.

'And don't forget Mystic Martha!' Shona reminded us. 'She's an absolute miracle-worker!'

'She's an absolute something alright,' Dad said.

'Mum,' said Megan, 'if Gordon's arm isn't fixed, can I give him one of mine?'

We all laughed.

'I don't know what you think is so funny,' she said. 'They can transplant all sorts of things – even hearts.'

'That's very kind of you, Megan,' I told her, 'but it'd be too small for me, wouldn't it?'

'I suppose,' she said, sounding disappointed.

Bill Quinlan, the surgeon who operated on my arm, stuck his head into the waiting room then and asked us to step into his office. In his hand, I noticed, he had a large X-ray. I cocked my head to try to see it, but then I didn't really know what I was looking to see.

'In you come,' he said. 'Sit down, everyone. Well, that's quite an entourage you've brought with you, Gordon!'

I couldn't wait. I just blurted out the question.

'Is it fixed?' I asked. 'Will I play rugby again?'

He held up the X-ray of my skeleton arm. I couldn't BELIEVE what I was seeing. The bones were held together by screws and bits of metal. It looked like a robot arm. I braced myself for bad news. But I was about to get a surprise.

'I'm very, very pleased with the way the bones have knitted together again,' he said, smiling.

I looked at Dad. I could see the delight written all over his face.

'Does that mean –' I began to ask.

'It means your arm is better,' Bill said.

'And I can play rugby again?'

'Yes, you can.'

'Yeeesss!' I shouted, jumping up in the air – it was as if I'd scored the winning try for the Lions against South Africa.

'I should warn you that it will take a little bit of time before you regain your full strength.'

'Thanks so much,' I said, heading for the door.

In my mind, I was already back at school, throwing the ball around with Conor and Peter.

'Er, haven't you forgotten something?' the surgeon said.

I stopped and turned around. I couldn't think of anything.

'Are you going to carry on wearing the cast as a fashion accessory?' Ian said, and he laughed.

The cast! Of course! I couldn't believe I'd almost walked out of there still wearing it!

I went back and sat down again. The surgeon produced a small, hand-held, electric saw. I was staring at the plaster and all of the words of wisdom that Aoife had written on it.

'Can I bring it home with me,' I asked, 'after you cut it off?'

'Of course, you can,' he said. 'It looks like there's a lot of good advice on it. I'll be careful not to damage it.'

Sixty seconds later, the cast was off – and I was in shock at the sight of my arm!

'Eeew!' Shona couldn't stop herself from saying. 'That's disgusting!'

The skin was loose and floppy – like it was too big for my arm. It seemed to have shrivelled in size. I put it next to my right arm and it looked so thin by comparison.

'It's almost half the size!' I said. 'It looks like . . . someone else's arm!'

'It's so long since you've used it,' he explained. 'There was bound to be a degree of muscle wastage. I'll give you some exercises to do to build it up again.'

'Within a few weeks,' Ian told me, 'you'll be doing one-armed press-ups, Gordon!'

'I've never been able to do one-armed press-ups,' I reminded him.

He could do them. It was seriously, SERIOUSLY cool.

'Then you should set that as your goal,' Ian said.

'Maybe I will,' I told him.

I thanked the surgeon. I bent my elbow a few times. It felt so good to be free of the cast. But, as I looked at my wizened left forearm, I knew that I still had a LOT of work ahead of me if I was going to make the Lions tour.

21 *An Impossible Choice*

'How does it feel?' Peter asked.

'It's definitely getting stronger,' I told him, then I showed him the left one next to the right one. 'Look, they're nearly the same size again!'

It was two weeks later and, for the first time since the injury, I was back in full training with the school team. There was a real buzz about the session as well. It was the last one before the big match. Clongowes were playing St Michael's in the final of the Leinster Schools Senior Cup the next day.

I wasn't expecting to play.

Peter moved over to Ciaran Finane, our scrum-half, and I heard him say that he was going to need to produce quicker ball from the ruck against Michael's. It was great to see how much Peter had grown in the past six months. He'd gone from being

157

this shy, studious character to this confident and highly vocal leader. I was so proud of him.

Mr Murray blew his whistle. 'Okay, everyone,' he shouted, 'you trained well today. I'm sure I don't need to tell you that tomorrow is match day – so the only thing you should be doing tonight is resting, okay?'

Conor sidled up to me then with a big grin on his face.

'What?' I asked, already nervous.

'Have you tried it yet?' he wanted to know.

I had no idea what he was talking about.

'Tried what?' I wondered.

'The one-armed press-up,' he reminded me. 'You said two weeks ago that that was your training goal.'

'No,' I told him, 'I haven't.'

'Well,' he said, 'there's no time like the present, is there?' and then he started calling out like a carnival barker: 'Roll up, roll up, ladies and gentlemen, boys and girls! For you are about to bear witness to an EXTRAORDINARY feat of ENDURANCE, not to mention SUPERHUMAN strength!'

'Stop it!' I said, at the same time laughing.

'You are about to see something that you have NEVER witnessed before,' he continued to yell, 'and will likely NEVER witness again. Gordon

D'Arcy, a boy from Wexford Town, is about to attempt something that us mere mortals would consider IMPOSSIBLE! I'm talking about ... THE ONE-ARMED PRESS-UP!'

Everyone cheered as they formed a circle around me. I was still laughing, but then the chanting started:

'D'Ar! Cy! D'Ar! Cy! D'Ar! Cy! D'Ar! Cy!'

And I had no choice but to drop to the floor – to even louder cheers this time.

I propped myself on my left arm, twisting my body to the side to place all my weight on it. Then I put my right arm behind my back. I took a deep breath.

'D'Ar! Cy! D'Ar! Cy! D'Ar! Cy! D'Ar! Cy!'

I bent my elbow slightly and, in slow, jerky movements, started lowering myself to the floor. My whole body shook with the effort it took. I managed to touch my chest off the floor.

That was the easy bit. Well, let's just say, it was the *easier* bit. Now I had to push myself back up again.

'D'Ar! Cy! D'Ar! Cy! D'Ar! Cy! D'Ar! Cy!'

159

I could feel the strain in my wrist, the pressure in my elbow, as I pushed hard against the floor and tried to lift myself up again.

'D'Ar! Cy! D'Ar! Cy! D'Ar! Cy! D'Ar! Cy!'

I raised myself one inch, then two inches, then . . .
'DOH!!!' I shouted, as I fell flat on my face!
Everyone cheered anyway. Conor helped me up.
'Good effort, Gordon!' he said. 'Next time, right?'
'Yeah, next time,' I promised myself.

As we were making our way back to the dressing room, Mr Murray asked if he could have a quiet word with me. Then he said something that I definitely wasn't expecting to hear.

'I want you to play against St Michael's tomorrow.'

'Tomorrow?' I asked.

'The Leinster Schools Senior Cup final,' he reminded me – not that I needed reminding. 'I want you to start.'

'But I haven't played rugby for seven months.'

'I saw enough of you today to know that you're ready,' he explained.

Hold on a second, I thought.

'Mr Murray, what position do you want me to play?' I asked.

'Your usual position,' he said. 'Inside-centre.'

Oh, no, I thought.

'But what about Peter?' I asked. 'He captained the team against Gonzaga.'

'Well, you can captain them against St Michael's,' he said.

'I can't,' I told him. 'I just . . . can't.'

'Gordon,' he said, 'it's my job as coach to pick the best fifteen players. Peter still hasn't proven himself.'

'But he was amazing in the semi-final. He stepped

up when Des got injured. We wouldn't be in the final if it wasn't for him.'

'I agree. He was brilliant – but you're still our best option at number twelve. Look, there's no room in rugby for sentiment, Gordon. You must have learned that in your time playing for Ireland and for Leinster.'

'But he's my friend. I'm not sure I could do it to him.'

'Look, if it makes your decision any easier, I probably should tell you that Clive Woodward is going to be at the match.'

'What?'

'I spoke to him this morning. He said he was keen to have a look at you in action before he announced the final Lions squad. I told him I was planning to start you against Michael's. I know it puts you in a difficult position, Gordon.'

'An impossible position,' I told him.

'Look,' he said, 'have a think about it anyway.'

22 *How Do You Want to Be Remembered?*

It was the longest night of my life. I didn't get a wink of sleep. For hour after hour, I kept poring over the dilemma in my mind. If I didn't play, then Clive Woodward would have had a wasted journey – and he wouldn't get a chance to see me in action before he announced the final squad for the tour of South Africa. If I did play, it would mean denying Peter his moment of glory – and he had worked so hard for it.

What made it worse for me was that Peter had no idea that his place was under threat. He was awake for most of the night too, as was Conor. They were discussing possible match scenarios – what they would do if X happened or if Y happened.

'The two Michael's centres are known as Bish and

Bosh,' Peter said. 'One tackles you hard to stop you dead in your tracks, then the other one tackles you to knock you down and take the ball from you. We're going to come up with a plan to stop them doing that, Conor.'

But there was one eventuality that he hadn't considered – that he might be watching it from the bench.

'This is how I prepare for exams,' he said. 'But I have to admit I'm more nervous about this match than I've ever been before any exam. There's going to be ten thousand people there! All my family are coming to see me lead the team out, including all my aunts and uncles, my cousins, my grandparents, then all my mum and dad's neighbours as well. They've hired a bus.'

I threw back my duvet and jumped down from the top bunk.

'Where are you going?' Conor asked.

'I'm going to go for a walk,' I told him, quickly pulling on my clothes.

'It's four o'clock in the morning,' he pointed out.

'Yeah,' I said, 'I think a breath of fresh air might do me good.'

'Do you want us to come with you?' Peter asked.

'No, thanks, I just need to clear my head.'

I stepped outside into the night air. It was cold and I watched my breath turn to fog as it left my mouth. I walked out of the gates of Clongowes and crossed the road to St Brigid's, the boarding school for girls that stood opposite. I headed for the dormitory block. Bending down, I scooped up a handful of gravel, then I started to throw it, piece by piece, at one of the windows.

PAP!
PAP!
PAP!

Inside, I heard urgent whispers, then a light was switched on. I was worried then that it was one of the nuns, so I dived head-first into some shrubbery and waited.

A few seconds later, a window opened above me and I heard a voice whisper, 'Who is it?'

It didn't sound like an adult's voice, so I stuck my head out of the shrubbery and said in a loud whisper:

'I'm looking for Aoife Kehoe!'

'This isn't her room,' the girl said.

'Yeah, I know that,' I told her. 'Can you go and get her for me?'

'But she'll be asleep. It's four o'clock in the morning.'

'Yeah, I know what time it is. Can you go and wake her for me?'

'What's your name?'

'It's Gordon.'

'Gordon who?'

'She'll know who I am.'

'And will she know what it's in connection with?' she asked.

'What are you,' I hissed back, 'a receptionist? Just go and get her, will you?'

Five minutes later, Aoife appeared at the window, looking bleary-eyed, which wasn't surprising given that it was the middle of the night.

'Gordon?' she said. 'Gordon, where are you?'

'Down here,' I told her, 'in the shrubbery!'

She looked down.

'What in the name of God are you doing here?' she asked.

'I have a dilemma,' I explained.

'Gordon, you'll have more than a dilemma if the nuns catch you here.'

'Mr Murray has asked me to play against St Michael's tomorrow.'

'What?'

'At inside-centre.'

'But Peter's been playing at inside-centre.'

'Mr Murray wants to put him on the bench and play me there instead. And he wants me to captain the team as well.'

'Oh my God! Is Peter upset?'

'He doesn't know yet. I told Mr Murray that I'd sleep on it.'

'Peter's put in so much work, Gordon.'

'I know – he's dedicated his whole year to this.'

'What are you going to do?'

'I don't know. But there's another complication. Clive Woodward is coming over for the match. He says he wants to see me play before he decides whether to include me in his final squad.'

Aoife was quiet for a long moment.

'Okay, I've thought about it,' she eventually said. 'Your dilemma is this. If you don't play, you run the risk of losing your place in the Lions squad. If you do play, you run the risk of losing a friend.'

'I know that!' I told her.

'But, having said that, there's a chance that Peter would understand. Mr Murray has to pick the team that he thinks has the best chance of beating St Michael's.'

'Aoife, all of his family are coming up from Wexford to see him lead the team out. His mum and dad. His cousins. His aunts and uncles. His grandparents. It'll be humiliating for him.'

'Gordon, you have a difficult choice to make. But let me ask you this question – how do you want to be remembered? As a great rugby player, or as a great friend?'

And, in that moment, I knew what I was going to do.

23 *The Best Man for the Job*

'A twinge?' Mr Murray said.

He sounded dubious.

'Yeah,' I told him, 'I felt it just after I got up this morning.'

'Where?'

'In the breakfast room.'

'No, I mean where *is* this twinge?'

'Oh, all the way down my arm,' I said. 'It starts in my elbow and then it goes all the way down to my, em, fingers.'

'So you won't be able to start?'

'Unfortunately not, no.'

We were standing in the corridor outside the dressing room. I could suddenly hear the roar of a helicopter overheard. It sounded like it was about to land on the pitch.

'Clive Woodward will be disappointed,' he said. 'He's come all this way just to see you.'

'I can't help it,' I shrugged. 'Like I said, it's a twinge.'

I knew he didn't believe me, but he nodded like he understood.

'I better get in the dressing room,' he said, 'and name the team.'

He pushed the door and I followed him inside. The boys were sitting around, waiting nervously to find out whether they were in the starting fifteen. As he called out the names, he handed each player a jersey.

Peter was given the number twelve and the captain's armband. He seemed oddly unexcited and I wondered if he was worried about the match. I was given the number sixteen jersey, which meant I was going to be a substitute.

When we'd changed into our rugby gear and put on our boots, Mr Murray gave us his pre-match talk. He told us to remember how hard we'd worked and how much we'd sacrificed to get here today. I felt like such a fraud, sitting there. I hadn't done anything to earn even a place on the bench.

Mr Murray told us to remember the things we'd worked on in training and to look out for each other on the pitch.

Then it was time to play.

As we left the dressing room, Peter asked if he could have a word with me.

'Yeah, what's wrong?' I asked.

'I know,' he simply said.

'Know what?'

'I know that Mr Murray wanted you to play instead of me. I saw the team sheet in his hand as we were getting on the bus this morning. He had you in at number twelve – and as captain.'

He looked so downcast.

'It's true that he wanted me to play,' I said. 'I told him I had a twinge in my arm.'

'Why?' he asked. 'Because you felt sorry for me?'

'No, it was because you deserve this, Peter. You've worked hard for it. I wasn't going to come in and steal your moment of glory.'

'But you should be in the team. It's Mr Murray's job to pick his best fifteen players.'

'He HAS picked his best fifteen players. Look, I don't want to be just given a jersey based on what I did in the past. I want to earn it – and I know I haven't. You're playing the best rugby of your life. You're the best man for the job, Peter.'

He brightened up a bit at hearing that. 'Do you really think so?' he asked.

'You're a brilliant inside-centre,' I told him. 'And an amazing captain. We're lucky to have you.'

'Thanks, Gordon,' he said.

'Now, haven't you got a match to win?' I reminded him.

He turned and followed the rest of the players out onto the pitch. As I made my way out to the substitutes' bench, I spotted Clive Woodward walking down the touchline towards me, looking confused.

'Gordon?' he said.

'Er, hi, Clive,' I replied.

'Meeting with Gordon D'Arcy,' he said, 'seventeenth of March, fourteen hundred hours and twenty-three minutes. Present at meeting – Sir Clive Woodward, Head Coach of the British & Irish Lions, and Gordon D'Arcy, of Clongowes Wood College, Leinster and Ireland.'

'And Wexford Wanderers.'

'And Wexford Wanderers. Gordon, what's going on? Your coach said you're not starting today.'

'No,' I told him, 'I felt a twinge in my arm.'

'A twinge isn't good news.'

'That's what I thought – so I decided that I'd maybe sit this one out.'

'Well, that's a real pity, Gordon, because I'm

picking the final squad tomorrow and I wanted to see for myself how your arm was bearing up.'

I felt bad, but I still knew I'd done the right thing.

'Oh, well,' I shrugged.

'Anyway, I might as well stick around for the game. I'll see you around, Gordon. Conversation with Gordon D'Arcy terminated.'

He took his seat in the stand and I took mine on the bench. As the match started, I couldn't stop thinking about his final words to me: 'I'll see you around, Gordon.'

Was that goodbye? Had he made up his mind not to bring me to South Africa?

But then I had to shut out those feelings because the match had started.

We got off to the best possible start. David O'Driscoll, who had replaced Des in the second-row, won a lineout right on their 22-metre line and our forwards immediately formed themselves into a maul. The vital thing when it comes to a maul is that all of the players joining it come in at the right height – first two around the standing player's waist, the next two below his hips – and in this case they got it absolutely perfect!

The St Michael's players were caught cold as it rolled forward. They did their best to slow it down, but they couldn't stop it crossing the line and Darren Kelly, our number seven, grounded the ball for a try.

James kicked the conversation and then, five minutes later, a penalty, and we suddenly had a ten-point lead.

But St Michael's settled themselves and started to play their way back into the match. Peter and Conor were playing well, but they weren't getting a lot of time on the ball. Peter was right about Bish and Bosh, the two gigantic Michael's centres. I didn't know which was Bish and which was Bosh, but the very moment Peter or Conor touched the ball, they would subject them to their two-part tackle.

One would go, BISH!

And the other would go, BOSH!

It meant we struggled to get our passing game going.

Then we started to give away penalties with mistakes in the scrum, and Michael's started to eat into our lead. Their kicker, Andy Dunne, was on fire. It didn't look like he was going to miss with anything. It was 10–3, then it was 10–6, then, just before half-time, it was 10–9.

Back in the dressing room, Mr Murray told the

players not to panic. He told them to try to cut out the errors in the scrum. He said Bish and Bosh would eventually miss a tackle and it would take just one little moment of magic from Conor or Peter to open the opposition up.

The second half was a lot tighter than the first. With only one score between them, it was as if both teams realized what they had to lose by making a mistake, so they tensed up. Instead of trying to play rugby, both teams resorted to box-kicking the ball back and forth into each other's territory. Simon Keogh, the Michael's scrum-half, would kick it into our half, then Ciaran Finane would kick it straight back. It was like a game of ping-pong, with the forwards stuck in the middle, not sure whether they should run into a ruck or not.

But it was one of those box-kicks that resulted in disaster for us. Ten minutes from the end, the ball was dropping out of the sky and James had to sprint to get underneath it. But, as he did, he pulled his hamstring. His face twisted in pain as the ball fell between his outstretched hands, hit the ground and bounced into the hands of either Bish or Bosh, who scored under the posts.

The Michael's fans were delirious. The ground seemed to shake with the roars from them. Andy

Dunne's conversion put their team into a six-point lead. But that wasn't the only bad news for us.

James was in no fit state to continue, which was disastrous because he was our designated kicker. As he limped towards the sideline, clutching the back of his leg, Mr Murray turned to me.

'That arm of yours?' he said. 'Still twinging, is it?'

'It's, em, not bad at the moment,' I told him. 'It sort of comes and goes.'

'Do you think it'd stand up to you playing the last ten minutes at full-back?'

I didn't need to be asked twice. I stood up, unzipped my tracksuit top and ran onto the field. As I passed Peter, he said, 'Good luck, Gordon!'

I took up my position. But I spent most of the next ten minutes doing not very much. St Michael's were determined to hold onto the ball, playing ruck after ruck after ruck, trying to run down the clock. The only time they kicked the ball at all now was to put it into touch.

Time was running out when Bish – or it could equally have been Bosh – tore through our midfield after a blisteringly quick exchange of passes and suddenly there was only me between him and a certain try.

I watched him hurtling towards me like an

articulated lorry. I thought about my arm and what had happened against Wesley. But then I thought about Clive Woodward, watching from the stand. I knew this might be my only chance to make an impression on him.

So I ran at Bish – or Bosh – and I struck him low with my shoulder and wrapped my arms around his legs. Down we both went. I got quickly to my knees again and managed to tear the ball out of his hands. I jumped to my feet. A few metres to my left, I could see that Conor was wide open. I thought about the offload. But I could also see three Michael's defenders coming towards me, so I didn't have time to get the pass off. Instead, I stepped inside the first defender, then outside the second defender. The third defender tackled me around the waist. But, as I fell, I got the ball to Conor with a flick of my wrists.

Conor ran thirty metres with it, then played a long, arcing pass wide to Peter, who caught it and, almost in the same movement, chipped the ball ahead of him. He ran through the last Michael's player, caught the ball as it bounced up, beat one player, then another and crashed over the line for a try.

Our fans went wild. I ran to Peter and we hugged each other.

'Didn't I tell you that you were the best man for the job?' I said, laughing.

But our happiness soon gave way to the realization that we still needed the conversion to win it – and our regular kicker was no longer on the pitch.

This seemed to dawn on all of us at exactly the same time.

That and the fact that the angle for the kick couldn't have been any harder. Everyone was looking around, wondering who was going to take on the responsibility. And that was when I saw Conor bend down and pick up the ball.

He started whistling – LITERALLY whistling – as he walked to the spot from where the conversion was due to be taken, spinning the ball in his hands.

'Conor?' I said. 'Are you sure about this?'

I was trying to remember if I'd ever seen him take a kick at goal before.

'Yeah,' he said, 'how difficult could it be, right?'

Well, that was my question answered.

'Conor,' I tried to explain to him, 'kicking the ball is a specialist skill.'

'I know,' he said, 'but I've seen Aoife do it enough times to have picked up a few tips.'

He started looking around him then, as if he'd mislaid something.

'Here,' he said, 'what do you call those plastic things that you sit the ball into?'

'Do you mean a kicking tee?' I asked.

'That's the one!' he said. 'I'm probably going to need one of those, aren't I?'

One of the other substitutes ran onto the pitch with the tee and handed it to him. Conor put it down on the ground and sat the ball into it – lying flat.

The Michael's players were looking at each other like they couldn't believe it.

'Wrong way!' Peter told him. 'It's supposed to

stand upright with the valve pointing towards the target.'

'Oh, that's right!' Conor said. 'It's all coming back to me now.'

Then he reset it.

'Is he joking?' I asked Peter. 'Please tell me this is one of his practical jokes and he's going to nail the kick.'

There was complete silence in the crowd. All I could hear was the sound of Conor whistling his happy tune.

'Conor,' I said, 'the Leinster Schools Senior Cup is riding on this. Maybe you should let someone else take it.'

'Yeah,' he replied, 'as if I'm going to take advice from someone who put the Liam MacCarthy Cup on a bus to France!' and he gave me a big, cheeky wink.

Peter pulled me away from him.

'Gordon,' he said, 'look around you. He's the one player out of all of us who has the nerve to take it. We always say it – he's not frightened of anything.'

Peter turned and called out to Conor, 'If you want to take it, then take it.'

I watched as he took four steps backwards, counting them out as he did so:

'One, two, three, four . . .'

And then he took three steps to the side:

'One, two, three . . .'

And then I heard a voice call from the crowd. It was Aoife.

'Kick THROUGH the ball, Conor!' she shouted at him. 'And make sure you finish with your toes pointing in the direction of the target!'

'Toes in the direction of the target!' he repeated without looking around. 'Righty-ho!'

By now, the Michael's players were looking at him like they thought he'd lost his mind.

'Okay,' he said under his breath, 'here goes nothing!'

Here goes nothing?

He ran at the ball and swung his foot at it. It took off like a rocket ship. Open-mouthed, we watched it trace a high arc through the air and then it started to come down again.

And the roars of the Clongowes supporters behind the goal told us that . . .

It was going between the posts!

The stadium erupted. Conor turned to me and Peter with an enormous smile on his face. He shrugged.

'I'll get better at that!' he said.

Conor was knocked to the ground in the celebrations and we all dived on top of him.

We had won! We had won the Leinster Schools Senior Cup!

Eventually, as I dragged myself out from under the pile of human rubble, I spotted Clive Woodward in the crowd. He was clapping. I caught his eye and I waited for some signal, an indication of what he was thinking. But I couldn't read anything from his expression.

Then he turned around and walked away in the direction of his helicopter.

Soon, it was time for the trophy presentation. The tradition said that the mother of the winning captain got to present the trophy to her son. I'd never seen Peter's mum look so proud of him. And she was proud of him all the time. But this was special.

First, the Michael's players walked up the steps to collect their runners-up medals. Then we went up to collect our winners' medals. Peter was the last in line because he was going to be presented with the famous trophy.

His mum handed it to him and kissed him on the cheek. We all cheered. Before he lifted it, he said he wanted to say a few words. He wanted to thank Michael's for giving us such a tough match – he said the victory mattered all the more for the fact that we'd had to fight for it against a great team who would have made worthy champions themselves. Standing around on the pitch, the Michael's players applauded this.

Then he thanked Mr Murray for having faith in him to lead the team. Then he thanked his teammates and his three best friends in the world. One of them, Aoife, wasn't in the team. Two of them, me and Conor, were.

'Just lift the thing,' Conor roared at him, 'before it starts getting dark!'

We all laughed. Then Peter grabbed the cup by its base, extended his two arms and thrust it up into the air.

I was so proud of him. I was so proud of us. It felt amazing.

24 *The Day of Reckoning*

There was a special assembly in school the following day, where the members of the victorious Clongowes team carried the famous silver cup onto the stage for the rest of the school to see it.

The roars almost lifted the roof clean off the Assembly Hall!

I stood at the back. Having played only ten minutes of the entire Cup run, I didn't deserve any of this adulation. No, the moment belonged to the two boys the Principal, Mr Cuffe, described as, 'Our two centres of excellence – Captain Peter Rackard and Conor Kehoe!'

My two friends took one side of the cup each and they lifted it above their heads. And the roar went:
   'YYYYYYEEEEEESSSSSS!!!!!!'

Mr Cuffe read out the names of every player individually then and each got a cheer. Mine was one of the last to be announced – and that's how it should have been.

My mind had already started to wander. Clive Woodward was announcing the final Lions squad that morning and my stomach was sick from the tension.

'And now,' Mr Cuffe said, 'back to class with the lot of you!'

There were groans throughout the hall.

'I'm only joking,' he added. 'You can all have the rest of the day off!'

That was more like it!

As we shuffled off the stage, I noticed Mr Murray in the wings waiting for me.

'It's today, isn't it?' he asked. 'Clive Woodward is announcing the final squad for South Africa?'

'Yeah,' I said, 'this morning, Mr Murray.'

'So, how do you feel?'

'Worried.'

He smiled and nodded. 'He didn't get to see very much of you,' he pointed out.

'I only touched the ball once,' I agreed.

'Well, it *was* an important touch.'

'Even so, I'm sure he didn't fly his helicopter all the way to Dublin just to see me make a tackle and then a two-metre pass.'

'It isn't always what you do with the ball that defines a great rugby player, Gordon. You can play the game of your life without ever getting your hands on it.'

There was a moment's pause.

'You know,' he said, 'what you did, Gordon, was a very noble thing.'

'Really?' I asked. 'I thought you were annoyed with me.'

'How could I be annoyed? We won the Cup. And you were right. Peter was outstanding.'

'I just felt like I didn't earn the right to play.'

'The great Willie John McBride used to say that being a Lion was about more than rugby – it was about solidarity, friendship and showing belief in your teammates. What you did in giving your place to Peter took selflessness, courage and, I think, real character. I hope Clive Woodward recognizes that those are the qualities that make a great Lion.'

Conor and Peter were waiting for me outside the Assembly Hall.

'So where are we watching it?' Peter asked.

'Watching what?' I wondered.

'The Lions squad announcement,' he said. 'It's happening this morning, isn't it?'

'Here, I've got a great idea,' said Conor. 'Let's go to the gym and watch it on the TV there. The rugby season is over for me and Peter, but you've got to stay in shape, Gordon.'

'I don't think Clive Woodward is going to pick me,' I said.

'Stop being defeatist!' Peter told me. 'Come on, the gym it is!'

Twenty minutes later, I was sitting on the rowing machine, pulling the oars while watching Sky Sports News on the giant TV screen on the wall.

'*Coming up in the next few minutes,*' the newsreader said, '*we're going to be bringing you the announcement of the fifty-man squad that Lions coach Sir Clive Woodward has selected to tour South Africa this summer . . .*'

I stopped rowing and I gulped. It was at that exact moment that Flash Barry walked into the gym.

'Knock, knock!' he said.

It had been two weeks since any of us had seen him. But he carried on as if nothing had ever happened.

'Where have you been?' I asked. 'Why haven't you been in school?'

'Hey, I'm a busy man, Darce!' he said. 'I've been

putting together this tour to South Africa. Lot of logistics involved – know what I'm saying?'

'You mean you've been hiding from people looking for their deposits back!' Peter said.

'Not so,' said Barry. 'Although, on that point, what's the inside track, Gordon – do you think you made the fifty?'

'I've no idea,' I said.

Then suddenly the words 'BREAKING NEWS!' flashed across the screen and, in a voice filled with excitement, the newsreader said: '*Now, we can bring you – live AND exclusive – the announcement of the Lions squad that will tour South Africa this summer. Sir Clive Woodward has named the fifty players he will take with him and here they are . . .*'

A list of names flashed up on the screen. I looked for mine. I couldn't see it.

'I'm not there!' I said. 'I'm not there!'

'They're the forwards,' Peter pointed out.

He was right. I read the names. Paul O'Connell was there. And Martin Johnson. He was going to be the captain, it said. And Lawrence Dallaglio. And Adam Jones.

The page changed. At the top, it said, 'BACKS' and I quickly scanned it, waiting for my name to jump out at me.

It didn't – but the words 'Jonathan Davies' did!

'Gordon,' Conor said in a sombre voice, 'I'm so sorry.'

My heart sank through the floor. Even though I hadn't expected to make the squad, I realized in that moment how hard I'd been hoping. And now the dream was over.

'Alriiiiighty!' Barry said. 'I'm out of here, Dudes!'

'Where are you going?' Conor asked.

'I've been thinking about changing schools for a while,' he said, at the same time switching off his mobile phone. 'If anyone comes to the room looking for me, can you guys tell them that Flash Travel has gone into voluntary liquidation?'

He gave us the guns one final time and said, 'Later, Dudes!'

Then he pulled the hood of his hoodie over his head, opened the emergency fire door, looked out to make sure the coast was clear and ran off.

I stood up from the rowing machine and headed for the door.

'Gordon!' Peter called after me. 'Gordon!'

But I wasn't in the mood to talk. I could feel the tears running down my face. I walked through the lobby of the school. It was full of happy faces and excited voices. Everyone was still buzzing about the school's victory in the Leinster Schools Senior Cup final.

I just wanted to be alone with my disappointment.

Then I heard the urgent sound of footsteps behind me. It was someone running. I turned around. It was Conor and Peter. They were smiling and out of breath.

'There was another page!' Conor said.

'What?' I asked.

'That's why I called you back!' Peter told me. 'I only counted forty-eight names!'

'There was another page,' Conor said, 'with two more names on it.'

'And?' I said. 'Please, you've got to tell me.'

And that was when I heard Mr Murray's voice across the lobby.

'Congratulations, Gordon!' he shouted. 'You made the final Lions squad!'

25 *Special Delivery*

Twenty minutes later, I walked into my dorm, along with Conor and Peter, to be greeted by a huge surprise.

There was giant, red bag in the middle of the floor. It was as long as a canoe. It had my initials – GD'A – embroidered in gold thread on the outside.

'It's from Clive Woodward!' Conor said.

We all looked around the room.

'How does he do that?' I asked.

I unzipped it. Then, with great difficulty, I managed to roll it onto its side and its contents spilled out onto the floor.

'WHOA!!!' we all said.

All the gear I would need for the next month in South Africa was there. There were training jerseys, shorts and socks for every single day – the date on which each was to be worn was printed on the outside of the bag. There were Lions tracksuits and t-shirts and water bottles. There were cufflinks and key rings and badges and stationery, all bearing the Lions crest. There were Lions toothbrushes and Lions toothpaste. There was a red Lions dressing-gown and red Lions slippers, which also had my initials embroidered on them.

There were three suits – one black, one navy and one grey – and they all had the Lions crest on the breast pocket. I tried on the navy jacket and it fitted me perfectly, which was strange because no one had taken my measurements or even asked me for them. Somehow, they just knew!

There was a Lions alarm clock, and Lions earphones, and Lions pyjamas, and a Lions iPod, and a Lions sleep mask, and – yes – even Lions underpants, a new pair for every day I was on the tour!

'Is that what I think it is?' asked Conor, pointing at a box.

I opened it. Inside was a brand-new laptop, which was red in colour, with the Lions crest on the cover.

'Wow!' Conor said. 'That's the coolest laptop I've ever seen!'

In another box, there was a smartphone, which was also red.

'They're collector's items,' Peter said. 'It's probably probably only the fifty players and the backroom team who have them.'

'I wonder is the phone like the Batphone,' Conor said, 'and only Clive Woodward can you ring you on it?'

I laughed as I switched it on.

'Whoa,' I said, scrolling down through the contacts. 'The numbers of all the other players are in here!'

'Come on,' Conor said, hurrying me along, 'open some of these other boxes!'

I pulled the lid off another box. Inside were two pairs of boots and two pairs of runners. I kicked off my shoes and I pulled on a pair of boots. They were so comfortable. They were like slippers.

'What's *that* thing?' Conor asked, pointing to something on the floor. It looked like some kind of face mask. It was similar to the *Star Wars* voice-changer toy that Shona bought me for Christmas a few years ago.

'I don't know what it is,' I said.

It had straps on it. I used them to attach the thing to my face.

'It's an altitude training mask,' Peter said.

'What does it do?' I asked.

I was disappointed to discover that it didn't have a voice-changer function to allow me to talk like Darth Vader – it merely muffled my speech.

'It re-creates the effects of trying to breathe at high altitude,' Peter said.

'Okay,' I told him, 'you might need to explain that to me.'

'Well, South Africa is a very high country. Parts of Johannesburg, for instance, are more than six thousand feet above sea level.'

'And how is that going to affect me?'

'Because the higher up you go, the thinner the air is. That's why mountain climbers often bring oxygen with them. At high altitudes, it becomes harder and harder to breathe, especially if you're running around.'

'So what exactly does this mask do?'

'It limits the amount of air that you can take in, thus mimicking the effects of training and playing at altitude. The idea is to get your body used to it before you arrive in South Africa."

I was suddenly feeling a bit light-headed, like I might be about to faint. I pulled off the mask.

'I could barely breathe in that thing,' I said.

'That's what it's going to be like when you're playing in South Africa,' Peter said.

'There's a letter,' Conor said then, pointing to an envelope with my name on the outside.

I tore it open, took out the letter and read it aloud. It said:

Dear Gordon,

Congratulations on your selection for the Lions squad. I am delighted that you are on board and we are very excited that you are going to be touring South Africa with us this summer. I hope it will be both an enjoyable and successful trip for us all.

Find herewith some items you will need during your month with us in South Africa.

You are now part of an extraordinary tradition. When you become a Lion, you stand on the shoulders of all those great players who have been Lions before you and will be Lions after you.

Remember, it's not just about being called a Lion. It's about being a Lion. Courage, pride and tenacity – those are our values.

I'm looking forward to working with you. I'll be in touch soon.

Regards,
Sir Clive Woodward

Dear Gordon,

Congratulations on your selection for the Lions squad. I am delighted that you are onboard and we are very excited that you are going to be touring South Africa with us this summer. I hope it will be both an enjoyable and successful trip for us all.

Find herewith some items you will need during your month with us in South Africa.

You are now part of an extraordinary tradition. When you become a Lion, you stand on the shoulders of all those great players who have been Lions before you and will be Lions after you.

Remember, it's not just about being called a Lion. It's about being a Lion. Courage, pride and tenacity – those are our values.

I'm looking forward to working with you. I'll be in touch soon.

Regards, CW (SIR)
Sir Clive Woodward

By the time I'd finished reading the letter, I was in floods of tears. I couldn't even speak.

'We're so proud of you,' Conor said, slapping me on the back. 'I only wish we could be in South Africa to cheer you on.'

It was at that exact moment that Flash Barry reappeared.

'Knock, knock!' he said, sticking his head around the door.

'What are you doing back?' Conor asked. 'I thought you said you were going to a different school?'

'A different school?' Barry repeated. 'I don't know where you got that impression!'

'You said it!' Conor reminded him. 'You took money from all those people and when you thought Gordon wasn't going to make the Lions squad, you decided to run away and leave him to deal with your mess.'

'I'm hurt,' he said, 'that you think I would do such a thing.'

'It's what you *did* do,' Peter pointed out.

'Look, guys – all's well that ends well, right? Gordon's in the squad. Which means the Flash Travel tour of South Africa can go ahead!'

'Barry,' Conor said, 'we don't want anything to do with you.'

'Don't be like that, Dude. We're friends.'

'We're not friends. As a matter of fact, I don't know about Gordon and Peter, but I don't want to share a dorm with you any more.'

'Okay, look,' Barry said, raising his hands in a defensive gesture, 'maybe I did have a bit of a wobble when it looked like Gordon wasn't going to make the squad. Let me make it up to you guys.'

'How?' Peter asked.

'How would you like to come to South Africa?'

'I'm not giving you two hundred and fifty euros,' Conor snapped.

'You don't have to give me two hundred and fifty euros,' Barry assured him. 'You don't have to give me anything. I'll take you and Peter to South Africa as special guests of Flash Travel.'

Conor and Peter looked at each other, their mouths wide with shock.

'Really?' they said at the same time.

'Really!' said Barry.

'What about Aoife?' I asked.

'Hey, I'm not made of money, you know,' he said. 'Okay, fine – she can come too.'

Conor punched the air. Peter looked pleased, if still a little doubtful.

'There better not be a catch,' he said.

'There's no catch,' Barry insisted. 'The whole thing is above board, guys! Trust me!'

26 Raw

'Gordon,' Mum said, 'will you please take that ridiculous mask off at the breakfast table?'

'It's not a ridiculous mask,' I pointed out. 'It's an altitude training mask. It's to help me adjust to the thinner air we're going to be breathing in South Africa.'

'Well, you're not in South Africa now,' she reminded me. 'You're in Wexford. And it's bad enough that you've been running around the town in it for the past two weeks. Poor Mrs Buttle dropped her shopping when she saw you coming down Summerhill Road. And poor Mr Mordaunt thought there'd been an alien invasion – he phoned the Guards in Clonroche.'

Dad lowered his newspaper and looked at me over the top of his glasses. 'They threatened to arrest him,' he chuckled, 'for making a prank phone call!'

'Okay, let's get some breakfast inside you,' Mum said. 'You've got a long day ahead of you, Gordon.'

The morning had finally arrived – a morning I thought would never come. After weeks and weeks of waiting, I was finally going to South Africa with the Lions.

'What are you going to have?' Mum asked. 'Do you want a bowl of Choco Choco Choco Puffs? You used to love Choco Choco Choco Puffs.'

'No,' I said, taking off my mask, 'I think I'll have eggs this morning.'

'You have eggs every morning.'

'They're very good for you – that's according to Clive.'

'Everything that comes out of your mouth these days is according to Clive,' she said. 'How do you want them?'

'Give Clive a ring on your red phone there,' Dad said. 'Ask him if you should have them boiled or scrambled.'

'Raw,' I said.

'What?' Mum asked.

'Raw,' I repeated.

'Now don't you start growling like a Lion in this house,' she said. 'You can save that for when you meet your pals.'

'No, I'm not saying "roar". I'm saying "raw" – as in, that's how I want my eggs.'

'You can't eat raw eggs,' Dad said. 'Have you lost your mind, son?'

'That's how Clive eats them,' I told him. 'He cracks them into a cup and he drinks them down.'

Mum and Dad stared at each other for about ten seconds, then Dad put down his newspaper, jumped up from the table and ran to the door of the kitchen.

'Ian!' he shouted up the stairs. 'Shona! Megan! Come down here! Gordon's about to eat raw eggs for breakfast!'

Suddenly, I heard the sound of my brother and sisters charging down the stairs like a herd of elephants. They burst into the kitchen, their faces filled with excitement, like they were expecting a show.

'I don't see what the big deal is,' I said.

But then I started to have second thoughts as I watched Mum crack one on the edge of the sink and tip the gooey contents into a cup.

'How many do you want?' she asked.

'He won't even be able to eat one!' Ian said. 'He'll puke – you watch.'

'Six,' I heard myself say.

What was wrong with me this morning?

'Six?' Mum said incredulously, then she cracked five more eggs into the cup.

She placed it in front of me then. The cup was full to the brim with a clear, oily liquid, with six perfectly round, bright yellow yolks swimming in it. It looked almost as disgusting as it smelled.

'I knew he wouldn't drink it!' Ian said. 'I knew he'd bottle it at the last minute!'

And, as everyone who's ever been called a chicken by their older brother knows, I had no choice now but to go ahead and drink those eggs down.

I put the cup to my mouth. The liquid felt thick and sticky on my lips. For a second, I thought I was going to gag. Then I decided that it was probably best that I didn't taste it. So I pinched my nose and lowered the contents of the cup into my mouth.

The eggs went down slowly. It was like drinking oil. I didn't bother biting the yolks. I swallowed them whole – and it felt like I was swallowing tennis balls.

When I'd emptied the cup, I wiped my mouth with the back of my hand. Ian, Shona and Megan were staring at me in absolute horror.

'I can't believe he did it!' Megan gasped.

I just shrugged. 'Not a big deal, little sis.'

'He's going to be sick,' Ian predicted.

'This is what top rugby players do,' I told him. 'You might almost say it's how we roll.'

Ian was right, though. I felt very, very sick. But I tried to put a brave face on it.

'Car should be here any minute,' I said, looking up at the clock.

'What's the itinerary?' Shona asked.

'I'm meeting Brian O'Driscoll, Paul O'Connell, Johnny Sexton and Seán O'Brien at Dublin Airport,' I said. 'We fly to London at thirteen hundred hours –'

'Thirteen hundred hours?'

'Oh, that's one o'clock in the afternoon. Then we meet up with the English, Scottish and Welsh players at Heathrow Airport for the flight to Cape

Town at seventeen hundred ... I mean, at five o'clock.'

'And how long is the flight?'

'Fourteen hours.'

'Fourteen hours?' Megan said. 'That's ages!'

Now that I said it, it did seem like a very long time. I'd never been in a plane for more than two hours before. I suddenly got sad then at the thought of being so far away from my family for so long.

'I wish you could all come with me,' I said.

And then, out of the corner of my eye, I saw Mum and Dad exchange a smile. As a matter of fact, they were all smiling.

'Will we tell him?' Dad asked.

'Tell me what?' I wondered. 'What's going on?'

'We're going to South Africa!' Mum said. 'To see you play for the Lions!'

'What?' I said, excited now. 'All of you?'

'All of us,' Mum confirmed. She opened a drawer. 'We booked it last week.'

She put a brochure down on the table in front of me. I read the name of the tour operator and my heart instantly sank.

'Flash Travel?' I said. 'You're going to South Africa with Flash Travel?'

'Yeah, a nice young man rang,' Dad said. 'He said he was a friend of yours, Gordon.'

'It's Flash Barry! He used to be my agent! He was the one who told me to stop training so hard and embrace the celebrity lifestyle!'

'Well, it seems he's a travel agent now,' Dad said. 'How can he do it so cheaply? That's what I keep wondering. Five hundred euros each for the whole trip!'

'Five hundred euros?' I said. 'It was two hundred and fifty a few weeks ago!'

I suddenly realized his game. He was charging them double to cover the cost of bringing Conor, Peter and Aoife.

'Dad,' I said, 'you're being ripped off!'

'Ripped off?' he said. 'Gordon, other tour operators are charging five times that amount! Look at the hotel we're staying in!'

'It's a five-star luxury suite!' Megan said.

It did look impressive alright. I read through all the features it contained. Four bedrooms. A kitchen, living room and dining room. Eighty-inch LCD televisions with surround-sound in every room. Super-king-sized double beds. Jacuzzi bath. Balcony.

Then, underneath, I spotted some tiny writing – so

tiny, in fact, that it was almost invisible to the human eye.

'What's that?' I asked.

'I don't see anything,' said Dad.

'There's some writing there, look.'

'That's not writing. Those are just toast crumbs.'

'Megan,' I said, 'go and get me your microscope, will you?'

Megan had got a microscope for her birthday. She went and fetched it for me. I put the brochure underneath it and I looked through the lens. And suddenly I could read what the small print said:

Actual hotel may look nothing like this whatsoever.

Mum and Dad didn't seem the slightest bit concerned when I read it out to them.

'They have to say that,' Mum said, 'just in case the first choice of hotel isn't available. Don't worry about us, Gordon. We'll be fine.'

I suddenly felt my stomach lurch. It was the eggs. They weren't going down without a fight.

'I think Gordon's going to puke,' Shona said.

'I'm not going to puke,' I insisted. 'Don't be ridiculous.'

I heard the sound of a car horn tooting outside.

'That'll be my lift to the airport,' I said.

I hugged Mum and Dad goodbye, then I hugged

Ian, Megan and Shona and told them I'd see them in a few days. Ian and Dad picked up my bags and they all escorted me outside, where a big surprise was waiting for me.

The car that was going to bring me to the airport was a red stretch-limo, with the Lions crest on the side of it.

But that wasn't the big surprise.

The big surprise was that the whole neighbourhood had come out to wave me off. They were holding banners that said 'Good Luck, Gordon!' and 'Wexford is Proud of its Lion!'

They gave me a big cheer as I stepped from the house. I was really overcome. Then I spotted Conor, Peter and Aoife in the crowd. I walked over to them.

'Thanks so much for coming,' I told them. 'What an amazing send-off.'

'Are you okay?' Aoife asked. 'Your face is green.'

'Just, em, something I ate,' I told her. 'It's not sitting right.'

I hugged them all goodbye.

'We'll see you before the first Test,' Conor said. 'That's provided Flash Barry keeps his promise.'

I climbed into the back of the limo. The seats were made of red leather. Dad and Ian put my bags in the back with me, then closed the door and waved me off. The driver looked at me over his shoulder.

'Dublin Airport,' he said. 'The first step of your journey to South Africa.'

'Could you do me a small favour?' I asked.

'Yes, of course.'

'As soon as we get around the corner, could you pull over and let me out? I'm think I'm going to be violently sick.'

27 Welcome to Africa

We took off for Cape Town in an enormous jumbo jet that was – like everything else connected to the Lions – red in colour.

The atmosphere on the flight was quiet. Clive took a step backwards and let the players get to know each other. But there wasn't a lot of mixing going on. For the first few hours, everyone stuck with the players they knew, which meant the Irish players, the English players, the Welsh players and the Scottish players all stayed in their own groups.

I was watching *Captain America* on my little screen while also watching the other players. I noticed that the Welsh players seemed super-friendly. They were all full of energy and enthusiasm and seemed to be constantly smiling.

The English players seemed super-serious by

comparison. They were a bit more stand-offish. They were all big, muscly men who looked like they spent a lot of time in the gym lifting weights.

The Scottish players seemed tough and rugged. A lot of them had big, wild beards and their accents made it sound like they were talking in a language that wasn't English.

The hours dragged by. As night fell, I decided to have a nap. I put on my eye mask, pulled my blanket around me and fell asleep. About twenty minutes later, I got the smell of food in my nostrils. The cabin crew were serving dinner. A moment later, I felt a tap on my arm. I pulled up my mask. A stewardess was smiling at me.

'We're serving dinner,' she said.

I told her I wasn't hungry. My stomach was still upset from the raw eggs.

'We do have some delicious chicken nuggets,' she said, 'for our younger passengers.'

'Younger passengers?' I replied, more than a little offended. I knew I was the youngest player in the squad by a distance, but I wasn't six years old! 'No thank you,' I told her – even though I loved chicken nuggets!

I nodded off again. I don't know how long I was asleep for this time, but the dinner things had been cleared away when I felt another tap on my arm. I pulled up my mask. It was a different stewardess this time.

'Would you like to visit the cockpit?' she asked.

'The cockpit?' I said, a bit cranky at having been disturbed from my sleep again. 'Why would I want to visit the cockpit?'

'Well,' she said, 'some children like to visit the cockpit to see how the plane is flown.'

'I'm not a child!' I told her. 'I'm on the Lions rugby team!'

'Oh,' she said, 'I'm terribly sorry.'

I pulled down my mask and went back to sleep again. Ten minutes later, I felt another tap on my arm. I pulled up my mask and there was yet another stewardess smiling at me. She put something down on the table in front of me. When I looked, I saw that it was a colouring book and a set of crayons.

'I'm sorry,' I said, very agitated now, 'do I really look that young to you?'

Suddenly, I heard a loud explosion of laughter behind me. The English, Welsh, Scottish and, yes, even Irish players were all in stitches. They'd put them up to it!

I couldn't help but laugh myself. They had well and truly pranked me!

Near the end of the flight, Clive Woodward made his way to the front of the plane. I noticed he had a large roll of paper in his hand, which looked like a map.

'Gentlemen,' he said, 'can I have your attention, please?'

We all looked up at him as he unrolled the map. It was another one of his tactical plays.

'It's a minute before half-time,' he said, 'and South Africa are leading 9–0. We've been awarded a penalty just inside their half. Owen Farrell, what are you going to do?'

'You're askin' me?' Faz said.

'Four . . .'

'What would I do?'

'Three . . .'

'Er . . .'

'Two . . .'

'I'd kick for t'goal – take t'three points.'

'Why?'

'Because it's better to go in at 'alf-time with summat on t'scoreboard. We come out for t'second half and it's a one-score game.'

'Correct answer,' said Clive, smiling his lopsided smile. 'What was Owen doing there, everyone?'

'Thinking Calmly Under Pressure!' we said in one voice.

Eventually, we landed in Cape Town. As I made my way to the door of the plane, I could immediately feel the heat on my face. It was as if someone had opened an oven. It was the middle of the day and it was very, very hot outside.

'It's lucky that all the matches are being played at night,' BOD said. 'We wouldn't last ten minutes in this heat.'

It wasn't just the heat. As we walked down the steps of the airplane, I understood what Peter had been talking about when he mentioned the thinness of the air. I felt like I couldn't catch my breath properly.

We made our way to the baggage hall to collect our luggage from the carousel. On the wall, I noticed an enormous mural of Nelson Mandela, in a Springbok jersey and baseball cap, presenting the World Cup to Francois Pienaar – the scene that Mr Stuyvesant had described to us in Physics class. And underneath it said:

Sport can create hope where once there was only despair. It is more powerful than governments in breaking down racial barriers. Sport has the power to change the world.

– Nelson Mandela

I noticed that quite a few of the other players were reading it as well. Everyone who did said the same thing:

'Wow!'

Once we'd collected our bags, Clive gathered us all together in the baggage hall and did a roll call. It turned out there was one player missing. It was Gavin Henson, the Welsh centre.

'He's probably in the toilets,' one of the Scottish players shouted, 'checking oot his hair!'

Gavin was famous for taking pride in his appearance. His hair was always immaculately presented and he was believed to be the first rugby player ever to wear fake tan. There were even rumours that he shaved his body. He was an amazing rugby player, though.

'Lol will find him,' said Lawrence Dallaglio, who always referred to himself in the third person and by his nickname. Then he headed for the men's toilets. Ten seconds later, he re-emerged. Gavin was with him, looking suspiciously well-tanned and with his hair freshly gelled. The English players wolf-whistled him.

'Just jealous,' he said with a big, bright smile.

We all made our way through the arrivals gate. And it was an amazing sight that greeted us on the other side. A huge group of Zulu warriors were there to welcome us to South Africa. They wore leopard-skin aprons and headdresses with feathers and they had come to perform for us a famous Zulu war dance called Umzansi.

About twenty of them had drums and they hit them so hard that the ground beneath our feet shook. And the others moved as one to the rhythm of the beat. It was incredible to watch.

When it was over, one of the Zulu leaders stepped forward. He was carrying a very large and – I couldn't help but notice – very alive snake! It writhed and hissed in his hands, its tongue kissing the air.

I'm sure I was thinking the same thing as everyone else: 'What's he going to do with that thing?'

For some reason, he instantly recognized Martin Johnson as our leader. He draped the snake around his shoulders. If it had been me, I think I would have fainted on the spot. But Johnno didn't seem bothered at all.

The Zulus looked at us and they said, 'Welcome to South Africa.'

And in that moment, I think we all felt very, very far from home.

28 *The Lap of Luxury*

There had been a mistake. That was the only explanation I could come up with. I picked up the phone and dialed 0 for reception.

'There's been a mistake,' I said. 'I've been given the wrong room.'

'What's your name?' the receptionist asked.

'It's Gordon,' I told her. 'Gordon D'Arcy.'

'And you're dialling from Room 1028. No, you're in the correct room.'

'It's just that, well, it's massive.'

'Yes,' she laughed, 'every member of the Lions party has a Superior Suite to himself.'

'It's about three times bigger than my mum and dad's house – and there are six of us living in that!'

'Well, what can I say except welcome to the Grand

Hotel Cape Town! Enjoy your stay, Mr D'Arcy!' she said, before hanging up.

I wasn't exaggerating. It was the biggest hotel suite I had ever seen in my life. And it had everything in it, including my own private sauna and steam-room and a jacuzzi so big you could bathe an elephant in it!

There was the longest dining table I'd ever seen – with twenty chairs around it!

There was a kitchen that was as big as one you'd see in a restaurant, with a two-door fridge and a walk-in pantry with enough food in it to feed the entire D'Arcy family for six months!

It had a home cinema with a screen covering one entire wall and a choice of ten thousand movies! It had twenty huge leather seats that reclined and lifted your feet in the air!

It had a pool table! And a table-tennis table! And an air-hockey table! And a six-foot-high chocolate fondue fountain! And a bar – stocked with only soft drinks and fruit juices, of course!

My bed was the size of a yacht! And, above it, the ceiling was made of glass, which meant you could fall asleep at night looking up at the stars!

There was a walk-in wardrobe that was as big as a clothes shop and a bathroom that was twice the size of the hotel room I stayed in when I played for Ireland in Paris!

All of my luggage had been unpacked and all of my clothes were either hanging or folded neatly in my wardrobe. I took the jacket of my navy Lions suit off the hanger and I put it on. Then I poured myself a glass of orange juice at the bar and stepped outside onto the balcony, which – like everything else in the room – was ginormous.

The evening was warm and bright. I could feel the sun on my face and hear the birds singing, but they weren't like the birds that you heard at home in Ireland. These sounded exotic, like the birds you heard in the aviary at Dublin Zoo.

In the distance, I could see a mountain that had a perfectly flat top. I knew from looking up facts about South Africa on the Internet that it was called Table Mountain. I stood there in my jacket, drinking my orange juice, watching the sun disappear behind it.

And there was one thing I knew for certain – I absolutely loved being a Lion.

29 *Dead on Our Feet*

'First Lions training session,' Clive Woodward said into his little microphone, 'third of June, oh nine hundred hours. Present: Sir Clive Woodward, Head Coach of the British & Irish Lions; Paul O'Connell, second-row, Ireland; Hamish Watson, flanker, Scotland; Shane Williams, winger, Wales . . .'

'He's no gonnae name every single player in the squad and staff, is he?' said Ross Ford, the Scottish hooker, in his thick accent. 'Hoo long is that gonnae take?'

Ten minutes was the answer. We stood around in the searing morning heat and we waited for the roll call to end.

'Okay,' Clive said when it was finished, 'let's do some work. But, first, members of the staff are going to be fitting each of you with one of these.'

He held up a small box that was attached by a wire to a circular, plastic disc.

'What is it?' BOD asked.

'It's a heart monitor,' Clive said, then he gestured to a man in a Lions blazer, who was sitting at a table on the sideline. He was tapping away on a laptop. 'All of your information will feed into that computer over there.'

'Why?' asked Gavin Henson.

'So we can tell how hard you're working,' Clive explained.

'I don't need a flipping computer to tell me 'ow 'ard *I'm* working,' Martin Johnson said. 'I can tell by 'ow much I'm sweating or 'ow tired I feel.'

'Look, just trust me on this one, Johnno,' Clive said. 'This is science, okay?'

A man in a blazer approached Johnno and asked him to pull up his training top. He handed him a disc, which had a sticky back on it, and told him to attach it to the left side of his chest, then he told him to clip the little box to the waistband of his shorts. Soon, we were all handed a heart monitor and told to follow Johnno's lead.

We started our warm-up with some stretching exercises, followed by two laps of the pitch. We had only run about ten metres when I heard a series of beeps going off. The discs on our chests were chirping away like a chorus of birds at dawn.

'Slow down,' Clive called after us, 'you're running too fast!'

'What's 'e on about?' asked Faz. 'We're 'ardly movin'.'

'Just remember,' Clive shouted, 'that the air is a lot thinner here. You're going to feel tired a lot more quickly.'

'Nuffink wrong wiv the air,' I heard Johnno grumble. 'Air is just air, innit?'

But, after running just one length of the pitch, it was as though I'd just run a marathon.

Paul O'Connell was running beside me. 'It's tough-going,' he said. 'I played here once or twice with Ireland. The first few days are the worst.'

'What's that horrible taste in my mouth?' I asked. 'And why does my windpipe feel like it's on fire?'

'That's lactic acid,' he said. 'It's produced by your muscles when you exercise. Usually, oxygen neutralizes it. But there's less oxygen in the air here, so your body is struggling to process it. So it comes up your throat.'

All of our monitors continued to beep. Clive was staring at the laptop screen and shouting, 'Gavin Henson, slow down! Owen Farrell, slow down! Hamish Watson, you're running too fast!'

I was halfway through my first lap when I noticed that one of my laces had come untied.

'I'd better see to this,' I said.

I stopped running and I dropped down on one knee to tie it. When I stood up again, I felt instantly light-headed, like I might be about to faint, so much so that I had to sit down on the ground. I noticed that more than half of the other players had also stopped. Some were lying face-down on the grass. Some were even doubled over, vomiting.

I was sitting on the ground for about sixty

seconds before I decided that I could trust my legs enough to stand up again.

Clive gathered us all together.

'You see?' he said, as all the players gasped for breath and took great, greedy mouthfuls of water from their bottles. 'That's why we have to respect the conditions here. They are going to be as much an opponent for us as the South African team. Those masks you were given – they're not toys for you to muck around with. They will help to slowly condition your body to need less oxygen. From now on, I want to see you wearing them at all times when we're in the hotel.'

I looked around me. We were all dead on our feet, including Johnno, who was red in the face and wheezing hard. And we hadn't even finished our warm-up yet!

'We are going to need a lot of energy,' Clive said, 'for the game-plan I have in mind, the game-plan that I believe will help us beat South Africa. It involves something called TME.'

'TME?' Ross Ford said. 'Does that have anything tae dae with teacups?'

'No,' Clive told him, 'Teacupping is a totally different thing. TME stands for Three . . . Minutes . . . of Excellence.'

'Three Minutes of Excellence?' BOD said. 'What's that?'

'It's one hundred and eighty seconds of absolutely note-perfect, keep-the-ball rugby, in which every pass is played with absolute precision, while under sustained pressure from the opposition. TME is going to be our other secret weapon against the Springboks. And we are going to practise it over and over and over again until we get it absolutely right.'

Clive arranged us into teams. One team would attack and the other would defend for three minutes.

He threw the ball to me, then he took a stopwatch from his pocket.

'The team that's attacking,' he said, 'I want to see three minutes of attacking rugby with no knock-ons, no dropped balls, no forward passes. I want to see phase after phase after phase. The team that's defending, I don't want you to hold back in the tackle.'

We lined up opposite each other.

'Aren't you going to ask me to dance?' Adam Jones said to Gavin Henson.

That got a huge laugh. As well as being a brilliant rugby player, Gavin was a great ballroom dancer and had competed in *Strictly Come Dancing*!

'Come on, concentrate!' Clive told us. 'You're going to attack for three minutes. If you happen to get over the try line, I will kick the ball back to the middle of the pitch and the three minutes will continue. Three Minutes of Excellence means NO ERRORS AT ALL! Let's see how close we can get to it.'

He blew his whistle and off we went.

It was my first morning training with the Lions and I was about to learn something new – that three minutes on a rugby pitch was a lot longer than I ever imagined! Usually, three minutes seems like no time at all. It's the length of time it takes to brush your teeth, or eat an ice cream, or boil an egg. Three minutes is an ad break in the middle of your favourite TV show. It's the time you spend waiting for the toaster to pop.

But three minutes on a rugby pitch, trying to play inch-perfect, keep-the-ball rugby while under constant pressure from the opposition, felt like an eternity!

It wasn't long before our exhausted limbs betrayed us. Johnny Sexton spilled the ball under pressure from Lawrence Dallaglio. I threw a ball that failed to find Jonathan Davies's hands. Adam Jones tackled

Gavin Henson hard around the waist and carried him AND the ball into touch.

When three minutes were finally up, Clive blew his whistle and we waited to hear how close we'd come to Three Minutes of Excellence.

'I counted FOURTEEN errors!' he said. 'Let's try it again.'

'Again?' I asked, because I was already exhausted. We all were.

'Have you ever wondered, Gordon, what makes the Springboks such a great team?' he asked. 'It's because when they discover something they're not good at, they practise it over and over again until they become good at it. Sometimes, they stay on for hours after training just to work on one small thing they can't get right. And when it gets dark, they bring their cars onto the pitch and they switch on the headlights so they can see the ball. And then they finally get that small thing right. And everyone thinks, Oh, South Africa are just good at that. But they're only good because they practised it hundreds, maybe thousands, of times.'

So we did it again. And again. And again and again and again. And at the end of every three minutes, Clive would tell us the error count:

'Twelve mistakes!'

'Eleven mistakes!'

'Nine mistakes!'

After two hours, we were all so tired, we could have lain down and fallen asleep on the training pitch.

'We will practise TME every single day,' Clive said at the end of the session, 'until we get it absolutely right.' Then he suddenly turned to Gavin Henson and said, 'We're 12–6 down against South Africa with a minute to go. They're attacking our twenty-two, but we've managed to turn the ball over and you have it in your hands. You can see Shane Williams in space on the wing, but it's a risky pass, because there's the possibility of an intercept. What do you do?'

'Errr . . .'

'Four . . .'

'Do you have a mep?'

'You don't need a map. Three . . .'

'Errr . . .'

'Two.'

'I keck it over the heads of the South Africa defence for Shane to ren onto et. Because I know Shane is fest enough to get to et first and et also

removes the resk of a South African player inter-
cepting the ball and scoring a match-winning try.'

'Correct answer. You know what you were doing
there, Gavin, don't you?'

'I was Thenking Calmly Under Preshare.'

'Thinking ... Calmly ... Under ... Pressure.
Right, let's go back to the hotel and recover.'

30 *EMMA*

We were all quiet in the coach. Physically and mentally, we had worked ourselves to the point of collapse. When we reached the hotel, we were directed to a room on the second floor, where a whole army of Lions staff was waiting to greet us, clipboards in hands.

'Gordon D'Arcy,' a man in a long, white coat said to me, sticking out his hand for me to shake it. 'Doctor Beckett is the name. I'm a sports scientist with the team.'

He was a tall, thin man, with a long chin and tiny, round glasses perched on the end of his nose.

'A scientist?' I said. 'Are you telling me the team has its own scientist?'

'No, I'm telling you the team has ten scientists,' he said matter-of-factly. 'You can see my colleagues scattered around the room, talking to your team-mates. It's our job to observe you all in training and to recommend such things as a recovery regime and a diet plan tailored to your specific needs on any given day. Do you understand?'

'Er, not really, no,' I admitted.

'Okay, for instance, I noticed that you nearly fainted when you bent down to tie your shoelace today.'

'It must have been the altitude. I could barely catch my breath and my legs felt unbelievably heavy.'

'Yes, you seemed to suffer from it much worse than some of the others. That's why I'm going to recommend you eat more foods that are rich in potassium – bananas, greens, avocados, dried fruits, potatoes and tomatoes.'

'So where would I get bananas?' I asked. 'And all the other things you just mentioned.'

'You're playing for the Lions now,' he said. 'You don't need to worry about that. You will all be individually monitored at every training session. Your information will be fed into the computer and your dietary requirements will be reflected in your meal plan, even as they change during the course of the tour.'

'Er, right.'

'Now, I couldn't help but notice that your right shoulder looked a little stiff when you went into contact during the Three Minutes of Excellence drill.'

'It's weird that you should say that,' I told him, 'because I think I slept on it funny last night. I woke up this morning and it was sore.'

'It's not weird that I should say it. We are here to notice these things. You hurt your left thigh as well, didn't you? When Martin Johnson tackled you?'

'I did!'

This man was good!

'Okay,' he said, 'let's get EMMA to look at those, will we?'

'Who's Emma?' I asked.

He smiled.

'EMMA,' he said, 'is our robot masseuse!'

'What?' I asked, struggling to believe what I was hearing. 'We have a robot . . . who gives massages?'

'Well, she's not a robot like C-3PO is a robot,' he said, 'or even Optimus Prime. Come on, I might as well introduce you.'

I followed him through a door into a treatment room, where a few of the players, including Johnny Sexton, Paul O'Connell and Stuart Hogg, were already gathered. They were staring in wonder at a piece of machinery that had two long mechanical arms with giant robot hands on the end.

'EMMA,' Doctor Beckett said, 'is an acronym, which is a word formed by the initial letters of other words. EMMA stands for Expert Muscle Manipulation Automaton – an automaton being any mechanical device that imitates a human function.'

'How does it work?' Paulie asked.

'I'll show you,' said Doctor Beckett. 'Let's start with a difficult one, shall we? EMMA, can you please conduct Igor Stravinksy's *L'Histoire du Soldat*?'

Immediately on Dr Beckett's command, without so much as a button being pressed or a knob being turned, the two robot arms came to life. First, they pointed upwards at the ceiling. Then the room was suddenly filled with music and the two arms started moving around in what looked like wild patterns.

'This is one of the most difficult classical pieces in the world to conduct,' Dr Beckett told us. 'And yet EMMA can do it with perfect timing and precision of movement. Stop!'

The second the word slipped his lips, the two arms ceased to move.

'She has been programmed to perform thousands of tasks,' said Doctor Beckett, 'everything from sign language to open-heart surgery.'

'Open-heart surgery?' I asked.

'Indeed, EMMA is capable of performing a heart transplant. Although hopefully we won't be needing that particular function on this tour. But I can attest to the fact that she gives the most rejuvenating massage you will ever receive. EMMA's fingers contain heat-sensitive pads, which can detect the muscle areas that are causing discomfort and apply just the right amount of pressure to help address the problem. Now, you're all carrying knocks from today, I take it. Who wants to go first?'

'Ah'm no gonnae go first,' Stuart said. 'Ah dinnae know if I'd trust it.'

'Darce, you go first,' Johnny said, taking a step backwards. 'You're not scared. You were the first to get into the cryogenic chamber with Leinster that time.'

That was true. And even the memory of it was enough to turn my body cold.

There was a bed next to the machine. I climbed onto it.

'Lie face-down,' said Doctor Beckett.

I did as I was told.

'EMMA,' Doctor Beckett announced, 'Gordon has a certain stiffness in his right shoulder. Could you see to it, please?'

Behind me, I heard the two robot arms come immediately to life, then a second later I felt EMMA's fingers touch my shoulder firmly. Nothing happened for a few seconds. It was as though she was reading my muscle to try to discover precisely where it was sore. Then I felt heat penetrate my skin and two sets of robot fingers began to work the muscle.

After sixty seconds, the pain had magically disappeared.

'We need one of these at Clongowes,' I said.

And suddenly, they all wanted a turn. Stuart Hogg shouldered Johnny out of the way and said, 'Ahm next!'

'I'm after you, then!' Johnny said.

But Paulie put his giant frame in front of Johnny and said, 'That might be how things work at Leinster, but you can get behind me. Show some respect for your elders!'

31 *A Piece of Paper*

Exhausted as we were by the conditions, we still had to hit the ground running. The first match of the tour was just two days away. We were going to play a club side called The Sharks. It would be followed three days later by a match against another team called The Bulls. Clive was going to use the two matches as an opportunity to see us all play before deciding which of us would be involved in the first Test.

We were all keen to play in the first match, to banish our nerves and to show Clive what we could do. And, hey, Lions versus Sharks had an exciting ring to it!

Between training sessions and team meetings, we killed the boredom by playing pool, or table tennis, or air hockey, while wearing our breathing masks.

The day before we played The Sharks, I was taking part in a mini pool tournament with BOD, Johnny and Paulie in my room.

We were all chilled out and enjoying ourselves.

'I have to admit,' I said, 'I find it very hard to understand what the Scottish and Welsh players are saying half the time. And some of the English players as well.'

They thought this was hilarious.

'They have the same problem with us,' Paulie said. 'And sure, didn't you struggle to understand me and Ronan O'Gara when you broke into the Ireland team that time?'

It was true. I did.

'The last time I played for the Lions,' Johnny said, 'I shared a room with Adam Jones. By the time I went home, I had a proper Welsh accent. No one could understand what I was saying for about a month!'

I'd forgotten that BOD, Paulie and Johnny had all played for the Lions before. I was the only one here who was new to the team.

'So when do we find out if we're in the team or not?' I asked.

'Ah, that's the exciting bit,' said BOD, who'd been

on three Lions tours. 'On the afternoon of the match, a piece of paper will be slipped under your door.'

'It's a Lions tradition,' Paulie said. 'It'll say nothing on it except your number. And from that you'll know if you're on the pitch or on the bench.'

'And what if you're not in the match-day squad at all?' I asked.

'No piece of paper,' Johnny said. 'I've been in that position before. And let me tell you, if you think Three Minutes of Excellence feels like a long time, it's nothing compared to three minutes of staring at the gap under your door, wondering is that piece of paper going to come through it.'

'Is that what you do?' I asked. 'Stare at the door?'

'You keep telling yourself you won't,' said Paulie. 'But when it comes to it, it's hard not to – you're listening out for footsteps in the hallway.'

I felt goosebumps just listening to him describe the experience. Right at that moment, my Lions mobile phone rang. I answered it.

'Hello?' I said.

'Hi, Gordon!' a voice said.

It was Dad. I couldn't remember when they were arriving in South Africa.

'Hey, Dad,' I said. 'Where are you?'

'Would you believe it if I told you that we were downstairs?' he asked.

I took the lift back down to the lobby, where Mum, Dad, Ian, Shona and Megan were waiting for me. It was so good to see them. I tore off my mask so I could talk to them properly.

'When did you get in?' I asked.

'The day before yesterday,' Mum said.

'And what's your hotel like?' I asked.

Megan was just about to say something when Ian silenced her with a look.

'Never mind our hotel,' Dad said, quickly changing the subject. 'Look at this place!'

'Our rooms are unbelievable,' I said. 'They're absolutely huge. I've got my own pool table, table-tennis table, sauna, steam-room and jacuzzi! There's even a six-foot-high chocolate fondue fountain!'

I noticed the look of longing in their eyes.

'Every need we have is looked after,' I told them. 'Oh, and there's a robot masseuse – called EMMA!'

'You're making that up,' said Ian.

'I'm not. It stands for Expert Muscle Manipulation Automaton. She fixed my shoulder. And my thigh.'

I was so happy to see them that it took me a few minutes to notice that something was wrong. They

242

all looked tired, like they hadn't slept. And, without wishing to be mean, they sort of stank a bit too, like they hadn't showered or changed their clothes in days.

'Is everything okay?' I asked. 'You didn't tell me what your hotel was like.'

Megan was about to speak again, but Dad interrupted her.

'You just focus on the tour, Gordon,' he said. 'You must be excited about the first match, are you?

Lions versus Sharks. Here, that sounds like a movie, doesn't it? Although, now that I think about it, a lion could never fight a shark – not in real life. I mean, a shark wouldn't last two minutes out of the sea. And lions are afraid of water, what with them being cats and everything.'

He was babbling. Which meant he was hiding something.

'Will someone please answer my question?' I demanded. 'What's your hotel like? Is it the luxury hotel that Flash Barry promised you in the brochure?'

'Please don't worry about us,' Mum said. 'Our accommodation is . . . adequate.'

And they all stared silently at their feet.

32 *A Waiting Game*

It was the day that the Lions were due to take on The Sharks. The match was being played at night. And, as I remembered from my time playing for Leinster, the day passes very slowly when you have a match that night.

I promised myself that I wasn't going to spend the afternoon staring at the door, waiting for the all-important piece of paper to be slipped under it – or not slipped under it, as the case may be.

Instead, I thought I'd spend the day shooting some pool by myself while checking the door maybe every hour – just in case Clive came around early with the notes. This soon changed to me checking the door every half-an-hour, then every fifteen minutes, then every five minutes, until I decided that it would be easier all round if I moved a chair out into the hallway and sat looking at the door for the entire afternoon.

So that's what I did, my eyes fixed, unblinking, on the little sliver of light underneath the door, concentrating on it like a lioness staring at a herd of wildebeest. I did this for about three hours – or maybe more. Eventually, my Lions phone rang and I could see from the screen that it was BOD. I answered it.

'Hey, Darce,' he said, 'you're not sitting, staring at the door, are you?'

I laughed.

'No!' I said, like it was the most ridiculous thing I'd ever heard. 'Are you staring at *your* door?'

'Of course not,' he said – although I suspected that he was lying, like me.

Suddenly, I noticed there was something obstructing the light coming through the gap under my door. Someone was standing outside my room. I noticed that my heart was beating at twice its normal rate. I was going to get a note!

'You still there, Darce?' BOD asked.

'There's someone standing outside my room,' I whispered.

'You *are* sitting, staring at the door!' he said. 'I knew it!'

That was when I noticed that whoever was standing outside my door was gone. They'd moved on. My heart sank. I stood up and turned away from the door and that's when I heard something behind me that sounded like someone whispering, 'Psssssst!'

I spun around and I saw it.

'I got a piece of paper!' I shouted. I felt like Charlie Bucket, finding one of Willy Wonka's golden tickets.

'What number?' he asked. 'Are you in the team or on the bench?'

I rushed to the door, bent down, picked up the note, which was folded in two, and opened it.

'Number twelve!' I told him. 'I'm starting at inside-centre!'

'Congratulations,' he said.

'What about you?' I asked.

BOD and I had played together for Ireland and for Leinster and we made a good midfield team.

'Nothing yet,' he said.

'I really hope you're playing at thirteen,' I told him.

And just then I heard a commotion outside in the hallway. There was shouting and screaming. Someone was either very, very happy about something or very, very annoyed. I opened the door and looked out. It was Gavin Henson. It turned out he was happy.

'I'm en, Darce!' he shouted, his two fists raised in triumph. 'I'm en the team!'

'Congratulations,' I told him.

'Thenks,' he said. 'I've got so mech to do now before I'm ready. I've got to do my tan, bleach my teeth, do my hair . . .'

'What position are you playing?' I asked.

'Nember thirteen,' he told me. 'Outside-centre.'

'Oh,' I said. 'I'm number twelve. It looks like we're playing alongside each other.'

'I don't mind,' he told me. 'Just remember, whatever you do, make me look good!'

33 *Eaten by Sharks*

I was sitting in the dressing room. My body was full of nerves. My right knee was bouncing up and down. This was the moment. I was already wearing my white shorts, my red socks and my boots. I was just waiting to be presented with my jersey.

My first Lions jersey.

'I want you to really savour this moment,' Clive told us. 'Because, like Jeremy Guscott told you, it's something you'll want to remember for the rest of your lives. I know that tonight is not a Test match. But I don't want you to think that it matters any less for that. I don't want you to think about this as a trials match or an opportunity to make an impression on me. I already know what you can do. That's why you're here. I want you to think of this as a match to be won.'

He walked around the dressing room then and handed a jersey to every starter and substitute. Each one was immaculately pressed and still warm from the iron. I opened mine out and laid it across my lap, just to savour the moment. I looked at the bright red fabric and I ran my finger across the embroidered crest with the emblems of Ireland, England, Scotland and Wales on it.

I thought about Dad's Lions video and all the legends of the game who'd worn the jersey in the past. And then I thought about all the players who'd never got to wear it. And I thought about Mum and Dad, and Aoife, Conor and Peter, and all my other friends from Clongowes who were here tonight. And I felt tears of pride well in the corners of my eyes.

I pulled the jersey on over my head. Then I stood up.

I was disappointed that I wouldn't be playing alongside BOD. But I was excited to get the chance to play alongside the great Gavin Henson.

The referee stuck his head around the door and told us that it was time.

Clive looked over at Martin Johnson. 'Do you want to have a word with them, Johnno?' he asked.

Johnno stood up. He was an absolute giant of a

man – almost as wide as he was tall. He was also a man of few words. So when he spoke, you tended to stop whatever you were doing and listen.

'Remember, you're playing for the Lions,' he said, 'some of you for the first time – and who knows, maybe even the only time. You don't want to look back and remember that you lost. So let's not lose.'

I took a deep breath and I stood up. Jonathan Davies was on the bench. 'Good luck, Darce,' he said, shaking my hand.

Even before he'd worn the jersey, it was clear that Jonathan Davies knew what it truly meant to be a Lion.

'I'm sure you'll play against The Bulls,' I told him.

'Whether I do or not,' he said, 'I'll be hoping you have the best game of your life out there tonight.'

But, as it turned out, I *didn't* have the best game of my life. None of us did. The Sharks were a lot better than any of us expected and they were determined to embarrass us in front of a passionate, mostly South African crowd. Which is what they did – they won 39–0. And, as Johnno said as he stormed off the pitch at the end: 'We was flippin' lucky to get flippin' nil!'

I don't know what happened. I struggled with the altitude – all those bananas and avocados that magically appeared at every meal-time seemed to have done absolutely nothing for my ability to deal with the altitude. But we couldn't just blame the conditions.

The truth was that we didn't click as a team. This shouldn't have come as a surprise to us. Most of us were still strangers to each other. We were all operating at different levels of energy and fitness. We were all coming from different rugby backgrounds. We had all worked under different coaches who had their own ideas of how the game should be played.

The result was that we were all on different wavelengths.

Whenever any of us turned to make a pass, the player you expected to be there was somewhere else instead. Or, if he was there, he was standing still with his hands by his sides, rather than running onto the pass with his hands raised.

Gavin and I didn't click as a partnership. The Sharks destroyed us in midfield – and every time we made a mistake, we were punished for it. Usually, if you give away a penalty in your own half, you don't have to worry about the kicker putting it over the bar, because it's almost impossible to find the distance from that far out. But at altitude, we discovered, it was totally different. Kicks travelled a good twenty metres further in the thin air – meaning every time we gave away a penalty, we were immediately another three points down.

When The Sharks kicked the ball out of play at the end, it felt like an act of kindness, to put us out of our misery.

I dreaded the bus trip back to the hotel. When you've had a bad match, one of the toughest things to do is to put a brave face on it in front of your teammates.

I was convinced that I'd played my first and last match for the Lions. I'd blown my chance.

I was walking back to the coach when I heard my name called:

'Gordon!'

I turned around. It was Aoife – and not only Aoife, but Conor and Peter as well. I was so happy to see my friends again, especially after a night like I'd just had. I gave them each a hug and told them I was delighted they were there.

'I'm just sorry you travelled all that way to see me play like that,' I told them.

'Don't be ridiculous,' said Aoife. 'It wasn't that you played badly. Anyone could see that you were struggling with the conditions – and you weren't the only one either.'

'I've no chance of making the team for the first Test now,' I told her.

'You don't know that,' said Conor. 'Anything could happen between now and the first Test.'

'Come on, Gordon,' Peter said, trying to cheer me up, 'you're not a quitter. You didn't think it was going to be easy, did you?'

'No,' I agreed.

'Being a Lion is hard – that's why it's the greatest honour in rugby. Look how far you've come. You wore the famous jersey tonight. You're already a Lion, no matter what happens from now on.'

He had a point, I supposed.

'Oh my God, though,' Aoife said, 'I would love to play rugby here – did you SEE the distance they were getting on those kicks?'

Suddenly, I spotted a large group of Irish supporters, many of them boys I knew from school. And in the middle of the group, I saw Mum and Dad, Ian, Shona and Megan. I called them and their faces lit up when they saw me.

'My brother!' said Ian, giving me a big bear hug. 'A Lion!'

'You played great!' Mum said.

And I thanked her, even though I knew she was just being kind.

I couldn't help but notice that they still looked exhausted. And, while I was loath to remark on other people's personal hygiene issues, I couldn't help but think that they all looked like they needed a good bath.

Now that I thought about it, Aoife, Conor and Peter looked – and smelled! – pretty awful too. As a matter of fact, the entire party did.

Clearly, something was wrong. Something was very, VERY wrong.

'I'm trying to think of a delicate way of putting this,' I said, 'obviously not wishing to hurt your feelings. But does your hotel have hot water?'

I noticed all of them exchange a look.

'Okay,' I said, 'you need to tell me what's going on right now.'

'Gordon,' Dad said, 'we don't want to burden you with our problems. You've enough on your plate.'

I looked at Aoife.

'Has Flash Barry put you in some dump of a hotel?' I asked.

'We're not even in a hotel,' Megan blurted out.

'What?'

Dad sighed.

'Look, we didn't want you knowing,' he said, 'because you should be focusing on your rugby. But, yes, let's just say that Flash Travel has failed to honour certain promises that it made.'

'What does Megan mean when she says you're not in a hotel?' I asked.

'We're staying in tents,' Megan said.

'Tents?'

'Hey, it's fine,' Conor said, trying to gloss over it. 'Camping has actually become pretty glamorous. Glamping, they call it now. You see it all the time at music festivals, don't you? Electric Picnic and all that.'

'Yeah,' Shona said, 'except at Electric Picnic, there's no danger of being eaten by an actual lion.'

'WHAT?' I said – unable to believe my ears. 'Where exactly are you camping?'

'Glamping,' Conor said. 'Remember?'

'Stop trying to put a positive spin on it, Conor. Where has Barry put you?'

'We're in the middle of the Royal Cape Wildlife Reserve,' Aoife admitted. 'Barry booked us on a safari trip. A very, very cheap safari trip.'

'And there's *actual* lions?' I said. 'Outside your tents?'

'Oh, they don't really bother us,' Mum said airily. 'They're more scared of us than we are of them.'

'Yeah, I doubt if that's actually true,' I told her.

'They just have a sniff around the tent and they go off with themselves.'

'Except you have to remember not to leave any

food inside,' Conor said. 'One of the lads from school had a Peperami in his sleeping bag and a lion chewed through the canvas to get it.'

'I can't believe this,' I said.

'Statistically,' Peter announced, 'lions kill a lot fewer people than you might think.'

'But then, there's also snakes,' Megan said. 'And crocodiles. And cheetahs.'

'I am going to kill Barry,' I declared in a loud voice. 'Where is he?'

'No one knows where he is,' said Aoife.

'What do you mean?'

'He saw how angry everyone was when they found out there was no hotel, and he ran off.'

'I think a lion probably ate him,' Megan said.

'I doubt it,' said Conor. 'He'll be in a luxury hotel somewhere, living it up on the money everyone paid him.'

'I still say he's been eaten by a lion,' Megan insisted.

'Don't say that,' Mum told her.

But I could tell they were all thinking it. And all I could do in that moment was gulp.

34 Solving the Puzzle

'SHARKS SWALLOW LIONS WHOLE.'

That was the headline the following morning in the *Cape Times*. To make matters worse, the newspaper had used a photograph of me to illustrate the article! Not a photograph of any of the five tries that The Sharks scored – a photograph of ME with my head in my hands!

The atmosphere around the team hotel the following day was like being at a funeral. Everyone was thinking the same thing – if that's what a South African club side could do to us, imagine what the South African national team would do!

I couldn't really think about the match, though. All I could think about was my family and friends and schoolmates sleeping in tents in the middle of a game reserve. I was worried about what might happen to them. I was even worried about Flash Barry. Yes, he'd ripped everybody off, but he didn't deserve to be eaten by a lion – if that's what had actually happened to him.

After breakfast, Clive called a team meeting. We sat there nervously, waiting for him to arrive. When he did, he got straight to the point.

'You didn't play like Lions,' he told us. 'That was the problem last night. It wasn't tiredness. It wasn't the altitude. It was because you played like England, Ireland, Scotland and Wales.'

'We didn't click,' Johnno agreed.

'The reason you didn't click,' Clive said, 'is because you're not thinking like a team. Whether you realize it or not, you have a bias towards your fellow countrymen. Which is understandable. In the heat of battle, your first instinct is to look around for the people you trust. When things started to go wrong last night, you reverted to doing the things you do when you're playing for your own countries. I saw Johnno and Lol doing things they do for England. I saw Gavin and Shane Williams trying out moves that have worked for Wales. Things that aren't even in our game-plan.'

I hadn't even thought about it. But now that I did, I realized that he was actually right.

260

'You have to stop thinking of yourselves as players from four countries,' he said. 'You have to start thinking of yourselves as Lions. Even now, when I look at you, I can see you're all sitting in your little cliques. Welsh players with Welsh players. Irish players with Irish players. Scottish players with Scottish players. English players with English players. When you're relaxing, playing pool or table tennis in your rooms, you're hanging out with the players you knew before. You haven't made the effort to get to know each other yet.'

He produced a box then. It had a picture of a lion on it. He removed the lid and turned the box upside-down, spilling its contents onto the table in front of him.

'A five-thousand-piece jigsaw,' he said. 'The players who played against The Sharks last night, I'm not going to keep you in suspense. You won't be playing in our second match against The Bulls. So I'm giving you a day off – and this is what you're going to do with it.'

'A flipping jigsaw?' said Martin Johnson. 'I 'aven't done a jigsaw since I was a kid.'

'The point of it, Johnno, is not the jigsaw itself,' Clive said. 'The point of it is to work together to produce something and, in the process, get to know a bit more about each other. Anyway, the pieces are there – all five thousand of them.'

'Is this what we 'ave to do,' Faz asked, 'for t'whole day?'

'It might not take you the whole day,' Clive said. 'You might discover that, when you start working together as a team, things come together a lot more quickly than you think. And remember, the quicker you finish, the quicker you can enjoy what's left of the day. Good luck, chaps.'

All of the players who'd started against The Sharks, and those who came on as substitutes, stayed behind while everyone else left. We made our way to the table.

' 'ow many pieces did he say?' asked Faz.

'Five thousand,' I reminded him.

'Five thousand? We'll be 'ere til flipping midnight.'

It did look like a BIG jigsaw.

Lawrence Dallaglio edged both of us out of the way then, keen to take charge.

'Lol has done loads of jigsaws in his time,' he told us. 'The first thing Lol does is he picks out all the pieces with flat sides on them. Lol always puts the border together first, then works inwards towards the centre.'

'I've an even bettare idea,' said Adam Jones. 'Why

don't we divade the pieces between us? Five thousend between twenty is only 250 pieces each. We make one pale for the edges, one pale for the lion's eyes, one for hes mouth, one for hes nose, one for hes ears, one for hes mane, and so on. Then we each take a pale and put our own lettle piece of the picture together. Then, when we're feneshed, we put all the lettle pictures together to make the lion.'

'Lol likes that idea,' said Lol.

So we did what Adam suggested. We divided up the pieces into twenty little piles and we each sorted through our own, saying, 'Edge!' or 'Nose!' or 'Mane!' or 'Tail!', before dropping each piece into the correct pile.

We chatted while we worked – a bit about rugby, but also about ourselves, where we came from, what kind of music we liked, things we'd seen on TV, our families. The conversation went back and forth.

I told them all about the sport of hurling, which they'd only heard about but had never actually seen. I told them about Wexford winning the Liam Mac-Carthy Cup, although I left out the bit where I accidentally put it on a bus to France. And I told them about my family and my friends, who'd come to South Africa to see me play, but who'd been swindled by Flash Barry.

'Who the 'ell is Flesh Berry?' Adam Jones asked, and I chuckled at the way he pronounced his name.

'He used to be my agent,' I told him. 'He nearly ruined my career, Adam.'

'Call me Bomb,' he said. 'All my friends call me Bomb.'

It was the perfect nickname for him. He was a big man, round like a cartoon bomb and – in addition to his famous mane of hair – he was known for his explosive power.

'Anyway,' I said, 'Flash Barry tricked over two hundred people, including my mum and dad, my brother and sisters, my friends and loads of people from my school, into thinking they were going to be staying in a luxury hotel. Instead, they're camping in a game reserve!'

'What do you mean,' asked Faz, 'in with t'animals?'

'Yeah,' I said, 'in with the animals.'

'Ain't you worried about 'em?' asked Johnno.

'I'm really worried,' I said. 'I don't want them to get eaten.'

We each finished making our section of the jig-saw. I did the eyes. Johnno did the roaring mouth with the sharp teeth. Faz and Gavin Henson did the border. Not surprisingly, Bomb did the lion's big, proud mane.

264

'I love his hair,' he told us. 'Thet's the look I'm going for mayself!'

Then we put all of our sections together. I looked up at the clock. We had managed to complete the entire jigsaw – in just one hour!

'We've got rest of t'day to us-selves,' said Faz. 'What are we gonna do?'

'I've got an idea,' said Johnno. 'Let's go on safari.'

'Sefari?' said Gavin Henson. 'I've never been on a sefari before.'

'Darce is worried abaaht his family and his friends,' said Johnno. 'We can go and check on 'em – and maybe see some animals while we're there!'

35 *Flattened*

We thundered along the bumpy dirt roads of the Royal Cape Wildlife Reserve, our wheels sending up large clouds of dust. We had borrowed one of the red, Lions-branded Land Rovers from the staff for the day and Lol was behind the wheel.

'Lol loves a Land Rover,' he told us. 'Lol drives nothing but Land Rovers back home in England.'

Also in the Land Rover were Johnno, Bomb, Faz, Gavin Henson, Stuart Hogg – and, of course, me.

The sun was beating down hard on our heads. Midday was probably not the cleverest time to go out into the baking hot African sun, especially with the roof down. But we were enjoying the sights anyway.

'Whoa!' said Gavin. 'Look et the zebras over there!'

'Where?' said Stuart. 'Ah cannae see them!'

'Over there,' Gavin pointed, 'with the long necks!'

'They're not bleddy zebras!' said Bomb. 'They're bleddy giraffes!'

'Well, I haven't got may contact lenses en,' said Gavin in his own defence.

'Shouldn't need contact lenses to tell the defference between a zebra and a giraffe,' Bomb insisted. 'One es a stripy horse, the other hes a messive, long neck, look.'

Lol pulled over so that we could get a better look at them. They crossed the road in front of us. I counted thirty of them altogether. For animals that looked so badly designed, each one moved with the grace and poise of a ballet dancer.

'They've got really heavy bodies,' I said, 'held up by long, bamboo legs.'

'Bit like you, Bomb!' said Johnno – and we all laughed.

One of the giraffes stopped in the middle of the road, momentarily blocking out the sun and casting a long shadow across us. She stared down at us, as if noticing us for the first time.

'Look at the eyelashes on her,' said Stuart. 'Ah cannae believe the length of them. Here, Gavin, they're like those fake ones you wore against us that time in the Six Nations!'

'They weren't feek,' said Gavin. 'Those were may real eyelashes, if you mest know.'

The giraffe lowered her neck and moved her face closer to us. Suddenly, her head was INSIDE the Land Rover and she was sniffing us.

'I think she lakes your aftershave, Gavin!' said Bomb.

And then, suddenly, a thick, black tongue emerged from the giraffe's mouth – and licked my face!

It was DISGUSTING!

The others hooted with laughter as the giraffe straightened up again and went on her way. I dried my face on the front of my Lions training top as Lol started the Land Rover again.

About twenty minutes later, we found ourselves driving along the banks of a river.

'Pull over!' said Faz, tapping Lol on the shoulder. 'Pull over t'jeep!'

Lol did what he was told.

'Look,' said Faz, pointing at a sign, which read: 'BEWARE OF THE CROCODILES!'

A cold shiver swept over us. We looked around. It was deathly quiet. There were no crocodiles to be seen – yet I couldn't shake off this uneasy feeling I had . . . that we were being watched!

'I've seen them on t'telly,' said Faz. 'What thee do is thee wait under t'water for summat like a gazelle or a wildebeest to come along and 'ave a drink. And then, all of a sudden . . .'

'What?' I asked.

'Two jaws,' he said, spreading his arms, then bringing his two hands together. 'SNAP!'

I shuddered.

'Is that one there?' asked Johnno, pointing to the middle of the river.

'Ah dinnae think so,' said Stuart. 'Ah think that's just a log, flooting in the watter.'

'Yeah, et's definetely a log,' said Bomb.

We stared at it for about thirty seconds. And suddenly, at one end of the log, a large eye opened. Gavin gripped my arm hard. But then I was gripping Bomb's arm. And Bomb was gripping Stuart's arm.

'Let's git oot ae here!' Stuart urged. 'Drave! Drave! Drave!'

'Lol thinks that's the best idea he's heard all day,' said Lol.

We took off again in search of the camp. We drove for about an hour until finally I spotted the multi-coloured tents in the distance.

'Over there!' I said, pointing.

'Okay,' said Lol, 'hold onto your hats, chaps – this is where we leave the road!'

He pulled sharply on the wheel and suddenly we were crossing a wide and bumpy plain, all of us bouncing up and down in our seats, as we got closer and closer to the camp. We were about fifty metres away when I realized that something was wrong.

The camp had been flattened. And circling overheard, I noticed, was a pack of vultures!

36 *Leader*

Lol pulled over.

'What the 'ell 'appened 'ere?' asked Johnno.

'It looks like a hurricane hit it,' I said.

'Either that or a toornado,' said Stuart.

Half of the tents had been completely destroyed and there were clothes and other items strewn everywhere. And the people were milling around like ants, everyone either in a daze or looking panic-stricken.

I felt a fear rising in me, thinking about my family and friends and schoolmates. Then I spotted my brother in the middle of the crowd.

'Ian!' I shouted. 'Ian!'

'Gordon?' he said, clearly surprised to see me.

'What happened?' I asked.

'There was a stampede.'

'Of what?'

'Elephants!'

'Elephants? Was anyone –'

I didn't even want to say the word.

'No one was hurt,' he said, to my great relief. 'It happened when we were at The Sharks game last night. We arrived back and it was like this.'

I looked around, open-mouthed. 'I can't believe elephants did all this damage,' I said.

'The tents that your mate Flash Barry rented for us were the cheapest that money could buy.'

'He's not my mate.'

'Not that any tent could stand up to an elephant stampede. But he set up our camp right in the middle of their migration path.'

I heard Mum's voice then.

'Gordon!' she said, sounding delighted to see me.

I ran to her and hugged her. Then, Dad and Shona and Megan appeared. I was so relieved that they were okay.

'Well, I don't think we'll be booking any more holidays with Flash Travel,' Dad said, putting a brave face on it.

'I want you all to meet some friends of mine,' I said, then I turned and gestured to my teammates.

'Wow, the great Martin Johnson!' said Dad – he was a fan.

'Johnno,' said Johnno. 'Call me Johnno.'

'And this is Stuart,' I said. 'Faz. Bomb. Lol. And that's Gavin Henson.'

'We know who Gavin Henson is!' said Mum. 'Everyone in the world knows who Gavin Henson is!'

Gavin seemed pleased by this news.

'We loved you on *Strictly Come Dancing*!' said Megan. 'We thought you should have won.'

'Thet's very nace of you to say,' said Gavin.

'Did you say you were camping in the middle of an elephant migration path?' Johnno asked.

'Yeah,' Shona said, 'they pass through here when they're looking for water. They were heading for the river.'

'Presumably,' he said, 'that means more will come?'

'It's a fair bet,' Dad agreed.

'Then you 'ave to move,' Johnno told him.

'Oh, don't worry,' Ian said, 'it's all being arranged. They say that in an emergency, there's always one person who steps forward to take charge. Well, that's certainly happened this morning.'

'Who is it?' I asked.

And then I saw her. She was wearing a green safari suit, which had short trousers and a short-sleeved jacket, and she had a red bandana tied around her head.

'Hi, Aoife,' I said.

'Hi, Gordon,' she replied. 'What are you doing here?'

Johnno stepped forward.

'We came out 'ere,' he said, 'to check on you lot. And it's a good job we did. Right, let's get these tents out of the path of them elephants.'

Aoife glowered at him. 'You might be the captain

of the British & Irish Lions,' she said, 'but *I* give the orders around here – do you understand?'

I could see that Johnno was a bit taken aback by this.

'Er, okay,' he said.

'If you want to help,' she said, 'by all means, help. But, as you well know, there can be only one leader here and that's me.'

I turned to my teammates.

'Everyone,' I said, 'this is my friend Aoife.'

They all said a polite hello.

'And Aoife,' I said, 'this is –'

'I know who they are,' she said, cutting me off. 'But we don't have time to talk about rugby now. We have to move this camp.'

'Where are you mooven et to?' asked Bomb.

'I went walking with Conor and Peter this morning,' she said, 'and we found an escarpment.'

'What's an escarpment?' I asked.

'It's a piece of raised ground,' a voice behind me said.

I turned around. It was Peter. He was standing there with Conor.

'We should be safer up there,' he said. 'It's out of the path of those elephants anyway.'

'So 'ow can we 'elp?' asked Faz.

Aoife looked us up and down like she was sizing up what our strengths might be.

'Lawrence Dallaglio,' she said.

'Lol,' he replied.

'What's so funny?'

'What do you mean?'

'You said Lol.'

'No, I mean that's what everyone calls me.'

'Right,' she said, 'we lost a lot of things in the stampede. There's a shop exactly two miles northwest from where we're standing. Can you drive there and pick us up some things?'

'Yeah, 'ang on,' he said, taking out his Lions phone. 'Lol will make a list.'

'Right,' Aoife told him, 'we need a brand-new barbecue and we'll need coals for it. We need a Primus stove and don't forget the gas. We need matches, water and tinned food – lots of it, because there's more than two hundred people here. And we need firewood. Did you get all of that?'

'Yeah,' he said. 'Lol got it all.'

'Take my credit card,' Dad said, handing Lol his wallet. 'I'll get the money back when I take Flash Travel to the High Court.'

'Bring Gavin Henson with you,' Aoife said.

'Gavin, I thought you were great on *Strictly Come Dancing*, by the way.'

'Thenks,' he said.

Aoife turned to Johnno then.

'Are you ready to help?' she asked.

'Er, yeah,' he told her, 'definitely.'

I couldn't believe it. The great Martin Johnson! A World Cup-winner with England! And here he was, taking orders from my friend Aoife!

'Most of the tents were flattened,' she said. 'Some of the tent poles were broken, but some were just bent out of shape. Can you see which ones you can fix?'

'Absolutely,' said Johnno.

'And Stuart Hogg will help you.'

She looked at the rest of us.

'Okay, Gordon, Owen Farrell and Adam Jones,' she said, 'will you help people to gather up their belongings and start bringing them up to the escarpment?'

'Yes,' we said in one voice.

'Well,' Faz said, 'aye.'

'Conor and Peter,' she said, 'you can help them. And you too, Ian.'

We all set to work.

'Here,' Conor asked at one point, 'why do you stink?'

'I got licked by a giraffe,' I said.

'You what?' Peter said.

'I can't say any more than that!' I told him. 'I don't want to relive the experience!'

'I wonder is that lucky or something?' said Conor.

'I didn't feel lucky at the time!' I told him. 'By the way, has there been any word from Flash Barry?'

'Nothing,' said Peter.

'Aren't you worried about him?' I asked. 'He might be on his own out there? He might be scared!'

'Believe me,' Conor said, 'he has far more to fear from us than he does from any lions, or crocodiles, or stampeding elephants that might be out there!'

While we worked, Aoife barked encouragement and instructions at everyone.

'We're going to need to work faster, people,' she said, clapping her hands together. 'We have to get the new camp set up before it gets dark. Adam Jones – a man who won three Grand Slams can carry more than that!'

Bomb smiled at me.

'Your friend,' he said, 'does she play regby?'

'She does,' I told him. 'She's on the Ireland School-girls team.'

'The captain, is she?'

'She is, yeah.'

'Thet figures.'

Lol and Gavin arrived back with all the provisions, then they helped with the job of moving everyone and everything up to the escarpment.

After four hours of hard work, the job was finally done. The unfortunate people who'd booked with Flash Travel had a new camp that was out of harm's way – certainly from stampeding elephants. Johnno and Stuart managed to fix every single one of the tents, bending the poles back into shape and taping the broken ones back together.

And the vultures had cleared off, realizing that there would be nothing here for them to eat tonight.

It had started to get cold. Conor and Ian lit a big fire and everyone gathered around it. Mum handed us each a mug full of baked beans and we ate them with a spoon as the sun went down and pitch-black darkness fell over the Royal Cape Wildlife Park.

'We'd better get back,' said Johnno. 'We've got to be up early for training tomorrow.'

'Thank you all for your help,' said Aoife. 'And I'm sorry if I was rude.'

'Hey,' he said, 'you can't be everyone's friend – especially if you're trying to get a job done.'

I could tell he was impressed by her. One leader recognizes another.

'Do you play rugby?' he asked.

'A bit,' she said with typical modesty.

'She plays for the Ireland Schoolgirls team,' I said proudly. 'And she's amazing.'

'Apparently,' added Bomb, 'she's the captain.'

'Makes sense,' said Johnno. 'They're lucky to have you.'

We said our goodbyes then. We climbed into the Land Rover and more than two hundred grateful campers waved us on our way.

We were all quiet during the drive back to the hotel. We were exhausted from the work we'd put in.

'Lol quite enjoyed that,' said Lol after a while.

'Aye, me too,' said Stuart. 'Ahm gonnae be pooting up tents in mah sleep noo, though!'

I looked around and I noticed that Johnno, Bomb, Gavin and Faz were all fast asleep. And I realized something in that moment. We were no longer just members of the British & Irish Lions squad.

We were teammates.

37 *You Can Feel the Greatness Coming Off Him*

Two nights later, the Lions played The Bulls – and they won! It wasn't even close either. The score was 48–3 and for the first time there was a feeling of real optimism around training.

After the false start of our defeat to The Sharks, it was like the Lions tour of South Africa had finally begun.

The bad news, from my own selfish point of view, was that Jonathan Davies, who'd replaced me at number twelve, scored a hat-trick of tries – and so did Brian O'Driscoll!

This time, the headline in the *Cape Times* was:

'WOODWARD'S BULL-FIGHTING
HEROES!'

And alongside it, there was a photograph of BOD and Jonathan Davies celebrating at the end. As playing partners, they shared this wonderful understanding on the field. There was no question that Clive had found his midfield pairing for the opening Test and I was resigned to the fact that I wasn't going to be a starter against South Africa.

I shook Jonathan's hand after the match – and again the next morning at training. I told him that I thought he'd played incredibly well and that if there was any justice, he would be playing at inside-centre against South Africa in three days' time.

Clive was a perfectionist. It didn't matter that his team had won, or even by how many points they had won, he would always find areas in which we could improve. Like, for instance, the ruck. Against The Sharks and The Bulls, he felt we were coming into it too high. So he came up with a novel way of teaching us to get in lower and give ourselves a better chance of stealing the ball off the ground.

At training, the day before the first Test against South Africa, he introduced us to a brand-new contraption that none of us had ever seen before. It looked like a giant trampoline, except that, instead of canvas, it was covered with a net made from thick rope. Underneath it, there was what Clive called a

Sausage Bag — a heavy, two-metre-long bag that looked like a punchbag from a boxing gym.

We were told to form a line, then each of us in turn had to run at it at full pelt, throw ourselves head-first underneath it, then drive the Sausage Bag to the other side as quickly as we could, before rejoining the line.

It was a lot harder than it looked, especially for the taller players, like Paulie and Johnno and Lol, who kept getting their ears or their noses caught in the netting!

We tried it about twenty times each before Clive decided that we'd learned enough from the exercise and we moved on to practising our Three Minutes of Excellence.

We were definitely getting better at it. Twice, we managed to get through three minutes with just seven errors. We were still nowhere near the zero mistakes that Clive demanded of us, but at least we were going in the right direction.

Part of the reason for that was because we were beginning to bond as a group. Now, when I walked into the hotel restaurant, or got on the team coach, I was as likely to sit beside an English player, or a Welsh player, or a Scottish player, as I was a player from my own country. And everyone else was the same.

We were even getting used to each other's accents. I didn't have to just nod blankly at Bomb or Stuart Hogg when they said something now.

We were coming to the end of training – our last session before we played South Africa – and we were all buzzing with excitement.

'Okay,' Clive said, 'we'll rest tomorrow. Those of you who'll be starting against South Africa or on the bench will get a note under your door during the afternoon.'

Then suddenly, out of nowhere, he turned to me.

'Gordon D'Arcy,' he said, 'it's a minute before the end of the third Test, with the series tied at one–all. The Lions are leading by two points, but South Africa have the ball. There's a Springbok player tearing up the wing, waiting to receive the ball. Do you tackle the man in possession, or do you wait to see can you intercept the pass?'

'Errr . . .' I said.

'Four.'

'I think I'd . . .'

'Three.'

'Er . . .'

'Two . . .'

'I'd maybe . . .'

'Time's up.'

'What was the right answer?'

'There's not always a right or wrong answer, Gordon. Sometimes, a situation just calls for a decisive action either way. You were caught between two options, both equally valid, but you couldn't decide which to take. Why? Because you weren't . . .'

'Thinking Calmly Under Pressure,' I said.

'Thinking . . . Calmly . . . Under . . . Pressure . . .' he repeated.

The reason I wasn't thinking calmly under pressure, though, was because – this is an awkward one to talk about – I needed to answer a call of nature. Eating bananas and avocados for breakfast, lunch and dinner can play havoc with your digestive system. I will go no further than to say that I needed the toilet very, VERY urgently.

While the rest of the squad began their warm-down at the end of training, I excused myself and ran back to the dressing room.

I was missing for ten minutes – fifteen at the very most. When I went back outside again, I sensed that something had happened. Something very significant.

The players weren't warming down, I noticed. They were standing around in silence, looking a little bit shocked.

'Ah cannae believe that just happened!' Stuart was saying to Paulie.

'The man has an aura!' I heard BOD say to Faz. 'You can actually feel the greatness coming off him.'

'I can't believe that Lol just shook the great man's hand,' said Lol.

Bomb spotted me arriving back then. 'Darce,' he said, 'where the 'ell 'ave you been?'

'I had to, em, quickly do something,' I told him.

'You messed hem, Darce!'

'What?'

'He was only 'ere for about ten menutes. Lended in a helicopter. Shook all of our hands and told us he wanted to wish us all the best against South Africa tomorrow.'

'Who are you talking about?'

And that's when he said it:

'Nelson Mandela!'

38 *Twenty-three*

I couldn't believe I'd missed the chance to meet the President of South Africa! I was still furious with myself the next day.

What had Mr Stuyvesant told me?

'It'll be one of the proudest moments of your life to say you shook the hand of one of the greatest men who has ever lived.'

And I didn't get to do it – all because I needed to go to the stupid toilet!

It didn't help matters that it was the only thing the others could talk about for the next twenty-four hours.

'He certainly knows his rugby,' said Lol. 'He was telling Lol that he saw South Africa play against the Lions in 1955 – and he cheered for the Lions.'

Why couldn't I have held on for even five more minutes?

'Will he be at the match tonight?' I asked.

'No,' said Bomb, 'he's flyen to London today – he's haven dinner with the Queen!'

Johnno held up his right palm.

'I shook Nelson Mandela's 'and,' he said. 'One of the greatest leaders of men who's ever lived and I shook his 'and! It's a story we'll tell our children one day. And our children's children. And our children's children's children.'

Okay, I thought. There's no need to rub it in.

It was the afternoon of the first Test and there was a large group of us gathered in Jonathan Davies's Superior Suite. We were all trying not to think about whether or not we'd get a note under our door that afternoon. Instead, there was a table-tennis tournament in full swing. Faz was playing Bomb in one semi-final. I was going to take on Jonathan in the other.

One of the things that Bomb was famous for – apart from his scraggy mane of hair – was his absolutely superhero strength. He seemed to have no real understanding of how hard he was hitting that little white ball across the table. Every time he served, Faz was forced to dive for cover like he was under enemy fire.

Jonathan and I were laughing our heads off

because Bomb and Faz kept bickering with each other across the table.

'You're flipping belting t'ball!' Faz pointed out.

'So?' Bomb replied. 'There's no rule thet says 'ow 'ard you can or can't het et, is there?'

'Supposed to be a friendly game,' Faz said.

'No such theng as a friendly game,' Bomb reminded him.

I had to agree with him on that point.

Bomb served again. It crossed the net at about two hundred miles per hour. Faz hit the deck again, then he went to retrieve the ball.

'Have a look,' he said, holding it between his thumb and forefinger. 'There's a dent in t'ball, look. That's how 'ard he's 'itting it.'

I turned to Jonathan and I said, 'I don't want to play Bomb in the final. If he wins this, I'm going to deliberately try to lose the semi-final to you!'

Jonathan laughed.

'It'll be the worst table-tennis match ever, then,' he said, 'because I'm going to deliberately try to lose to you!'

That was when Lol, who'd been watching the match, looked up and noticed something.

'Jonathan,' he said. 'A piece of paper just came through your door.'

Everybody turned and looked at the door.

Lol was right – it had!

Jonathan made his way to the door, trying to look cool, although I'm sure he didn't feel it inside. He picked it up and opened it.

'Twelve,' he said.

He would be playing inside-centre in the first Test. Which obviously meant that I wouldn't be.

A strange silence descended on the room then. I could tell that everyone was thinking the same thing: if Jonathan had got a piece of paper under his door, then maybe they had too.

Faz put down his table-tennis bat.

'We, er, might finish this some other time,' he said to Bomb, walking backwards towards the door. 'I just need to go back to my room to, er, check summat.'

'Yeah, Lol needs to do the same,' said Lol.

'Yeah, me too,' said Gavin Henson. 'There's thengs I need to check as well.'

Within sixty seconds, the entire suite had cleared out and it was just me and Jonathan left.

'I'm delighted for you,' I told him, shaking his hand. And I was – even though I was disappointed for myself. 'You were brilliant against The Bulls. You deserve it.'

'Thet's very nace of you to say,' he said. 'Are you

gonna go back to your room to check did you get pecked?'

'I probably should,' I said.

Even though I wasn't hopeful, I still had to know. I stepped outside into the hallway. As I was passing Faz's door, it was suddenly thrown open.

'Darce,' he said. 'I'm playing number ten!'

Number ten? I thought. Johnny Sexton will be disappointed.

'I'm delighted for you,' I said.

Again, I was telling the truth.

Gavin's door opened then and he stepped out into the hallway.

'Number twentay,' he said, waving a piece of paper in the air. 'I'm a substitute.'

He sounded like he didn't know whether this was a good or a bad thing.

'That's great news,' I said. 'You'll definitely get on at some point.'

'What about you?' he asked.

'I don't know yet,' I told him.

I made my way back to my room. As I put my key card in the slot in the door, I realized that my heart was pounding. I didn't know why. Jonathan was playing number twelve and I couldn't see myself fitting in anywhere else in the team.

But when I pushed the door open, I still made a point of looking down. And, to my great surprise, there was a folded-up piece of paper on the floor.

I bent down to pick it up, my hands trembling. I opened it. On it, was written the number twenty-three!

I was on the bench!

My heart leaped. Just at that moment, my Lions phone rang. I took it out of my pocket. I could see from the screen that it was BOD. I answered.

'Hey, BOD,' I said, 'did you get good news?'

'Yeah,' he said, 'number thirteen – outside-centre. What about you?'

'I'm on the bench,' I said.

'That's great news,' he reminded me.

'Yeah,' I said, 'not quite as good as starting, but at least I'm in the match-day squad.'

'Darce,' he said, 'it's a long tour. Trust me – anything can happen between now and the end.'

I had no idea at that moment just how right he was about that. And, looking back, I wonder did he?

39 *The Bomb Squad*

'Team talk,' said Clive into his headset mic, 'by Sir Clive Woodward, Head Coach of the British & Irish Lions. First Test versus South Africa, Cape Town, the tenth of June, nineteen hundred hours. Present at team talk . . .'

I zoned out. We were sitting in the dressing room, but I was listening to the crowd beyond the door. The atmosphere in the stadium crackled like live wires touching and you could see it reflected in the faces of the players. Everyone was tense.

The Springbok fans had not come to cheer on the Lions. It was clear from the noise they were making that they wanted to see us taken apart!

'If we are to win this match,' Clive told us, 'we will have to win it twice.'

We all looked at each other. Win it twice, we thought? What's he talking about.

'We will have to win the first sixty minutes,' he said. 'Then we'll have to win the last twenty minutes – like it's a totally different match. And it will be a totally different match.'

'Why?' asked Faz. 'What 'appens after t'sixtieth minute?'

'They're going to bring on the Bomb Squad,' Clive replied in a grave voice.

We all looked at each other.

'What's the Bomb Squad?' asked Paulie.

'According to my sources,' said Clive, raising one eyebrow, 'the South Africans have developed a crack unit of forwards with one mission in mind – to beat you up!'

'Beat us up?' Jonathan asked.

'Within the rules, of course,' said Clive with a lop-sided smirk. 'They're going to keep them on the bench for the first hour of the match. Then, with twenty minutes to go, when you're tired and out on your feet, they're going to bring them on.'

''ow many of 'em?' said Johnno.

'Six,' replied Clive.

'What? That's nearly the entire pack!'

'Precisely. They're going to swap one set of forwards for another set of forwards. The second set have been trained for the sole purpose of – let's just say – increasing the physicality of the game in the final quarter.'

'We'll be ready for 'em,' Johnno said, standing up and looking around the dressing room. 'Right, lads?'

We all nodded, even though some of us were probably less certain than others.

Johnno threw open the door.

'You lot coming or not?' he said – like we were late for school, rather than going outside to face the mighty South Africa!

All of the other players stood up and followed him. I just had time to wish BOD and Jonathan all the best, then we stepped outside into the hostile atmosphere of the stadium.

I took my seat in the stand along with the other substitutes as the players warmed up. We stood for the anthems, then everyone assumed their positions, the referee blew his whistle and Handre Pollard, the Springbok number ten, drop-kicked the ball into our half of the pitch.

It travelled a huge distance and seemed to hang forever in the thin South African air, before Stuart Hogg, our full-back, finally rose to catch it.

I remembered a lesson I learned from Joe Schmidt when I was playing for Leinster – that just because you're not on the pitch, doesn't mean you're not involved. Joe taught me that, as a substitute, you have to focus on the match as if you were actually on the pitch yourself. That way, if you do have to go on at short notice, you understand the pattern of the game and what is required of you.

So I studied the match really closely, so much so that when the ball was kicked, my foot moved involuntarily. When the ball was passed, I found myself flicking my wrists. And when a player was tackled, I braced myself like it was my own body on the line.

The first ten minutes were cagey. Neither team was giving anything away. But then we scored a try! BOD and Jonathan Davies were on the short side of a ruck, close to the left-hand touchline. Mike Phillips, our scrum-half, pulled the ball out of the ruck. He made it look as though he was going to pass it to the right, but then he flicked it to the left to Jonathan, catching the Springbok defence by surprise. Jonathan sidestepped one defender, then drew another towards him, creating space for BOD to run into. He used his quick hands to play the pass to him – I performed the motion myself – then BOD ran thirty metres to put the ball down under the posts.

The Lions supporters occupied just one tiny section of the stadium, but they went absolutely wild. Faz kicked the conversion and we were winning 7–0.

Handre Pollard kicked off again – and that was when disaster struck.

The ball seemed to take an eternity to come down. And, by the time it did, the Springbok players had charged forward, determined to win the ball from the restart. BOD looked up and could see it falling towards him. He raised his two hands, leapt into the air like a salmon and caught the ball firmly.

However, as he did so, he fell forward, over the back of Schalk Burger, the Springbok blindside flanker, and head-first to the ground from a height of over six feet. BOD let out a roar:

'AAARRRRRRGGGHHH!!!'

And I could tell instantly that something was seriously wrong. The referee could tell too. The match was stopped and the Lions medics ran onto the field. It was just as bad as I suspected.

'Gordon,' Clive said, 'warm up – you're going on.'

'Me?' I asked.

I was surprised. I wasn't a number thirteen. I was sure he was going to ask Gavin Henson, who was a more logical replacement for BOD.

I warmed up quickly.

I was worried about my friend, who was being carried from the pitch on a stretcher, clutching his shoulder, his face gripped in pain. But I didn't have time to think about it – or even the fact that I had never even played at outside-centre before!

I had a job to do.

We had lost our best player. It was a big blow, and you could almost see some of the belief leave some our players in that moment. I got my hands on the ball a few times and tried to make something

299

happen. I figured that if we scored another try very quickly, it might help settle everyone down again, but I could see that everyone was thinking about BOD and his injury. It was as if some kind of collective depression had descended over the team.

We started to give away penalties for silly infringements. Handre Pollard kicked three of them to ease South Africa into a 9–7 lead.

It could have been even worse just before half-time when Makazole Mapimpi, the brilliant Springbok winger, found himself with the ball in his hands and nothing but thirty metres of clear field between him and our try line. Mapimpi was an absolute flier – one of the fastest runners I had ever seen. I chased after him. While I knew he was too quick for me, Mr Murray had taught us to never give up chasing the ball-carrier, even if a try looked inevitable.

'Rugby is a game of unexpected twists,' he liked to say. 'That's why we don't play it with a round ball.'

So I kept up my pursuit. When he was ten metres from the line, I noticed a sudden change in the way he was running. He'd somehow tweaked a muscle and slowed down to the point where I was sure I had enough time to tackle him. So I launched myself at him:

BANG!

And I dragged him into touch.

'Well done, Darce!' said Bomb, pulling me to my feet and almost tearing my arm out of its socket in the process. The man really didn't know his strength!

'You just saved us seven points,' Johnno told me.

It was a nice moment. I felt like I'd finally arrived as a Lion.

But we were still losing by two points and we'd lost our most inspirational player. We were all hugely relieved when half-time arrived.

When we got back to the dressing room, all anyone wanted to talk about was BOD.

'Hoo is the lad daeing?' asked Stuart Hogg.

'He's dislocated his shoulder,' said Clive. 'They've taken him to hospital for an X-ray. But, difficult as it is, we need to put him out of our minds now. What happened was an unfortunate accident, but Brian wouldn't want it to cost us the first Test. We need to get back into the lead as quickly as we can because, remember, the Bomb Squad is coming for you.'

We all looked at each other.

'When they arrive, I want you to give me Three Minutes of Excellence,' Clive said.

'We've not even managed that in trainen,' Gavin Henson pointed out.

'Three Minutes of Excellence will show them

that we have the technical ability to more than match their physicality. Johnno, do you want to say anything?'

Johnno stood up.

'Yeah, we've 'ad a blow in the first 'alf,' he said, 'losing Brian like that. He was our main attacking threat. But we know we're not a one-man team. Certain players need to step up now and fill the gap he's left.'

I was sure he was talking about me.

'Right,' he said, 'let's go out there and get some points on the board quickly. Then we'll see abaaht this so-called Bomb Squad of theirs!'

As usual, Johnno was the first player out the door and we followed after him out onto the pitch.

Ten minutes into the second half, Lol jumped the highest to steal the ball from a Springbok lineout. When he landed with it, our forwards were set perfectly for the maul. They started to power forward like a great human tank, with Mike Phillips shouting directions from the back. South Africa tried to slow them up, but they couldn't. When the maul crossed the line, Johnno touched the ball down.

As we celebrated with him, I heard one of the Springbok players mutter, 'Yeah, you won't do that to the Bomb Squad!'

Faz kicked the conversion and now we were winning the first Test by 14–9.

And not long afterwards, the lights went out. Literally. The floodlights were switched off, casting the entire stadium into darkness. I could barely see Jonathan standing five metres away from me.

Silence fell over the crowd.

'What the 'ell is going on?' I heard Johnno ask the referee.

Suddenly, we could hear the sound of drums through the PA system – loud, ominous-sounding drums that whipped up the crowd into a cheering frenzy.

Six of the South African forwards started running for the sideline. 'You're in big trouble now!' one of them shouted in my general direction.

A spotlight suddenly lit up the area where the Springbok players were sitting. We could see the outline of six players, who were standing on the sideline, waiting to come on. And one thing was immediately clear . . .

THEY WERE ENORMOUS!

The floodlights came on again and the crowd

roared even louder. The stadium announcer said their names:

'The substitutes for South Africa are Malcolm Marx, Steven Kitshoff, Vincent Koch, R.G. Snyman, Franco Mostert and Francois Louw.'

They looked big enough from a distance – up close, they were GIANTS, bearing down on us like we were their little brothers.

The game restarted. And it was instantly clear that everything had changed.

Every time we got our hands on the ball, the Bomb Squad hit us hard. Lol caught a high ball and . . .

BANG!

Faz was about to kick the ball deep into the Springbok half and . . .

BANG!

Jonathan was about to dummy a pass to me and . . .

BANG!

We had no time to settle on the ball. And because I'd never played at outside-centre before, I wasn't one hundred per cent sure what I should be doing. Brian was great at timing the angle of his runs to always be in a position to receive the ball. My strength was my ability to sidestep and jink my way through tackles. But, remembering what Johnno had said about filling the gap left by BOD, I found myself trying to imitate him, instead of just sticking to the things that I was good at. The Bomb Squad had done their homework on BOD and figured out how to stop his runs, so they had no trouble stopping me.

The result was . . .

BANG!

The first time I was tackled by one of the Bomb Squad, it felt like I'd been hit by a speeding truck. Malcolm Marx hit me around the midriff and I found myself lying on the flat of my back, winded and with no idea what had happened to the ball. Although that question was answered about ten seconds later when I heard the stadium erupt and I found out that the Springbok full-back, Willie le Roux, had scored a try.

The Bomb Squad totally outmuscled our forwards too. Every time either team was awarded a scrum, it resulted in a penalty to South Africa. And with the ball cutting through the air like a rocket, Handre Pollard had the perfect kicking day. Everything he put his foot to sailed over the bar.

'TME!' we heard Clive shout from the sideline as we chased the game. 'TME!'

But we'd found it impossible to pull off even one full minute of excellence in training. Now, we couldn't string more than three passes together without running into the brick wall of their pack.

In the end, South Africa won 48–14.

I could see the Springbok players laughing and shrugging, like they couldn't believe how easy it had been.

'We'll finish the job next week,' I heard one of their players say.

We trooped off the pitch with our heads down.

'Lions?' Faz said to me. 'It were more like lambs we were.'

'Yeah,' I agreed. 'Lambs to the slaughter.'

40 Change Nothing, Nothing Changes

We all went to bed early that night, hoping that things would seem a little better in the morning.

They didn't.

As a matter of fact, they were worse.

We came downstairs to the news that BOD was going home. The doctors said he could be out of the game for up to a year.

It was hard to know what to say to him as I helped him pack his bags. It had all happened so quickly. The night before, he was lining out to play for the Lions. Now, he was going home with his arm in a sling, not knowing when he'd play again.

Rugby could be so cruel.

'I'm sorry,' I told him. 'It must be hard.'

'It's all part of the game, Darce,' he said. 'It can't be helped. Good luck with the rest of tour.'

He must have seen something in my face in that moment.

'What's wrong?' he asked.

'The rest of the tour?' I said. 'We were destroyed last night.'

'So?'

'They're too good for us.'

'There's no such thing as too good for us.'

'But the Bomb Squad –'

'Forget the Bomb Squad! Every team is beatable. One team comes up with a secret weapon, like the Bomb Squad. Then it's up to everyone else to come up with something to neutralize that weapon. It happens all the time in rugby. That's why no team dominates for very long.'

'I suppose.'

'There's no suppose about it, Darce.'

'It's just, I've never played outside-centre before.'

'Come on, stop looking for excuses to lose and start looking for reasons to win. Outside-centre and inside-centre aren't that different.'

'I was trying to do all the things you do.'

'Don't.'

'What?'

'Clive didn't pick you because he wants you to be me. He picked you because he wants you to be you. Just do the things you're good at, okay?'

'Okay.'

'Now, give me a hand with these bags, will you? I've only got one good arm here, remember?'

I helped him carry his bags to the lift, then downstairs to the hotel lobby. A car was waiting outside to take him to the airport and a flight back to Dublin.

All of the players in the squad had come down to the lobby to see him off. They gave him a round of applause. I could tell he was embarrassed by it.

'Remember what I said,' he told me, as I put his bag into the boot of the car. 'You can still win the two remaining Tests.'

Then he climbed into the car and he was gone.

Clive had called a meeting of all the players for that morning. We were told to report to the second floor before we'd even had our breakfast.

We all sat around, comparing our war wounds, while we waited for Clive to arrive. The Bomb Squad had really bashed us up and there wasn't a Lions player who'd come off the pitch without a few bumps and bruises for souvenirs.

Clive had been furious with us after the match — and his anger hadn't cooled that morning.

'You didn't Think Calmly Under Pressure,' he said. 'You didn't give me Three Minutes of Excellence. The Bomb Squad came on and they softened you up like they were tenderizing meat.'

'No, they didn't!' a voice at the back of the room suddenly said.

All of the players turned around to see who had spoken.

It was Johnno.

'South Africa didn't soften us up,' he said. 'We was soft to begin wiv.'

'What do you mean by that, Johnno?' Clive asked.

'Look, as the captain, I feel it's my responsibility to say these fings. I mean, look at this 'otel.'

'What's wrong with this hotel?' asked Clive. 'It's the best hotel in Cape Town. It's got seven stars.'

'That's the point,' said Johnno. 'I came back to my room last night and someone had run me a bath and filled it with rose petals. Everything we need has been provided for us. And a lot of things we don't need. There's a flipping chocolate fountain in my room.'

Everyone laughed. I liked the chocolate fountain, but I decided to say nothing.

'We're not royalty,' Johnno said, 'or famous Hollywood actors. We're supposed to be a rugby team. But with all this luxury around us, we've gone soft.'

'So what are you proposing?' Clive asked. 'You think we should move into a six-star hotel?'

'What I'm suggesting,' Johnno said, 'is that we don't stay in an 'otel at all!'

Everyone turned and looked at each other.

'What are you talking about?' Clive asked, speaking for us all.

'Darce's family and his friends and all his schoolmates are camping out in the bush. What I'm suggesting is that we offer them our rooms here in the hotel. And we take their tents.'

Clive looked at Johnno like he thought the man had lost his mind.

'I'm serious,' Johnno said. 'There's an old saying – change nothing, nothing changes. If we're going to take on the Bomb Squad, we are going to have to toughen up as a group. That's not going to happen while we're dipping marshmallows into chocolate and getting massages from a robot called EMMA.'

'But wouldn't it be dangerous?' Clive asked. 'Presumably, there are animals in this wildlife reserve?'

'There's a friend of Darce's,' said Johnno, 'a girl called Aoife – captain of the Ireland Schoolgirls rugby team – and she's the one who got me thinking this way. Their camp got trampled by an elephant stampede –'

'An elephant stampede?' said Clive, horrified. This clearly hadn't figured in his extensive preparations for the tour.

'– and this Aoife didn't sit around like us here this morning, feeling sorry for herself. She decided, right, I'm going to own this. She organized everyone and directed the rebuilding of the camp in a safer location.'

'But is it not dangerous,' Clive asked, 'living outdoors?'

'Of course it's dangerous,' Johnno insisted. 'That's why I'm suggesting it. We need to sharpen our senses. We need to be 'arder.'

Clive looked around the room at the rest of us.

'Well,' he said, 'how would you feel about moving out of this hotel and spending the rest of the tour living in tents, surrounded by deadly animals, out in the bush?'

One by one, we all nodded our heads and said, 'Yeah, let's do it.'

41 *Halt! Who Goes There?*

We flew over the wide-open plains, looking down on herds of zebra and wildebeest as they grazed. We saw elephants taking a bath at a watering hole, hippopotamuses rolling around in the mud and rhinoceroses lolling around under the hot African sun.

I had never been in a helicopter before and it was so exciting.

'This is Sir Clive Woodward,' Clive said into his little headset, 'coach of the British & Irish Lions. We are currently cruising at an altitude of two thousand feet and vectoring towards the encampment of Flash Travel in the Royal Cape Wildlife Reserve. With me on board is Martin Johnson of Leicester and England and Gordon D'Arcy of Clongowes Wood College, Leinster, Ireland –'

'Wait!' I shouted.

'Yes, I was about to say Wexford Wanderers,' Clive said.

'No,' I told him, 'I've just spotted something.'

Down below us, in the middle of small cluster of trees, I could see a red tent.

'Can you land this thing?' I asked Clive.

'Roger Wilco,' he said, which was obviously pilot speak for yes, because he started to bring us down.

'What is it?' asked Johnno as we finally touched the ground and waited for the rotor blades to stop spinning.

'There's a tent,' I said, 'among those trees over there.'

'Who's in it?' he asked.

'I don't know for sure,' I told him, 'but I could take a good guess.'

When the blades were finally still, we opened our doors and climbed out. It was a hot morning. The sun was beating down on our heads. We started to make our way towards the trees.

'You were right,' said Johnno as we got closer. 'There *is* a red tent in there.'

A moment later, the three of us were standing directly in front of it.

'Hello?' I called out. 'Hello?'

Suddenly, behind us, we heard the sound of a twig snapping, then a voice said, 'Halt! Who goes there?'

We spun around. And standing there, pointing a sharpened stick at us, with two black stripes painted on either cheek and a wild look in his eyes, was none other than Flash Barry.

'Who *are* you?' he asked, a crazy edge to his voice. 'Have you come to kill me?'

'Er, no,' I told him, 'we haven't come to kill you.'

He showed the pointed end of the stick to each of us in turn.

'If you're not happy with the accommodation,' he said, 'you can ring Joe Duffy and talk to him about it. But he'll probably tell you what I'm telling you – you should have read the terms and conditions.'

He was wearing leopard-skin long johns and no shirt and he had a bandana tied around his head.

'Barry?' I said. 'It's okay, Barry – it's me! It's Gordon!'

'Darce?' he replied, narrowing his eyes to better to take me in. Then, once he was satisfied that he wasn't hallucinating, he relaxed. He even sounded pleased to see me. 'Darce! What are you doing here?'

'I was about to ask you the same thing,' I told him. 'Why are you camping out here on your own?'

'Oh,' he said, 'I don't know if you heard, but one or two people on the tour were a bit unhappy with the accommodation that was provided for them.'

'One or two people?' I repeated. 'Try more than two hundred people! Including my family! Barry, you promised them a luxury-hotel experience! They're living in tents in the middle of a wildlife reserve!'

'Hey,' he said, 'it clearly stated in the brochure that the accommodation shown might not be the one offered.'

'It didn't clearly state it,' I reminded him. 'I had to use my sister's microscope to read it.'

'That's why it's called the small print, Dude,' he said. 'Anyway, like I said, not everyone was happy with the alternative accommodation offered, which was why I decided to, er, take the business offline temporarily.'

He stuck out his hand then and introduced himself to Clive and Johnno.

'Barry,' he said. 'I'm a friend of Gordon's.'

'He's not a friend of mine,' I told them. 'Quite the opposite, in fact.'

'I'm a tour operator,' he said, shaking first Clive's hand, then Johnno's. 'I also do a bit of agenting work. Can I ask you, Johnno, do you have representation at the moment?'

'Er, yeah,' said Johnno, 'I do.'

'Because if you *were* thinking of switching, I would be more than happy to add you to my roster of clients. I represent a diverse range of athletes across a whole range of sports, helping them to manage their careers while maximizing their earning potential.'

'I think he's suffering from heat stroke,' said Clive.

'No,' I told him, 'this is what Barry is like all the time.'

'Sign up with me,' Barry continued, 'and I will get you some major moolah. You know what I'm talking about when I say moolah? I'm talking about coin. I'm talking about boodle. I'm talking about cha-ching. If you're looking for references, Gordon here will vouch for me.'

'I won't,' I said.

'He'll tell you what I did for him and I've no doubt he'll do it in glowing terms.'

'He nearly ruined my life, Johnno. Don't sign anything he offers you.'

'What about you, Clive?' Barry asked. 'Do you have an agent? Sorry if I came across as a little crazy earlier. It's just I haven't really slept for a week, what with the fear of being torn apart by wild animals and dissatisfied customers –'

'Barry,' I said, interrupting him, 'we're here today because we want to move into your camp.'

A smile suddenly illuminated his face.

'You want to be a part of Flash Travel's Tour of South Africa?' he asked. 'Hey, I think I can offer you guys a competitive rate.'

'We have no intention of paying,' I told him. 'We're doing you a favour here, Barry.'

'How do you work that one out, Dude?'

'We're offering our suites in the Grand Hotel Cape Town to all the customers you let down.'

'What if I said I could let you have the tents for a thousand euros per man? I'm just thinking of my overheads here.'

Clive turned around and started to walk back to the helicopter. 'Well, this has been a wasted journey,' he said.

'Alright,' said Barry, 'seven hundred and fifty euros per man. Those are good tents – they're elephant-proof!'

'They're not elephant-proof!' I told him. 'One thing they're definitely NOT is elephant-proof!'

Johnno started walking back to the helicopter then and I followed him.

'Okay,' said Barry, running to catch up with us. 'On behalf of Flash Travel, I would like to accept your offer to swap accommodation.'

'Good,' said Clive.

'Can I just ask you one tiny favour? Can I break the good news to my customers?'

'What,' I said, 'so you can claim the credit for them getting to stay in a seven-star hotel?'

'Well, yes,' he admitted. 'They were very angry the last time they saw me. I can tell them it was all a big mix-up and the Grand Hotel Cape Town had rooms for them after all.'

'I don't mind who tells them,' said Clive.

Barry climbed into the helicopter with us. He rubbed his hands together.

'You can say what you want about Flash Barry,' he said, 'but he always delivers in the end!'

42 A Noise in the Night

'There's nowhere to pleg in may hair-drayer.'

I was sharing a tent with Gavin Henson, who was quickly discovering the disadvantages of living outdoors.

'Of course there's nowhere to plug in your hair-dryer!' I told him. 'We're in the middle of the bush! There's no electricity!'

'But how can I look may best if I don't have access to may hair-drayer?' he asked. 'There isn't even a mirror in here!'

'I don't think having access to our home comforts is what this tour is about any more,' I said.

I climbed into my sleeping bag and I zipped it up. I was exhausted after the match the night before and the job of packing up all my things and moving out of the Grand Hotel Cape Town. Mum and

Dad took my suite. Ian took Johnno's. Shona and Megan took Faz's. Conor and Peter took Paulie's. And Aoife took Gavin's, which she was thrilled about, firstly because she was a huge fan, and secondly because he left her all of his good shampoo and moisturizers.

Flash Barry, of course, took Clive's suite and he didn't waste a moment in letting everybody know that he was responsible for the sudden improvement in their living conditions.

'I told you I wouldn't let you down,' I heard him telling the tour party as he showed them into the spectacular lobby of the hotel. 'At Flash Travel, we care passionately about the comfort of our customers.'

I just thought, let him have his moment.

'So what's the point of livven in a tent like this?' Gavin asked.

'Johnno thinks we've all gone soft,' I reminded him. 'He thinks living like this will toughen us –'

Suddenly, from somewhere outside, we heard a loud, blood-curling animal roar. It went:

RrroooOOOAAARRRRRR!!!!!!

I felt my heart quicken in my chest.

'What the hell was that?' Gavin asked.

'I don't know!' I told him.

'It was Bomb,' he said. 'He's playing a treck on us! Bomb, was that you?'

Bomb and Jonathan Davies were in the tent next to ours.

'It wasn't me, I swear,' he said. 'But I heard it – same as you boys.'

A second later, we heard it again:

RrroooOOOAAARRRRRR!!!!!!

Except it seemed to come from closer by this time.

'Alright,' shouted Faz, 'I wanna know oo's doing that? Whoever it is, knock it off, alright?'

'No one's doo-en et,' Bomb said in a loud whisper. 'It's an animal. And lower your blooming voice, Faz. Whatever et es, et might be hungray.'

We all lay there then, completely silent, and frozen with fear. But whatever it was that roared had obviously gone because we didn't hear it again.

As tired as I was, I found it very difficult to get to sleep after that. After a few hours of trying to make myself comfortable on the hard dirt ground, while convinced that every noise I heard outside was

an animal coming to eat me, I finally managed to drift off.

I don't know how long I'd been asleep when I suddenly woke with the urge to pee. Clive had told us that we all needed to increase our intake of fluids now that we were living outdoors. I'd drunk a pint of water before I went to bed and it had gone right through me.

I thought I'd maybe try and hold it until the morning – or at least until it got a little bit brighter outside. But, after ten minutes of crossing my legs and trying not to think about it, I realized that it was no good – I couldn't hold it for any longer.

'Where are you gowen?' Gavin asked me as I slipped out of my sleeping bag.

'Call of nature,' I told him.

'You're gowen outside, are you?'

'I have to. I need to pee.'

'You must be mad.'

I unzipped the tent and stuck my head out. I had never seen darkness like it. I was suddenly very, very scared.

'At least take may head torch,' Gavin said.

Gavin threw it to me. I strapped it onto my head and switched it on.

'Go on, then,' he urged me. 'The quecker you go, the quecker you'll be back, Darce.'

I crawled out through the opening in the tent, then I stood up. It was pitch dark. I looked down and the light from the torch lit up the ground in front of my feet.

Slowly and silently, determined not to become a midnight snack for whatever might be out there, I crept over to the area of long grass – six feet high – at the back of the escarpment.

I did the necessary and felt an instant sense of relief that caused me to forget all about my fear.

I looked up and I trained my beam of light onto the grass in front of me. I swept it backwards and forwards. And, in that moment, I almost passed out with the fright.

Because all I could see, staring back at me from the darkness of the thick grass, were dozens and dozens of pairs of eyes.

43 *A Tablespoon of Concrete*

'Who were that screaming in t'middle of t'night?' Faz asked as we warmed up for training the following morning.

I said nothing. I knew he was talking about me, but I hoped that nobody else had heard.

'It was Darce!' said Gavin. 'Loud enough to wake the sheep in the Ogmore Valley!'

'Yeah, Lol heard you as well,' said Lol. 'What was it all abaaht?'

'Oh, nothing,' I insisted.

'Tell 'em,' said Gavin. 'Tell 'em what you told me. Listen to thes, boys.'

Everyone stopped stretching then and gathered around me. So I had no choice but to tell them.

'I got up for a pee in the middle of the night,' I

said, 'just in front of the long grass at the back of the escarpment.'

'And?' said Faz. 'What 'appened?'

'I let the beam of my head torch sweep backwards and forwards. And all I could see were –'

'What?' said Paulie.

'Eyes,' I said.

'Whose eyes were they?' asked Johnny Sexton.

'I've no idea. They could have been anything.'

'Hey, did you 'ear what 'appened to me?' asked Bomb.

'No,' I said, 'what?'

'It were about four o'clock in the mornen and something was sniffen around outside may tent.'

'What was it?'

'Some kind of animal. I bopped hem on the nose.'

'You did what?'

'Hit him. On the nose. Not too 'ard – just 'ard enough so as to frighten hem off.'

I had to laugh. Bomb was frightened of absolutely nothing.

'Well, I don't know abaaht you lot,' said Johnno, 'but I 'ad the best night's sleep I'd 'ad since we arrived in South Africa.'

Some of the players were clearly braver than others!

Clive had decided that since we were so keen to live on the wildlife reserve, we might as well train on it as well. So he had the Lions staff paint the outline of a rugby pitch on the hard dirt ground, then they cut down lengths of bamboo and tied them together to make two sets of goalposts.

'Good morning, gentlemen,' Clive said. 'I trust you all enjoyed your first night sleeping outside in the wilds of Africa. This morning, I thought we'd practise our Three Minutes of Excellence –'

'No,' snapped Johnno.

'No?' said Clive. 'What do you mean, no?'

'Look, no disrespect, Clive, but we're going to need something more than that to counteract the Bomb Squad. We got bashed up in the first Test. Bashed up badly. Especially our backs.'

Clive looked at me, Jonathan and Faz.

'I'm not sure if our boys have what it takes to match the Bomb Squad for physicality,' he said.

'Isn't that why we're out 'ere,' said Johnno, 'sleeping under the sky? To toughen everyone up? So let's do it!'

'What are you suggesting?'

'At Leicester,' Johnno said, 'we do a drill called "A Tablespoon of Concrete".'

Tablespoon of Concrete? I already didn't like the sound of it.

'I've got a bad feeling about this,' Faz said to me out of the side of his mouth.

'Me too,' I said.

Johnno called for the ruck pads, which only increased my fear. He handed them out to all of the forwards – Lol, Bomb, Paulie, Cian Healy, Hamish Watson, Alun Wyn Jones, Richard Hill, Neil Back. He kept one for himself.

Then they positioned themselves so that they were standing two by two, one metre apart, forming a sort of tunnel. They held up their ruck pads like they were riot shields.

'Alright, Darce,' said Johnno, who was standing at the front next to Bomb, 'run at us and try to muscle past us.'

'What?' I asked. 'Why?'

'You're gonna relive the experience of what it's like to run into the Bomb Squad,' he said. 'And you're going to do it over and over and over again, so that it 'olds no fear for you. The rest of the backs, form a queue. Alright, Darce, let's go, mate!'

There was no point in arguing with him. Johnno was the captain of the team after all. So I took a deep breath and I ran at them. Behind their pads, they braced their shoulders for the impact.

I ran into Johnno on one side and Bomb on the other and I bounced off them and landed on the flat of my back.

'Up you get, Darce!' Johnno told me.

'What are we supposed to be learning from this?' I asked, picking myself up from the ground.

'You're learning 'ow to use your footwork, rather than brute force, to find a way through the Bomb Squad,' he said. 'You're learning 'ow to use your body angle to change the point of contact so you can get past 'em.'

'Right.'

'Go to the back of the queue, Darce. Your head should have cleared by the time it's your turn again. Johnny Sexton, you're next. Don't look so worried, Darce, we'll only do this for abaaht two hours – no longer than that!'

44 *A Sneak in My Tent*

It was the morning of the second Test. We were sitting around the campfire, eating a breakfast of sausages, which we stuck on the end of pointed sticks and held over the flames to cook, and cold baked beans straight from the tin.

We'd been living outdoors now for six nights. And I'm going to admit something – I didn't miss my chocolate fountain at all. Or, in fact, any of the comforts we'd enjoyed in the Grand Hotel Cape Town.

Like most of the other players, I'd also gotten used to the strange noises we heard in the night. The roars. The screeches. The howls.

Even when I woke up and felt an animal's nose pressed against me through the canvas of the tent, I would just say, 'Oh, go away, whatever you are!' before rolling over and falling asleep again.

Six nights sleeping outdoors had toughened us up in other ways as well – especially the backs. We practised A Tablespoon of Concrete for two hours every day. And something happened – just as something happens whenever you practise something over and over again. We got better at it. Which is to say that we started to squeeze through the tiny gap in the ruck pads.

We learned not to look at the four men standing there, barring our way, and to concentrate instead on the space between them. Faz was the first one to get through. Then Jonathan. Then me. Then Gavin. And soon we were able to get through the gap once out of every three times we tried it.

We were almost finished with breakfast when Clive stepped out of his tent, looking neatly turned out and well-rested. That was one of the great mysteries of our time living in the bush. We all looked rough. We were dirty and our breath stank and probably so did we. Everyone looked tired and had a good growth of stubble on their face – except me, of course, given that I was still a boy. But Clive emerged from his tent every morning, clean-shaven, wearing a fresh white shirt, along with a cravat, and neatly pressed trousers. And he always looked like he'd just had the best sleep of his life.

'Morning, gentlemen,' he said. 'I trust we all enjoyed our breakfast, did we? I'm going to break slightly with Lions tradition today. I'm not going to tell you who's in the team for tonight by slipping a note under your door – mainly because you don't have doors. Telling you to all go back to your tents and then posting your number through the flap seems a bit silly. So I'm going to put you all out of your misery now.'

He named the team for the second match against South Africa. It was the same fifteen players who'd

started the first Test – except I was starting at outside-centre instead of BOD.

'I trust you men,' he said, 'because after last weekend, you understand the enormity of the job facing us. You know what it's going to take to beat South Africa. Be ready in an hour – the flight leaves at midday.'

The second Test was taking place in Durban, a huge city on the other side of South Africa, on the Indian Ocean coast, in the province of KwaZulu-Natal.

Clive turned to walk away, then he spun around, pointed at Bomb and said, 'Adam Jones. It's the last minute against South Africa and they have a scrum ten metres from our line. When you engage with the opposition loosehead, you realize you've jarred a nerve in your back and you're in agony. What do you do?'

Bomb didn't get the opportunity to answer because Gavin Henson suddenly appeared and there was a loud cheer from everyone. Gavin was famous for his lie-ins and the players would bet money on what time he would surface each morning.

'I weren't t'one who said nine o'clock!' declared Faz. 'You owe me a tenner, Lol.'

'Whoo do we knae it's even hum?' said Stuart Hogg.

This was another running joke. Since we'd moved outdoors, Gavin had begun to look less and less like himself every day. Back home in Wales, he was a part-time model, but he looked far from it now. His hair was a mess and he looked strangely pale.

'Boys,' he said, 'there's semthen I 'ave to tell you. There's a sneek in my tent.'

'A sneak?' I asked, thinking, for a horrible moment, that he was referring to me.

'No, not a sneak,' he said. 'A sneek. It's a long, limbless reptile that 'as fangs full of venom.'

'What?' I asked, jumping to my feet. 'How long has he been in there?'

'I 'ave no idea,' he said. 'I just woke up and saw the thing staring at me from the other side of the tent with 'is 'orrible, unblinken eyes.'

'How big is it?' I asked.

'At a guess, I'd say about six metres.'

'Six metres? Are you serious?'

'It's probably an African rock python,' said Clive. 'It's the biggest snake in Africa.'

'Is it poisonous?'

'No, nothing to worry about there – all pythons are non-venomous.'

'Thank God for that.'

'Pythons kill by constriction.'

'Constriction? What's that?'

'They wrap their bodies around their prey and crush it to death.'

Johnno jumped to his feet.

'What are we,' he asked, 'a bunch of cowards? Come on, let's see how tough this snake is.'

We all got to our feet then, left the safety of the campfire and followed Johnno to the tent. The snake was just emerging through the flap when we arrived.

Gavin was right. He was enormous. As he slithered out of the tent, there seemed to be no end to him and he was as thick as the branch of a tree. He looked up and he saw us all standing there, contemplating him. He stared at us for a long moment with his cold, dead eyes, while flicking his tongue at us.

Then, suddenly, he reared up, lifting the top part of his body off the ground, so that his head was now at the same height as Paulie's. He hissed at us. Instinctively, we all took a step backwards – except Johnno, who was staring him down.

'Right,' he said, 'I'm going to tackle him.'

'What?' I asked. 'Are you out of your mind?'

'I'll 'it 'im first, up front, just to shock 'im,' Johnno said, 'then a second later, Lol will grab him around the middle just to 'old 'im, then after that Bomb will grab him by the tail to make sure he can't do no damage wiv it. What do you fink, boys?'

'Alrait,' said Bomb. 'I'm up for et if Lol is.'

'Lol is up for it,' said Lol. 'Lol is always up for it.'

'Okay,' said Johnno, 'one . . . two . . . three . . .'

He threw himself at the python, knocking it to the ground and holding its jaw closed with one of his giant hands. In almost the same moment, Lol grabbed the snake around the mid-section and held on tightly to it, while Bomb dived on the tail, just as the snake lifted it with the intention of clobbering Johnno and Lol with it.

The snake struggled for all it was worth, bucking and writhing to try to throw the three of them off. But they held on tightly and, after about thirty seconds, the snake had been fully subdued.

'You can let go now,' said Johnno.

'But he's still alave,' said Bomb. 'He's still mooven, look.'

'It don't matter,' said Johnno. 'The fing is, 'e knows who's boss now. It's awright – you can let 'im go, boys.'

So they did let him go. And, just as Johnno suggested, the snake, looking chastened, slid away on his stomach, having clearly learned his lesson.

The rest of the players were all looking at each other, seriously impressed by what we'd just seen.

And Johnno smiled like he'd suddenly been hit by a thunderbolt of an idea.

'I've just figured aaht,' he said, '' 'ow to beat the Bomb Squad!'

45 *How to Beat the Bomb Squad*

'Explain et to may again,' said Bomb.

'Well, if I shouted the words "Ninety-nine" during a match, what would you lot fink?' Johnno asked.

'I'd think you were talking about an ice cream with a Flake sticking out of it,' I said, 'but I don't see how that's going to help us against the Bomb Squad.'

Everyone stared at me open-mouthed. I began to suspect that I had got the wrong end of the stick.

'The Ninety-nine Call,' Clive said, 'was something the Lions came up with during the 1974 tour of South Africa. It was a way of responding to rough play from the Springboks. It was a "one-in, all-in" policy, which meant that all the Lions players had to bail out any teammate who was in trouble – once he

341

shouted, "Ninety-nine!" – in the knowledge that the referee couldn't send the entire team off.'

'And there was definitely no ice cream involved?' I asked.

'No, it has nothing whatsoever to do with ice cream,' said Clive.

Johnno looked around the dressing room.

'After an hour, when the Bomb Squad arrive, we need to turn up the temperature on 'em,' he said. 'Except we're not gonna shout Ninety-nine. We're not gonna shout anyfing, in fact. As soon as one of the Bomb Squad gets 'is hands on the ball, that's the call for the three players nearest to him to – BANG! BANG! BANG! – 'it 'im like we 'it that snake!'

Ross Ford smiled. 'If we're gonnae beat South Africa,' he said, 'we're gonnae have tae hammer the hammer!'

''Ammer the 'ammer!' Johnno agreed.

'I know I'm only on the bench,' Gavin Henson told Clive, 'but if I heppen to be on the field in the last twentay minutes, you will not find me hi-denn.'

'That's good to know,' said Clive. 'Right, does everyone know their roles tonight?'

'Yes,' we all told him.

'And you don't need me to remind you what's on the line. Lose tonight and the series is over. Win – and it gives us a chance of going into the final Test next weekend. And remember the two things we've learned. Try and give me Three Minutes of Excellence when I ask for it – and keep Thinking . . . Calmly . . . Under . . . Pressure.'

Johnno stood up.

'Right, lads,' he shouted, 'let's be 'avin' you!' and he marched with purpose towards the dressing-room door and tore it open so violently that I thought it might snap off in his hand.

We ran out onto the pitch to a chorus of boos from the home crowd. The weather was just as hostile towards us. It was a wet night. The rain had been bucketing down ever since we'd stepped off the plane that afternoon and there were giant pools of water all over the pitch. The referee was considering cancelling the match. He called Johnno and the Springbok captain, John Smit, together and asked them if they were happy to play in the conditions.

'Don't even fink abaaht calling it off,' Johnno told him.

John Smit agreed. 'Lit us just git on with ut,' he said in his South African accent.

One thing was for sure – it wasn't going to be a match of exciting, running rugby.

'What do you think?' I asked Jonathan as we took

up our positions and waited for the game to start. 'Have you ever played rugby in weather like this before?'

'I come from Wales,' he reminded me. 'I've played in worse than this – plentay of times. Just don't teek any unnecessary resks, Darce.'

Faz kicked off, booting the ball deep into the South African half. It didn't even bounce. It came down and landed with a dull splat in a puddle right on the opposition twenty-two. Zane Kirchner, the Springbok full-back, picked it up, shook the water off it and kicked it back in the direction it had come from.

And so began perhaps the worst forty minutes of rugby anyone in the stadium had ever seen. The only excitement for the crowd was when a player lost his footing on the wet ground, as I did three times in the first forty minutes. But in a funny way, the weather played into our hands. In conditions like that, it's easier NOT to have the ball. So we let the Springboks have loads of possession and we tackled them hard as the rain continued to fall in sheets.

When half-time arrived, neither team had scored a single point. The crowd was growing restless. They had come to see South Africa finish us off, but the first half was so boring for them and they had to watch while getting absolutely soaked to the skin.

When we got back to the dressing room, Clive told us we were doing great.

'This is going to be a one-score match,' he said. 'And, from the evidence of the first half, we're the team most likely to get it. Just keep Thinking Calmly Under Pressure and give me those Three Minutes of Excellence when I ask for them.'

But then the referee stuck his head around the door of the dressing room and said that if the rain didn't stop by the time the second half started, he was going to abandon the match and declare it a 0–0 draw. Our hearts sank. A 0–0 draw meant that we couldn't win the series. Even if we won the final Test, the best we could hope for would be a draw.

'Forget abaaht the rain!' Johnno said. He was pacing the floor of the dressing room like a caged animal, determined to get out there again. 'Let's focus on the fings we can control – and let's not forget that, right now, they're winning. A draw 'ere tonight means that we can't win the series – but they still can. So we 'ave to win the match or we might as well go 'ome tomorrow.'

He looked at me and Jonathan. 'We need a bit of magic from one of you two to turn this match,' he said. 'And don't forget – twenty minutes' time, we've got the Bomb Squad coming on. I hope we're tough enough for them this time.'

A few minutes later, we walked back out onto the pitch. To our great surprise, the rain had stopped and the air had turned warm, even tropical.

This change in the conditions resulted in a shift in the mood of both sets of players. Suddenly, we both started playing more hopeful, optimistic rugby, putting passing moves together and running with the ball, trying to beat players. It was like a completely different match.

We won a five-metre scrum. The ball shot out to Mike Phillips. Jonathan and I ran flat lines, but Mike hit Faz on the short line off the scrum. No one saw it coming. Faz beat two players and managed to get over the line for a try. But the referee went to the TMO and decided that the ball had been held up by Duane Vermeulen, the South Africa number eight, and the score stayed at 0–0.

Then, shortly afterwards, South Africa were convinced that they were going to open the scoring when Cheslin Kolbe, their brilliant winger, chipped the ball over the heads of our players and over the try line. But the ball bounced over the end line just before he could touch it down.

The minutes whizzed by. Then, suddenly, the

stadium floodlights went off and we could hear the sound of drums through the PA system again – the same loud, ominous-sounding drums that had signalled the arrival of the Bomb Squad in Cape Town. The crowd went wild.

Six of the Springbok forwards made their way off the pitch and I could see the six substitutes waiting to come on, lit up by a spotlight.

'The substitutes for South Africa,' said the stadium announcer, 'are Malcolm Marx, Stephen Kitshoff, Vincent Koch, R.G. Snyman, Franco Mostert and Francois Louw.'

The crowd roared even louder as they took to the field and the floodlights clicked on again. And then the chant went up:

'BOMB! SQUAD! BOMB! SQUAD! BOMB! SQUAD!'

Johnno didn't need to tell us what to do in that moment. A simple look said all that needed to be said.

We decided to let them have the ball. Instead of them tackling us, WE were going to tackle THEM. And we would do it hard!

A few seconds later, Stephen Kitshoff had the ball in his hands and he tried to power his way through our midfield. I was the nearest Lions player to him, so I went in low, chopping at his knees . . .

BANG!

Then Bomb arrived from the other side and hit him around the waist . . .

BANG!

. . . so that Kitshoff sort of tottered, looking like he might fall at any moment, before Paul O'Connell arrived and administered the final knockout.

BANG!

It all happened in a split-second. And Kitshoff was so shocked that he dropped the ball right into Jonathan's hands, who performed a brilliant spiral kick to find touch five metres from the Springbok try line.

Johnno slapped me on the back. 'That's 'ow you do it, Darce!' he said encouragingly.

We could see the shock on the faces of the Bomb Squad. They hadn't been expecting us to hit back like that.

From the lineout, it happened again. Franco Mostert had the ball and set off on a big, arcing run. Johnno tackled him hard, followed by Bomb, followed by Lol, all in quick succession. They drove him back fifteen metres and we ended up being awarded a scrum.

This happened five or six times and I could see the Bomb Squad looking across to Rassie Erasmus, the Springbok coach, as if to say, 'What do we do here? They're not scared of us!'

There were five minutes remaining and the score was still 0–0. We had possession of the ball. But unless we made something happen very quickly, we wouldn't be able to win the series. Jonathan ran at the Springbok defence. As he was tackled, he flicked the ball, back-handed, to me, which opened up space in front of me.

I raced ahead and I noticed four members of the Bomb Squad – Marx, Louw, Snyman and Kitshoff – standing in front of me, like a brick wall, seven foot high and seven foot deep. And maybe I was Thinking Calmly Under Pressure in that moment. Or maybe I was just remembering the Tablespoon of Concrete drill I'd practised hundreds of times that week. But I knew immediately what I was going to do.

I was going to go THROUGH them!

From Johnno's drill, I knew it was about coming in at the right angle. My body jolted as I hit Marx with my left shoulder and Snyman with my right, then in the same movement I was barging my way through Kitshoff and Louw and now all I could see in front of me was a clear route to the line.

I ran with all the strength that was left in my legs. Five yards from the Springbok line, I felt myself

being firmly tackled from behind and pulled to the ground. As I fell, I twisted to my right and Jonathan was right behind me. I managed to bundle the ball into his hands. He ran on and dived underneath the posts to score a try.

Shortly after Faz converted it, the match was over. We fell to our knees. We'd done it. We'd beaten South Africa. Now the series was level.

But, even more importantly, we knew that we no longer had anything to fear from the Bomb Squad!

46 *Humbling*

We flew back to Cape Town that night and returned to our tents in the wildlife reserve – swapping the noisy commotion of a packed stadium for the eerie quiet of the bush.

It was three o'clock in the morning when we got back to our camp. But no one wanted to sleep. We were still buzzing with excitement after the events of the night.

Johnno lit a fire and we all went off and gathered armfuls of wood to feed it. We pulled our chairs around it in a large circle. Then Lol lit the barbecue and soon we were eating hamburgers and sausages and reliving the match.

'Here, Darce, I thought Marx and Snyman were gonna absolutely cream you!' Faz laughed.

'Tablespoon of Concrete!' Johnno said, at the same time raising one eyebrow to me.

'Tablespoon of Concrete!' I agreed – because it was practising the move over and over again that had made it second nature to me.

We stayed up all night, telling each other more about where we came from and exchanging funny stories. We really bonded around that campfire. And it wasn't just the players who were on the pitch in Durban – it was the entire squad. There was a real togetherness about us.

Paulie came up with the idea that we should each do a party-piece – sing a song, or tell a joke, or perform a trick, for the entertainment of the rest of the group.

Bomb went first. He could juggle. Not only could he juggle – he was the best juggler any of us had ever seen! He started off juggling three Coca-Cola bottles, then he called for someone to throw another one to him. Johnny Sexton threw one and, in a rapid flash of hands, Bomb caught it and added it to the others he had spinning in the air. Everyone clapped and cheered at this amazing feat.

'Oh, you ain't seen nething yet, boys,' he told us, then he started calling for more and more bottles.

I threw one to him. Johnno threw one to him. Faz threw one to him. He caught them all and, barely breaking rhythm, incorporated each one into the juggle, while we cheered every time. Eventually, he was juggling FIFTEEN Coca-Cola bottles. And when he'd decided we'd seen enough, he put them down on the ground, one by one, while continuing to juggle the rest.

It was seriously, SERIOUSLY impressive.

Then it was Lol's turn. He announced that he was going to sing 'All Things Bright and Beautiful'. I didn't expect him to have a good voice. I don't know why. Perhaps it was because he was so tough on the pitch. But when he opened his mouth, out came this amazing tenor voice:

'All things bright and beautiful,
All creatures great and small . . .'

Next up was Gavin. He told us he was going to show us his Paso Doble – which, it turned out, was a fast-paced Spanish dance that he'd performed on *Strictly Come Dancing*.

'Okay, I need a partner,' he said.

There were no volunteers, but Paulie threw him a tackle bag.

'This will do perfect,' Gavin said.

A moment later, he was Paso Dobling his way around the camp, striking bullfighter poses and swinging the tackle bag around like it was a matador's cape. The man could really move! When he finished, he received a standing ovation from the rest of us.

Next, it was me. But I'd been too busy enjoying everyone else's acts to think what I might do when my turn came. I didn't have a party-piece. I couldn't sing, or dance, or juggle for that matter.

I stood up.

'Alreet,' said Stuart, 'what are yee gonnae dae for us?'

'I don't know,' I told him honestly.

'Come on,' Johnno said, 'there must be summat you can do.'

And that was when I said it:

'I can do a one-armed press-up.'

The words were out before I'd even thought about them.

'A one-eermed press-up?' asked Stuart.

He sounded impressed. So did everyone else.

'Whoooaaa!!!' they went, rubbing their hands together in anticipation.

'Alreet, Darce,' said Stuart, 'let's see this one-eermed press-up so.'

I dropped to the ground – to the cheers of the other players. I propped myself on my left arm, twisting my body to the side to place all my weight on it. Then I put my right arm behind my back. I took a deep breath. The entire group started chanting:

'D'Ar! Cy! D'Ar! Cy! D'Ar! Cy! D'Ar! Cy!'

I bent my elbow slightly and, in slow, jerky movements, started lowering myself to the ground. My whole body shook with the effort it took. I managed to touch my chest off the floor.

That was the easy bit over. Now, I had to push myself back up again.

'D'Ar! Cy! D'Ar! Cy! D'Ar! Cy! D'Ar! Cy!'

I could feel the strain in my wrist, the pressure in my elbow, as I pushed hard against the ground and tried to lift myself up again.

'D'Ar! Cy! D'Ar! Cy! D'Ar! Cy! D'Ar! Cy!'

I raised myself one inch, then two inches, and then, with one final push . . . all the way up!

Everyone cheered. I climbed to my feet again and accepted everyone's congratulations, quietly delighted with my achievement, but not daring to tell anyone that it was the first time I'd ever done it.

But I HAD done it! A one-armed press-up! I couldn't wait to tell Conor, Peter and Aoife! I couldn't wait to tell Ian either!

Soon, the sun came up and we all started to yawn and think about heading for our tents to get some much-needed sleep. That was when we heard movement in the bushes behind us, then suddenly a zebra appeared, followed by another, then another, then another.

There were sixteen of them in all. They started to eat the grass next to us. We all sat and watched them in silent wonder, no one saying a word. It was so quiet that all we could hear was the sound of them munching away.

And they didn't pay us the slightest heed. The night before, we had played a rugby match and it felt like half the world was watching us. But to these beautiful animals, it was like we didn't even exist.

'It's humbling,' I heard myself whisper.

47 *We Shook His Hand!*

After our victory over South Africa, Clive told us we could have a day off. Some of the players went on a safari. Others headed for the beach. I decided to go back to the Grand Hotel Cape Town to find out how my family and friends were getting on.

The first person I saw when I stepped into the lobby was Flash Barry. He was much changed from the last time I'd seen him. Gone were the leopard-skin long johns and the bandana and the black lines painted on his face. He was wearing a suit now – and not just a suit, but the most expensive-looking suit I'd ever seen.

He was talking to a couple of older boys I recognized from Clongowes. They were raving about the chocolate fountain in their room.

'Well, at Flash Travel,' Barry told them, 'our focus

is your comfort. The idea of the first few days was to allow you to experience Africa with all of your senses. It was always my plan to bring you here afterwards.'

I was going to let it go until I heard him add:

'By the way, if you're interested in watching Darce play for Ireland in the World Cup, Flash Travel is currently taking bookings for France. It's three hundred euros, all-inclusive. And I know what you're thinking – how can he do it for that cheap?'

I couldn't help myself. I let out a roar at him:

'Barry!'

He turned his head and saw me for the first time.

'Speak of the devil,' he said, 'here's my business partner now!'

'I am NOT your business partner!' I told him as I grabbed him by the suit lapels and pulled him to one side.

'Hey, watch the new threads,' he said. 'Okay, you're not my business partner in the sense that I'm going to share the profits with you. But we probably wouldn't be staying in this hotel if it wasn't for you, Dude.'

'There's no *probably* about it,' I pointed out. 'You'd still be hiding in a tent in the wildlife reserve.'

'Hey, this suit cost me a lot of money, Darce.'

I let go of his lapels and he straightened his jacket.

'Okay,' he said, 'let's talk about this like two civilized people. What's up?'

'What's up?' I asked incredulously. 'Why are you telling people that I'm going to be playing for Ireland in the World Cup?'

He looked at me like I was insane.

'You are!' he said.

'You don't know that,' I told him.

'Given the way you played last night,' he said, 'you'll definitely be on the plane to France. And I want as many people as possible to see the great

Gordon D'Arcy perform on the biggest stage of all! It's a compliment to you, Darce.'

'Barry, you have to stop this!'

'I'm just giving the people what they want, Dude. Hey, do you think your old pair would be interested in going?'

I was so angry, I couldn't talk to him any more. So I brushed past him and went looking for my family and my friends.

Mum and Dad were having lunch with Ian, Megan and Shona.

'Gordon!' they all shouted at me from the other side of the restaurant. 'Come and join us!'

I walked over to them and gave them all a hug.

'You were brilliant last night!' Dad said. 'How did you squeeze through that gap to set up the try?'

'Yeah,' Ian added, 'I was convinced that Marx and Snyman were going pulverize you!'

'Well,' I told him, 'that wasn't the only amazing feat I performed in the last twenty-four hours! I did a one-armed press-up!'

'No! Way!' said Ian.

'I did!' I told him. 'I swear!'

I sat down at the table in the empty seat next to Megan.

'So, em, how's the camp?' she asked.

I laughed.

'It takes a bit of getting used to,' I told her. 'Especially with all the random noises you hear in the night.'

'All those cackles and roars!' she said. 'I don't miss those.'

'And then, of course, all the eyes looking at you from the long grass!'

'What?' Mum said.

'Yeah,' I told her, 'the one lesson I've learned is don't drink so much water that you need to get up in the night for a pee!'

'What kind of animals do these eyes belong to?' Shona asked.

'Anything and everything,' I told her.

I watched them all shudder.

'I think I'll have a massage after lunch,' Mum said.

'Another one?' Dad asked. 'You've already had one this morning!'

'Well, I'm going to have another one,' she replied. 'I'm on my holidays! There's a robot masseuse upstairs called EMMA.'

'Yes,' I said, 'we've met.'

'She gives the best massage I've ever had. I said to your dad, they'd want to get one of those in the Ferrycarrig.'

I heard my name called from the other side of the restaurant then:

'Gordon!'

I turned around and it was Aoife, along with Conor and Peter. It was so good to see them.

'You were BRILLIANT last night!' Aoife said. 'I have no idea how you squeezed through that gap! When I saw you running at Marx and Snyman, I turned away!'

'We did too!' Conor laughed. 'I can't wait for the third Test now! And you're bound to be in the team after setting up the winning try like that!'

'Er, Gordon,' Peter said, 'I don't quite know how to tell you this, but Flash Barry is telling people you're going to be playing for Ireland at the World Cup in France.'

'Yeah,' I replied. 'I asked him to stop.'

'Is he doing packages?' Dad asked.

'We are NEVER booking with Flash Travel again,' Mum reminded him.

'I don't understand,' Megan said, 'why would any-one trust him again?'

'Because most of the people on the trip have no idea that we gave them our hotel suites,' I explained. 'Barry's telling them that the week of camping was just to allow them to experience Africa with all their senses and that it was always part of the plan to bring them here.'

'What an absolute chancer!' Dad said. 'How much is he charging for the World Cup – just as a matter of interest?'

'We are NOT giving any more money to Flash Barry,' Mum said, 'and that's the end of the matter.'

'Sit down!' I told Aoife, Conor and Peter. 'We can all have lunch together!'

They all pulled up a seat and the waiter came and handed us each an enormous menu.

'So,' I said, 'how are you all enjoying the hotel?'

'It's unbelievable!' Conor said. 'There's a pool table in our room! And a table-tennis table! And a chocolate fountain!'

'We love it,' said Peter. 'But Aoife misses the great outdoors.'

'I'm not saying I don't appreciate the chocolate fountain,' she said, 'or the robot masseuse. I'm just scared that I might go soft here.'

I laughed. She was such a bad-ass.

'If you hadn't been staying here,' Conor said, 'you wouldn't have met *him*!'

'Who?' I asked. 'Who did you meet?'

'We didn't *just* meet him!' Conor said. 'We shook his hand! AND we got a selfie with him!'

He took his phone out of his pocket. I noticed Peter subtly shaking his head at Conor, trying to tell him to shut up.

'Oh, sorry,' Conor said. 'I forgot you haven't met him yet.'

'He just happened to be in the hotel last night,' Aoife said, 'for a meeting.'

'Who are you talking about?' I asked.

'President Mandela,' Peter told me, almost apologetically.

'You met Nelson Mandela?' I said, hearing a note of jealousy in my own voice. It seemed like everyone had shaken Nelson Mandela's hand except me. 'So what was he like?'

'He was the most amazing man I've ever met,' Aoife said.

'Cheer up, Gordon,' said Peter. 'I'm sure you're going to get to meet him.'

But I wasn't so certain. If I was being honest, I thought that my chance of shaking the hand of Nelson Mandela had slipped away.

48 Back to Work

It was the day before the third Test and there was an air of nervous excitement about training. We were looking forward to the match, but we weren't frightened of it, even though Clive assured us that South Africa would come back at us even more strongly the next time.

'Their pride is bound to be hurt,' he said, 'especially after what you did to their Bomb Squad. You totally destroyed them – and no one has ever done that to them before.'

Suddenly he turned to Paulie and said, 'Paul O'Connell, there's five minutes to go in the third Test and we're trailing South Africa by two points. We have a lineout on the South African twenty-two – where's the ball going to go?'

'Right into my hands,' he said, as quick as a flash.

'Then I'd try to get it back to Faz for the drop at goal.'

'Good answer,' said Clive. 'You know what you were doing there?'

'I was Thinking Calmly Under Pressure,' said Paulie.

'You were Thinking ... Calmly ... Under ... Pressure,' Clive confirmed. 'And I hope we're all going to be doing that tomorrow night.'

The third and deciding Test was to be played in Johannesburg, the biggest city in South Africa and another plane ride away from where we were staying.

'The atmosphere is going to be very hostile towards us,' said Clive. 'South Africa don't like losing at home and their fans will want to see us not only beaten, but beaten well. I know we haven't managed to do it yet, but I have a feeling that this is the match where we'll need those Three Minutes of Excellence. That's why we're going to practise it again this morning.'

Once again, he didn't get the full Three Minutes of Excellence from us, but we were edging closer to it. We practised it for an hour and we managed to get through three minutes with only two errors.

Being a perfectionist, though, Clive was disappointed and insisted that we practise it for another hour. It was just after this second hour started that the incident happened.

I had the ball in my hands. Bomb tackled me – hard but fairly. As I fell, I looked around to see who I might throw the ball to. But I landed on my elbow and I felt the most savage pain shoot down my left arm. For a moment, I was convinced that I'd broken it again. I didn't even want to look at it.

Bomb grabbed my arm – the sore one – and pulled me to my feet. As he did so, he watched me grimace.

'You alright, mate?' he said.

'I just, em, banged my funny bone,' I told him.

I could see the look of concern on Clive's face as well.

'Gordon, is your arm okay?' he asked. 'Do you need some ice for it?'

'No, it's fine,' I told him, returning to action.

But it wasn't fine. Though the pain eased, I started to become self-conscious of it. Going into contact, my first thought was to protect it at all costs, even if it meant dropping the ball.

We had gotten the closest we'd been yet to Three Minutes of Excellence, but suddenly we couldn't hold onto possession for more than thirty seconds – and it was usually me who lost it.

'Are you sure that arm is okay?' Clive asked me when we decided to give it up altogether. 'You seem to be worried about injuring it.'

'It's fine,' I told him. 'I'm not worried about it at all.'

The thing was, though . . . I was lying.

49 *The Fear*

The third Test was five minutes old and we had gotten off to the worst possible start. South Africa had scored three tries in the first five minutes and we were all just running around in shock.

The score was 21–0 and the Johannesburg crowd was going wild. They knew their team was well on the way to winning the third match and the series.

Out of the corner of my eye, I could see a lot of activity on the side of the pitch. The substitutes were warming up. Clive had the board in his hand. And on the board, I could see my number – the number thirteen. I'd only been playing for six minutes and he was taking me off!

The embarrassment of it! With my family and friends in the crowd! With half of Ireland watching!

I had to do something. I had to do something quickly.

Lood de Jager, the South African second-row, had the ball tucked under his arm and he was making a lot of yards. He stepped into my channel and he was running straight for me with his head down.

Instinct took over – my absolute need to stop him from going past me. I stretched out my left arm to tried to grab him around the waist – but, as he sped past me, the point of his elbow struck my forearm hard. I fell to the ground, letting out a loud, piercing scream, like an animal roar:

RRRRRRAAAAAAGGGHHH!!!

I sat up again. Relief slowly washed over me as I realized that it had all been a dream. I looked to my left. Gavin was fast asleep in his sleeping bag, having an altogether happier dream judging from his mutterings:

'Dancing the Samba, it's Mid Glamorgan's very own Fred Astaire. Ladies and gentlemen, let me hear it for . . . GAVIN!!! HENSON!!!'

I lay down again and tried to get back to sleep. But it was no good. All I could think about was my arm. Clive was right. I *was* suddenly worried about hurting it again – and it was affecting the way I played.

I'd heard that this sometimes happened to players who came back from career-threatening injuries. The fear of it happening again started to eat away at them. As I lay there in the dark stillness of the tent, I realized that it had happened to me.

I had lost my nerve.

And I realized something else too. I was bursting for a pee again. I tried to focus on something else.

Gavin was still happily dreaming one of his *Strictly Come Dancing* dreams:

'Gavin,' he said, in an Italian accent, 'what can I say? That was a Samba FULL of pecs appeal!'

No, there was no use trying to put it off. I needed to go and I needed to go urgently!

I picked up Gavin's head torch and I strapped it to my forehead. Then I unzipped the tent and stepped out into the chilly, pitch-black night. I made my way to the long grass at the back of the escarpment, the light from my torch illuminating the ground beneath my feet.

This time, I decided I wouldn't train my beam of light on the long grass for fear of seeing those creepy eyes again.

Moments later, as I performed the necessary task, I thought about everything. I didn't want to let my teammates down. But I was so concerned about hurting my arm again that that's what was going to happen if I played in the third Test.

I came to a decision. I was going to tell Clive the truth – that I had lost my courage. And that he should pick someone else instead.

At that exact moment, I heard a movement in the long grass in front of me. Then I felt the ground start to shudder. Suddenly, the grass parted like a curtain – and all at once I found myself standing face to face . . .

. . . with a lion!

My first instinct was to scream. But when I opened my mouth, no noise came out. My next instinct was to run. But when I tried to move my feet, I discovered that they were rooted to the ground.

The lion gave me a long, cold stare. I could hear a low grumble coming from deep inside him – like the sound my tummy made when I was hungry, except a thousand times louder.

Then he opened his mouth and he let out a roar that almost blew me back off my feet. I could see his incisors – as sharp as knitting needles – and saliva dripped from his jaw.

From out of nowhere, I found myself whispering:

'I'm not scared of you. I'm not scared of you. I'm not scared of you.'

I don't know where it came from. I just felt the urge to say it. And I continued to say it, even when the lion emerged fully from the cover of the grass and I saw the size of him.

He was HUGE!

I looked at his muscular front legs, and his enormous paws, and his razor-sharp claws, and I continued to whisper my mantra:

'I'm not scared of you! I'm not scared of you! I'm not scared of you!'

And in that moment, I thought about Mystic Martha. I remembered what she had told me about my spirit animal being a lion.

He stepped forward, never taking his eyes off me, until our faces were about three inches apart. He was so close to me now that every time he exhaled, I could feel my hair being parted in the middle.

'I'm not scared of you!' I whispered. 'I'm not scared of you! I'm not scared of you!'

He sniffed my face. And, as he did, I noticed something that surprised me. My breathing was completely normal. My heart wasn't even beating fast. I really WASN'T scared of him!

And something unbelievable happened then. Without taking his eyes off me, the lion started to back away. Then he turned his back on me and, with one final look at me over his shoulder, he disappeared into the long grass again.

A calm resolve had settled over me. I realized that I wasn't frightened of injuring my arm any more. I'd just come face to face with a lion and lived to tell the tale. Except I didn't tell the tale – not to my family, not to my friends, not to my teammates. As a matter of fact, I've kept it to myself until now.

But, from that moment on, how could I be frightened of anything?

50 *Thinking Calmly Under Pressure*

'Pre-match team talk,' Clive said into his little mouth-piece, 'delivered by Sir Clive Woodward, coach of the British & Irish Lions. Third Test. Ellis Park Stadium, Johannesburg. This is it, guys. This is the culmination of months and months of hard work. It all comes down to what happens here tonight. This is the match that will decide whether you'll be remembered as winning Lions . . . or losing Lions.'

I looked around at my teammates – at Johnno, and Paulie, and Lol, and Faz, and Bomb, and Stuart, and Gavin, and Jonathan. I thought about all we'd been through together over the past few weeks and how much we'd bonded as a team. A month ago, most of us were strangers to each other. A group of players from Ireland, England, Scotland and Wales who had to learn to play as a team and think as a team. And we'd done it.

Sleeping outdoors in the African wild, surrounded by animals who regarded our camp as a giant buffet, had toughened us up, just as Johnno said it would. It had brought us closer together too.

'Remember what Jeremy Guscott told you,' Clive said, 'about the moment when he kicked the drop goal that won the series against South Africa in 1997. He said his entire rugby career flashed before his eyes. That's how much it means to be a winning Lion. Don't forget the things we've learned out there today. Three Minutes of Excellence and Thinking Calmly Under Pressure. Johnno, do you want to say something?'

Johnno stood up to his full height.

'Yeah,' he said, 'I wanna say summat. 'ow much do you lot want this, eh? 'ow much? Because that's the question you're gonna be asked out there tonight. And when it gets tough, you're gonna ask the question yourselves. 'ow much do I really want this?

'Being *picked* for the Lions is the easy bit. To win a series – that's the ultimate. Sir Clive said that tonight will decide if we're remembered as winning Lions or losing Lions. Let me tell you summat. No one remembers losing Lions. No one talks about them.

And unless we win tonight, no one will talk about us. We'll just be a bunch of fellas who went on 'olidays togevver.'

I had butterflies in my stomach. Beyond the dressing-room door, we could hear the excited roar of the crowd as the South African players walked out onto the pitch. Above our heads, we could hear the sound of thousands of South African fans stamping their feet.

'Do you 'ear that?' Johnno asked. 'They've come for one fing and one fing only – to see their team finish us off. And maybe they will. Losing doesn't bovver me. We've all lost rugby matches – loads of times. To put in a performance, that's the main fing. So right from the off, let's get in their faces. Let's outjump 'em. Let's out-ruck 'em. Let's out-tackle 'em. Let's do summat tonight that people will talk about for the rest of our lives.'

We all stood up and followed Johnno outside. We warmed up. I felt nervous. But then I remembered Joe Schmidt telling me once that nerves were the body's way of telling you to be ready.

We stood in line to listen to the South African national anthem. But, before it started, a hush descended over the stadium.

'What's going on?' I asked Jonathan, who was standing next to me.

'I thenk the President is arriving,' he said.

I looked up at the stand in front of us and I saw a small figure appear, flanked by security guards. It was Nelson Mandela. He was wearing a green Springbok jersey and baseball cap. The roar from the crowd was ear-splitting. He smiled and waved at his people. And they chanted:

'Nel! Son! Nel! Son! Nel! Son! Nel! Son!'

After the anthems, we all got into our positions. Pollard got ready to kick off and the other fourteen Springbok players fanned out on the ten-metre line, staring straight ahead with military focus. The referee blew his whistle and Pollard sent the ball high into the air.

From very early on, it was obvious that this was going to be a completely different game from the second Test in Durban. It was a warm, dry evening – the perfect conditions for free-flowing rugby – and it was clear that the crowd wanted to see a show. More than anything, they wanted to see their team win.

The Springboks were really keen to get a fast start. And they did, scoring a try after just six minutes.

Stuart Hogg, our full-back, kicked the ball straight

into the hands of Cheslin Kolbe, who was an absolute flier – and he was almost impossible to tackle. He broke through our defensive line and touched the ball down under the posts.

But five minutes later, we struck back with a try of our own. It came from a lineout on the Springbok twenty-two. Paulie rose higher than anyone to claim the ball with the tips of his fingers and, when he landed, the forwards got the maul going. We followed the maul, watching it closely, waiting for the ball to pop out. But it didn't. Somewhere deep in the moving mass of bodies, I could hear Johnno roaring like a lion as they pushed the Springbok pack backwards, metre by metre. Just as they reached the line, Bomb emerged, holding the ball in his armpit, and bashed his way over the line for a try. Faz kicked the points to put us level.

Not long after that, the Springboks struck back. After a short lineout, Duane Vermeulen carried the ball into midfield. Jonathan and I both went with him. He played the ball to Faf de Klerk, who quickly offloaded it to Jean de Villiers, the brilliant South Africa centre, who scored an amazing solo try down the short side.

But then, six minutes later, I scored my one and only try in a Lions jersey. It was all down to

Jonathan's hard work. He beat two players, drew two more on him, then, just before he was tackled, somehow anticipating exactly where I'd be, he played an unbelievable no-look, backhand pass to me. I caught it, wrong-footed the Springbok full-back Willie le Roux by going one way, then suddenly changing direction, and I crossed the line to score.

It felt different from all the other tries I'd scored for Ireland, Leinster, Clongowes and Wexford Wanderers. It was somehow more precious.

This was how it continued for the rest of the first half. We matched each other score for score. Handre Pollard kicked a penalty for the Springboks, then Faz kicked one for us. Mapimpi scored a second try for the Springboks, then Jonathan scored a second try for us.

We were like two heavyweight boxers slugging it out.

At half-time, the score was 30–30 and the crowd was loving it. *They* might have been – but Clive most definitely wasn't.

'What are you doing out there?' he asked, sounding utterly exasperated.

'We're trying to outscore 'em,' Johnno told him. 'That's the object of the exercise, innit?'

'You've got to tighten things up,' Clive insisted.

'We're not here to provide entertainment for the crowd. I don't care if the second half is the worst half of rugby anyone has ever seen – as long as we win, okay?'

The Springboks had obviously had a similar talk from Rassie Erasmus because the second half was far more cautious. No one was playing that risky pass or trying to go around one man too many.

At the start of the second half, when we had possession of the ball, Clive shouted, 'Three Minutes of Excellence, Lions! Three Minutes of Excellence!'

We managed to give him about Two Minutes of Excellence before I knocked the ball on under the weight of a tackle from the Springbok second-row, Eben Etzebeth, who left me feeling like I'd been caught in an elephant stampede!

But still, it focused our minds on doing the simple things right, even if the crowd were baying for more tries.

Midway through the second half, a buzz of excitement went around the stadium as the Bomb Squad prepared to make their entrance.

But they didn't hold the same fear for us as they did in the first Test.

'''ere comes the cavalry!' I heard Lol say with a

laugh when we saw them lining up on the side of the pitch. 'Bring it on. Lol loves a scrap.'

They were going to make their entrance the next time there was a break in play. I'm not sure if this was what disrupted the Springboks' concentration, but I sensed that they'd slackened off a little bit. I managed to intercept a pass. Gavin Henson had replaced Jonathan Davies, who'd had to go off with a dead leg. And, while we had been on two different wavelengths against The Sharks, Gavin and I had developed an almost psychic understanding after all that time sharing the same tent.

He knew what I was going to do almost as soon as I knew what I was going to do myself. I dropped a perfectly weighted kick into the space behind Kolbe. The moment the ball left my boot, Gavin was already haring after it. He beat Willie le Roux, the Springbok full-back, to the ball. It bounced up into his hands. He wrong-footed le Roux and crashed over the line, grounding the ball in the corner to give us a five-point lead with twenty minutes to go.

The crowed booed and hissed at us, but we celebrated.

The only downside was that he gave Faz a difficult angle for the conversion. Faz picked up the ball and put it in the tee, then went through his usual pre-kick routine, measuring his steps backwards, then to the side, then sizing up the posts out of the corner of his eyes. He took one step, then he ran at the ball and kicked, sending it towards the posts in a high arc.

'It's going over!' I told him. 'It's going over!'

But it didn't go over. At the last second, it veered slightly to the left, struck the post and bounced out of play.

'I 'ope that don't cost us,' Faz said to me worriedly as he ran back to his position for the restart.

The Bomb Squad made their entrance. And the crowd roared:

'BOMB! SQUAD! BOMB! SQUAD! BOMB! SQUAD! BOMB! SQUAD!'

I watched our forwards stare them down as they entered the field of play, just to let them know that they weren't intimidated.

'Three Minutes of Excellence!' Clive demanded of us when the Springboks had the ball just inside our twenty-two. So we defended with everything we had. We gave him Three Minutes of Mostly Excellence, breaking up the South African momentum and forcing them into phase after phase, at the end of which Johnno was penalized for a high tackle on Snyman and the Springboks were awarded a penalty directly in front of our goal. Pollard split the posts right down the middle and cut our lead to two points with only five minutes remaining.

Then disaster struck. There was a minute left and we were struggling to hold on. The Springboks had won a scrum just inside their own half. Faf de Klerk, the Springbok scrum-half, put the ball in. A second later, the scrum went down like one of Flash Barry's so-called elephant-proof tents.

The referee blew his whistle. And suddenly I watched Johnno and Paulie and Lol and Faz climb to their feet with their heads in their hands. The referee had penalized us for deliberately collapsing the scrum – and now Pollard had another kick at goal, to put South Africa into the lead.

The only hope for us rested on the distance and the conditions. He was more than fifty metres from the goal and a stiff breeze had been blowing since just after half-time.

The stadium fell silent as Pollard placed the ball in the kicking tee, then measured his steps backwards and to the side. He looked at the goal, then at the ball, then at the goal again, then at the ball again. He stood there motionless, for what seemed like forever – but that was understandable. This kick, he knew, would probably decide the series.

Finally, he moved. He ran at the ball and struck it cleanly. It was so silent in the stadium that we could hear the sound of leather hitting leather. And the ball took off and soared through the air in the direction of the posts. The kick had the accuracy. The only question was whether he had struck it hard enough. It started to come down . . .

. . . down . . .

. . . down . . .

. . . down . . .

. . . down . . .

. . . and it cleared the bar by about three inches.

I watched our players' heads fall. Faz, in particular, was devastated.

'If I'd kicked that conversion,' he said, 'we'd still be in t'lead.'

But Bomb grabbed him by the front of his shirt and said, 'I'm not listenen to thet rubbesh. There'll be plenty of tame for craying after the final whestle. You can cray for the rest of your lafe for all I care. But the metch ain't over until it's over – do you hear me? And until the referee blows that whestle, we're still en et. So make sure it's a good keck, there's a good lad.'

We had to win the restart. If we didn't, South Africa would keep the ball, wind down the remaining seconds and then kick it out of play. So Bomb was right. We had to win the restart, which meant we needed the perfect kick from Faz.

And that's what we got.

He put his boot to the ball and it went high in the air, travelling about ten metres before dropping towards de Villiers. I outjumped him and beat him to the ball.

Now we had possession. The eighty minutes were up. Clive was on the sideline, shouting, 'Three Minutes of Excellence! Three Minutes of Excellence!'

It would have to be Excellence. Because the next time we made a mistake, the match would be over and the series lost.

We started putting phases of play together, inching our way over the Springbok twenty-two and towards their try line. We didn't make a mistake. Every pass found a pair of hands. When a player was tackled, he quickly presented the ball. When a move broke down, we reset our positions and went again.

'That's it!' Clive roared. 'That's Three Minutes of Excellence!'

And maybe it was the thrill of having done it for

the first time that led Faz to do what he did next. He got the ball in his hands and, with a quick swivel of his hips, he cut through a gap in the Springbok defence and made a run for the line. He was pulled down about a metre short of it and Mike Phillips retrieved the ball from the ruck. All of the Springbok backs fanned out, waiting for the ball to be passed down the line.

In that moment, I suddenly thought about Jeremy Guscott on Dad's Lions video. I remembered what he had said to us in the Vale of Glamorgan, how he had no idea that he was going to be the hero of the series until the very moment arrived. And now, it was as if I heard him talking to me – down the years, one Lion to another.

'*Get in the pocket!*'

I didn't question it. I didn't stop to think about it. I just put my trust in the jersey.

I ran backwards for a few metres. Mike looked around him. He spotted me standing in the position where Faz would normally be. I watched the surprise register on his face.

But all I could think about was getting that ball in my hands.

'Give it to me!' I told him with my eyes.

'Nail et!' he said. 'Do you understand may?'

He released the ball. Like Jeremy, I had never, EVER attempted a drop at goal in my entire life. But I was completely calm as the ball arrived, even with four Springbok players charging towards me with their arms raised. A feeling of sweet serenity had come over me, like this was my destiny. I caught the ball in my two hands and, in the same movement, dropped it on one of its pointed ends. As it bounced, I put my foot under it.

It wasn't the cleanest strike, but I got enough of my boot on it to send it wobbling through the air . . .

And in that moment, I understood EXACTLY what Jeremy Guscott meant when he said that his entire rugby life flashed before him. Because that's what happened to me! I saw myself at five years old, holding a rugby ball for the very first time, unable to even get my two arms around it. I saw myself playing for Wexford Wanderers and my battles with Conor Kehoe before we became friends. I saw myself playing for Clongowes and for Ireland and for Leinster. And, yes, it really did feel like all of those moments were leading up to me . . .

. . . standing there . . .

. . . with my mouth open . . .

. . . watching . . .

. . . as the ball . . .

. . . sailed through the air . . .

. . . and flew . . .

. . . right between the posts!

The stadium fell silent. All I could hear was the sound of our players roaring with delight.

The referee blew his whistle.

We'd won!

We'd beaten the mighty Springboks on their own turf and we'd won the series!

I felt myself being lifted off the ground. I was suddenly sitting on Lol and Paulie's shoulders. I raised my hands in the air in triumph.

Clive Woodward was standing beside us. I looked down at him. With one of his big, lopsided grins, he said, 'You know what you were doing there, Gordon, when you received the ball, don't you?'

'I was Thinking Calmly Under Pressure,' I told him.

'Yes, you were!' he said, giving me a wink.

'Thank you,' I told him, 'for having faith in me. And for sticking by me even after I broke my –'

But I couldn't finish my sentence because the emotion of the moment got to me and I burst into tears – tears of pure, unadulterated joy.

Paulie and Lol carried me over to the corner of the stadium where all the Lions supporters were sitting. All of the other players were standing beside us – this amazing group of people, most of whom I hadn't known until the morning Clive ordered us to do a jigsaw together. And now they were my friends. We'd achieved something that would mean we were bonded together for life.

We all stood there, trying to pick our families, our friends and our loved ones out of the crowd through our tear-filled eyes. I suddenly spotted Mum and

391

Dad, and Ian and Shona and Megan, and sitting beside them were Conor and Peter and Aoife, and they were all clapping and laughing and wiping away tears.

I felt such a surge of love for them – and for everyone who'd helped me on my journey here, a huge stadium in Johannesburg, on literally the other side of the world to Wexford. I couldn't even bring myself to be angry with Barry, who, I noticed, was taking money from a few of the Clongowes boys, almost certainly as a down-payment for the World Cup.

We'd done it. We'd beaten South Africa. We were now part of the legend of the British & Irish Lions. And who knows, maybe one day I'd be invited to tell my story to the young Lions of the future?

As we celebrated on the pitch that night, I knew that nothing had ever felt so good. And I wondered would anything ever again?

51 *Testing Time*

There were more scenes of jubilation back in the dressing room. Clive asked us where we wanted to stay that night. Did we want to spend our final night together in the luxury of the Grand Hotel Cape Town? Or did we want to spend one last night sleeping under the stars amidst the lions and the elephants and the zebra and the wildebeest and the giraffes and the snakes and the baboons of the wildlife reserve?

'Darce scored the points that won it,' Bomb announced. 'Let hem be the one who decides.'

I didn't even hesitate.

'Wildlife reserve!' I said – and everyone cheered.

Clive told us that we'd done ourselves proud and that this group of players would always be mentioned whenever the great Lions teams were being discussed.

Then he had some amazing news for us.

'They're hosting a reception for us at Johannesburg City Hall in an hour,' he said. 'I've been told that the President would like to meet you all.'

My heart nearly burst out of my chest.

It was finally going to happen! I was going to meet Nelson Mandela!

And that's when the knock on the door came.

A man stepped into the dressing room. He was wearing a suit and carrying a clipboard.

'I'm looking for Gordon D'Arcy,' he said.

'I'm Gordon D'Arcy,' I told him proudly – I thought he was looking to interview me for TV.

'You've been selected for a random drug test,' he announced.

'What?' I said. 'Why me?'

'It's just routine,' he said. 'We draw the name out of a hat – one player from each side. Shouldn't take more than a few minutes. Would you come with me, please?'

I followed him outside. I spotted Mum and Dad in the corridor. A security guard had let them through because they wanted to tell me how proud they were of me. They saw me being led off.

'Where are you going?' Mum asked.

'He says he wants to drug test me?' I replied.

'Drug test him?' Mum said, absolutely furious. 'My son's not on drugs!'

'The players are selected purely at random,' the man with the clipboard argued.

'How dare you! My Gordon? On drugs?'

Dad tried to intervene.

'It's just routine,' he argued with her. 'It's to ensure that no one's cheating.'

'Oh,' Mum said, 'he's not only on drugs, he's a cheat now as well, is it? I'll not listen to this for a moment longer!'

She suddenly swung her handbag at the man with the clipboard, catching him on the side of the head.

I laughed. I couldn't help myself.

'Mum,' I said, 'it's fine. This is just part of sport. It's to make sure everyone competes on the same level.'

'There's nothing to worry about,' the man said, rubbing his head. 'Unless, of course, he *is* on drugs.'

Mum swung her handbag at him again, but he managed to duck away this time and Dad managed to wrestle the handbag off her.

'Here,' the man said, handing me a little plastic bottle. 'Just pee into that and then you can go.'

He showed us into a little room, which had a sofa and TV in it, and a small en suite just off it. Mum and Dad sat down and Dad found a channel that was showing highlights of the match.

'I can't wait to see your kick again,' he said.

'I'll be long gone by the time that comes on,' I told him. 'I'm going to City Hall to meet Nelson Mandela.'

But suddenly it was the exact reverse of what happened at night in the tent. When the last thing in the world I wanted was to have to get up to go to the toilet, I was bursting. Now that I desperately wanted to go, I couldn't.

'You're probably dehydrated,' Dad said. 'Hang on, I think your kick is coming up soon.'

I started drinking water – pint after pint after pint of the stuff. But it was no good. I still didn't have the urge to pee.

After about forty minutes, Clive stuck his head around the door of the room. He said they'd have to head to City Hall without me – the President didn't have a lot of time – but he'd leave a Lions car outside that would bring me straight there as soon as I was finished here.

Fifteen minutes passed. Then another fifteen minutes. Then another fifteen minutes.

And still nothing.

'I'm not going to get to meet him,' I said. 'Mr Stuyvesant told me that I had to meet Nelson

Mandela and shake his hand. All of the other players have already met him. I missed him because I was bursting for the toilet. Now I'm going to miss him because I'm *not* bursting for the toilet. It's so unfair.'

'The more you think about it,' Dad said, 'the more unlikely it is to happen. Oh, here comes your kick! Brilliant! Even better the second time around!'

It was more than an hour and a half before I finally peed. I handed the bottle to the man with the clipboard, hugged Mum and Dad and told them I'd see them at the airport, then I raced down to where a red Lions car was waiting for me.

I jumped into the back.

'City Hall?' the driver asked.

'Yes,' I said. 'And can you please drive like some idiot has accidentally put the Liam MacCarthy Cup on a bus to France and you're trying to catch it?'

'The Liam Who Cup?' the man said.

'Doesn't matter,' I told him. 'Just drive like the clappers.'

'I will drive like the clappers,' he said, 'but I have to drive within the legal speed limit.'

Another one like my dad!

It took half-an-hour to reach City Hall. I opened the door before the car had even come to a stop. Then I jumped out and ran into the building.

'The reception,' I said to a woman standing behind a desk, 'for the Lions players?'

'Main function room – top of the stairs,' she told me, pointing the way.

I took the stairs two at a time – up four flights – and raced into the room. All of the Lions and Springbok players were in there, dressed in their suits, mingling with each other, enjoying a laugh now that the series was over.

I overheard Johnno telling the Bomb Squad about the python that was in our tent.

I ran around the room, looking for him.

Faz spotted me.

'Darce?' he said. 'Why aren't you in your suit, mate?'

I looked down. It was only then I realized that I was still in my Lions gear.

'I got here as quick as I could,' I said. 'I wanted to meet Nelson Mandela.'

'You've missed 'im,' Faz said. 'If you'd got 'ere five minutes earlier, you'd have seen 'im.'

I was devastated.

'He were asking for you 'n' all,' Faz said. 'Said he wanted to meet t'kid who scored t'winning drop goal.'

'I don't believe it,' I told him.

'Are you 'aving a Coke or summat?' Faz asked.

'No,' I told him, 'I just need to pop outside for a minute.'

With my shoulders slumped, I stepped out of the room. I needed to get out of there before anyone could see how sad I was. I couldn't be bothered taking the stairs down, so I headed for the lift at the end of the corridor.

I stepped inside and I pressed the button for the ground floor. And then I heard a voice shout, 'Hold the lift!'

I stuck my foot between the doors and they opened again. And five seconds later, a figure appeared in front of me. I heard myself gasp.

It was Nelson Mandela.

'I always get lost in these big buildings,' he said. 'It probably has something to do with spending half of my life in a six-foot-by-twelve-foot cell.'

I tried to speak, but no words came out of my mouth.

'So,' he said, pressing the button to close the doors, 'you are Gordon D'Arcy, who kicked the drop goal to win the series?'

I didn't answer. I couldn't.

'What you did took a lot of nerve,' he said, 'and a lot of courage.'

And I wanted to tell him that what he did took a lot of nerve and a lot of courage too. But I was so in awe of him that I couldn't even move my lips. I couldn't do anything except stare dumbly at him.

It was so embarrassing. But he offered me a look of understanding.

'You know,' he said, 'I've always said that people can say far more with their mouths closed than they can with a thousand words.'

We reached the ground floor and the doors opened. He stepped out of the lift, then he turned and held out his hand. And I shook it. I shook the hand of Nelson Mandela.

GORDON D'ARCY

Gordon D'Arcy was first called up to play for Ireland while he was still at school. He won his first cap in 1999 and his final cap in 2015, making him Ireland's longest-serving international player. Shortly after making his first appearance for his country, he fell out of favour with management because of his 'attitude problems'. But he returned three years later, a better and more mature player. In 2004, he was named the Six Nations Player of the Tournament. He played a total of eighty-two times for his country, scoring seven tries. Partnering Brian O'Driscoll in the centre, he was a vital part of two Six Nations Championship-winning teams, including the Grand Slam team of 2009, and starred in four World Cups. He was also a member of two British & Irish Lions squads. With Leinster, he won three European Cups, a Challenge Cup and four Celtic League Pro14 titles.

I hope you enjoyed reading *Lion's Roar*. The first two books in this series, *Gordon's Game* and *Blue Thunder*, were a huge success and lots of you got in touch to tell me you loved them – thank you very much! Some of you also asked me some fantastic questions. Here is a selection, answered as best I can.

Q1. Who was the hardest person to tackle?

Q2. Who tackled the hardest?

Setanta, age 10, Ballinteer, Dublin

A1. At the start, it was always my big brother, Ian. We used to practise on the upstairs landing, but when we nearly broke the banisters, we decided it might be better to take it outside. Otherwise, it was a guy called Jean de Villiers of South Africa. He had a way of dropping his shoulder into me, even when I went super low, and was so hard to tackle.

A2. Everyone from Samoa! I toured there once and I met a man at the airport in New Zealand. He asked where we were going and I said, 'Samoa, to play rugby.' He smiled and said, 'When you've passed the ball, brace yourself! The Samoans hit hard and not always when you have the ball.' Turns out he was right!

Or Neil Best, who played for Ulster and Ireland. He wasn't a big fan of the ball in rugby, but he loved to tackle! His timing was incredible and he made some of the biggest tackles I've ever seen. I got hit by him once, and I was able to taste my lunch from the previous day!

Q1. **What is the most embarrassing thing that ever happened to you at school?**

Q2. **Was Graham Bull really as mean as you said he was?**

Páidí Mac Cormaic, age 9, St Senan's RFC

A1. There were a lot. And I do mean a LOT! The worst was the time when I was in the dinner hall and I was holding my tray with my lunch on it. A 'friend' of mine came up behind me and pulled my trousers down! I was waddling around like a penguin with my trousers around my ankles, trying to put my tray down so I could pull them back up! Everyone got a laugh out of that one! I always laughed at practical jokes – even when I was the victim. And, let's be honest, with Conor Kehoe around, I had a LOT of practice!

A2. He was really mean to me, wasn't he? I think he didn't want to lose his place and he behaved really badly. The only way he knew to try to stay in the team was to be mean to me. By doing that, he hoped I would go away. Often, when people are being mean, they are insecure about something else. When you stay strong, they are the ones who wilt away.

Q1. Do you have any tips for an inside-centre like me?

Q2. What song did you sing when you made your Irish debut?

Q3. How did you cope when you lost?

Cillian, Barnhall U-11s

A1. Of course. Make sure you are the best passer of the ball on the team – even better than the number ten! It is the best skill to have as a twelve. It will get you out of more trouble than anything else. And the most important thing is to enjoy your rugby. The practice. The matches. Enjoy it all with a big smile on your face. Playing rugby should be fun, first and foremost.

A2. Would you believe it if I told you that I didn't sing when I won my first cap, as players are required to do today? I made my Ireland debut during the World Cup in 1999 and we didn't celebrate first caps the way the players do now. If I had to sing a song, though, it would one hundred per cent have been 'Friends in Low Places' by Garth Brooks. Your mums and dads will tell you about it!

A3. Losing is never easy, and it is different for everyone. If I had done my best in training, and in matches, I was never too upset if we lost. I knew I had done my best. Even if I made mistakes, that was enough. I always want to win games, but you also have to lose games – that is sport. I'd always try to look myself in the mirror after a game and know I'd done my best.

Q. Craig Casey sang 'Careless Whisper' by George Michael on his first Irish cap. What did you do on your first Irish cap?

Matthew Fletcher, age 10, County Waterford

A. Thanks for your question, Matthew. As I said above, to my great regret, I didn't get to sing a song in front of all my Ireland teammates! Who knows, I might get to sing my favourite Garth Brooks song as the half-time entertainment at the RDS one day!

Q. If you didn't play in the centre, what position would you have liked to play?

Adam O'Donnell, age 9, Terenure College RFC U-10s

A. That's a great question, Adam. Well, I started life as a hooker, until my coach shouted at me, 'If you're going to hang back there like Keith Wood, go play as a back!' I moved to number ten, which I absolutely loved. Then we needed to get our best players on the pitch, so I moved to full-back. When I joined Leinster, I found a home on the wing, and then, when Brian O'Driscoll got injured, I ended up in the centre. So the moral of the story is, play everywhere and enjoy it! You never know where you'll end up!

Q. How many times did you win the Six Nations and the Pro14 (formerly the Celtic League)?

Liam, age 8

A. Not enough times, I think! I'm pretty sure I won the Pro14 four times, the Six Nations twice and the European Cup three times. But I played for so long that I'm not quite sure! Will you do me a favour and check?

Q. Did you prefer playing for Ireland or Leinster?

Caoimhe, age 9

A. That is so tough to answer, Caoimhe. Playing for your country is an incredible honour. But I also grew up in Leinster as a hugely proud Wexford man and Leinster was everything for me. I also couldn't have played for Ireland without playing for Leinster, because you only get picked for Ireland by playing for your province. So I don't think I could ever pick between them. Playing for both teams was a privilege to me.

Q. Are you still friends with Conor, Aoife and Peter? And who was your closest friend in the Ireland and Leinster teams?

Mikey, age 11, Kilkenny

A. I'm still friends with all of them. Conor is still playing practical jokes on me, Peter is still the brains of the outfit and Aoife is still putting me straight on things when I go a little wobbly. My closest friend in the Ireland and Leinster teams was Malcom O'Kelly – although we are not that physically close. I'm 5'11" and I think he might be close to 7 feet tall, which possibly makes him even taller than big Devin Toner!

409

Q. Are you still friends with Conor and Peter? Do you know what Conor's job is?

Con, age 9, North Meath RFC

A. Yes, I'm still really good friends with all of them. Rugby is a great way of forming long-term friendships. Conor now works as a clown – and is available for weddings, parties and other private functions!

Q. What was it like being a rugby player?

Logan, age 10 (whose dad jumped the Gollymochy)

A. Honestly, it was the best fun. I got to train every day outside and do something that I loved from the time I was really young. I would have played rugby for free. And I got to do it with my friends. How cool is that?

Q. I love playing rugby and my favourite part of the game is tackling. Who was the hardest person to tackle in your rugby career? And why?

Niall, age 8, Garryowen RFC

A. As I said earlier, Niall, it was either my brother, Ian, or Jean de Villiers of South Africa. Both of them really made you feel that you'd been in a match!

Q. What number were you originally going for, or were you happy to get number twelve?

Charlie, age 10, Ballincollig RFC

A. I played in many different positions over the years. I wasn't built to play in the second-row, but if it was the difference between playing and not playing, I'd have definitely given it a go! I wore quite a few different numbers before I settled at twelve. But I found that the more experience I had of other positions, the more understanding I had of how difficult every player on the team's job could be.

411

Q. In your first book, you said that you went to your uncle and auntie's farm. My grandad has a farm too. Did you like it on the farm? Were you very friendly with Conor and Peter? Were you nervous when you were buying the fake tan?

Tadhg, County Carlow, but living in Jeddah, Saudi Arabia

A. Great questions! I loved growing up on a farm. There was so much to do and every day was different. I really HATED picking eggs, though. Those chickens had my hands pecked to pieces! Conor and Peter are still my friends today. They are so funny. They always have my back. And they tell me when I'm being a little silly – which is something we all need from time to time! As for buying the fake tan, I don't think I have ever been so nervous in my life! I kept thinking, what if someone sees me? But then everybody knew I was wearing it once I put it on. Let's be honest, they couldn't miss it!

Q. When you played for Leinster, who was your favourite teammate and why?

Ryan, age 11, Ranelagh, Dublin

A. Two of my favourite people to have played rugby with are Andrew Dunner and Simon Keogh. They were like twins but looked nothing like each other and behaved completely differently. So not very twin-like, but they were there at the same time. We played on loads of teams together and they were super fun, and very exciting rugby players. The perfect mix – nice people with infectious smiles who loved rugby.

Q. I want to play second-row like Paul O'Connell. What is Paul like?

Jack, age 11, Sligo RFC U-11s

A. Paul is so nice. You'd love him. On the pitch, he was the guy you could always rely on – big, strong and very committed. Off the field, he is a lot of fun. He likes to talk with everyone and anyone over a cup of tea (like, really, REALLY chatty). He was a really hard trainer, but also a really good teammate.

Q. You said at the end of your book that your wife's name is Aoife – by any chance would that be Aoife Kehoe? What was the most embarrassing thing Conor did while you were playing for Wexford Wanderers? And, finally, what is your favourite burger from McWonderburger (without gherkins, of course – yuck!)?

Ava, age 11, County Offaly

A. Very well spotted, Ava. Yes, you are correct – Aoife is now my wife. Conor once put Deep Heat in my underwear and Vaseline in my shoes after a match. I didn't speak to him for a week – until I saw the funny side of it! I've eaten every burger on the menu in one sitting – but, I always insist, no gherkins! Yuck!!!

Q. Who was the hardest team to beat and who was the hardest coach you ever had?

James, age 9, Dublin

A. There is only one team that's hard to beat – and that's New Zealand. I never managed to beat them. I got close twice but, unfortunately, we weren't good enough – although not long afterwards, an Ireland team did finally beat them after more than a century trying! I don't think of coaches as being hard or soft – they are good teachers or they aren't. I've had some brilliant ones and learned something from every single one of them. Sometimes, rugby isn't just about winning. It can be about learning and becoming a better player.

Q. Which team did you like playing for the most: Leinster, Ireland or the Lions? And which trophy did you treasure the most?

Aaron, age 9, Loughrea RFC

A. As I said earlier, it's impossible to answer. I loved playing for them both equally – just as I loved playing for the Lions. I won my first European Cup with Leinster in 2009 – that had been a huge goal for the team for such a long time and I loved winning it while playing alongside so many friends. I had also been a professional rugby player for eleven years at that stage, so it was important that I won something!

Q. Do you have any advice for anyone who wants to make a career as a rugby player? And how did you cope with the exercise and health regime when you were called up to the Ireland and Leinster Academy?

Ruairí

A. The best career advice I can give anyone who wants to be a rugby player is to keep practising and learning. As for the exercise, you can always get fitter. You can always get faster. You can always get stronger. Believe it or not, they are the easy bits. But they are also the least valuable in rugby. Trust me when I say, the most skilful will always be more successful. It is harder to try to develop your skills as you get older. When you're young, focus on passing, kicking and evasion – be the best at that and get fitter, faster and stronger later on. But, most importantly of all, make sure you enjoy your rugby.

Q1. What was your favourite jersey when you were a kid?

Q2. If you played a different sport, what would it be?

Paddy Smith, Westmanstown RFC U-9s

A1. My favourite jersey was the All Blacks jersey from the 1990s. It was very basic – just black with a white fern. But it was SO cool.

A2. I would have one thousand per cent played hurling – and hopefully for Wexford!

Q1. Who was the funniest player you played with?

Q2. Who is the best dancer at Leinster?

Charlie Smith, age 7, Westmanstown RFC

A1. I think Donnacha O'Callaghan is possibly one of them. I remember when we were meeting President Mary McAleese, and he pretended to trip when walking up the steps to meet her!

A2. Mike Ross, when he got in the groove, could do a very good breakdance. He needed plenty of room, but it was awesome!

Q. Who is the best and most encouraging captain you have ever trained under?

Tom Quinn, Seapoint RFC

A. I think that would have been Paul O'Connell. He knew how to be a great captain on the pitch and a good friend off the pitch. He knew when you needed a kick up the bum or an arm around the shoulder.

Q. Who is physically the strongest player you have ever played against or with?

Darragh, age 8, Blarney, Cork

A. I think that is Cian Healy. When he does a squat with weights on it, the weight is so heavy it bends the bar on his shoulders!

If you'd like to put a question to Gordon, go to gordonsgamebook@gmail.com.

ACKNOWLEDGEMENTS

Gordon D'Arcy's acknowledgements:

The third book in the *Gordon's Game* series has been so enjoyable again, great people coming together to create something that we are all so proud of. Paul Howard and Rachel Pierce – thank you both for your continuous support and belief in this series. Paul, I don't know how you do it and where you find your magic from, but I'm so thankful that you bring this to life every time. It has genuinely been superb working with you. Rachel, the eyes that we don't have and that see all the little and important details. Thank you again. Alan Nolan playing an absolute blinder with the illustrations, a pleasure to work with you again.

Faith O'Grady, thank you again for believing in this series and all your support along the way. To

Patricia Deevy, Michael McLoughlin and everyone at Sandycove, we could not ask for a stronger team. The passion you have for books is inspiring, and the way you have supported *Gordon's Game* has been incredible – especially Louise Farrell, to whom we owe a big thank you!

There were two and now there are three – welcome baby Meadow to the gang, it's a little crazy, but we have lots of fun. So to my gang, Soleil, Lennon and Meadow, I hope you love reading these books in years to come.

And, finally, to my wife, Aoife, thank you for being amazing, for being you and helping me to be me.

Paul Howard's acknowledgements:

Enormous thanks to Gordon D'Arcy for making this collaboration such a pleasurable experience. I've loved every minute of plotting and writing these stories with you. Thanks to Alan Nolan for your amazing artwork, which makes these books sing! Thanks to our wonderful editor, Rachel Pierce, for all your expert guidance and never-less-than-excellent advice. Thanks to our agent, Faith O'Grady, for supporting this idea from the very start. Thanks to Erris McCarthy, our most diligent reader, whose feedback we value so much. Thanks to Michael McLoughlin and Patricia Deevy of Sandycove for seeing the potential in these books from the outset. And thanks to the entire Sandycove team of Louise Farrell, Cliona Lewis, Brian Walker, Aimee Johnson, Carrie Anderson and Brendan Barrington. And a special word of thanks to my wonderful wife, Mary.

a seriousfun camp

Childhood stops for seriously ill children, at
Barretstown we press play on childhood

www.barretstown.org

Missed the first book in the series?

GORDON'S GAME

is available in paperback now!

A rugby-mad boy. A huge game. And a chance for an epic win . . . or an epic fail!

Gordon D'Arcy is an ordinary boy, but he's not so ordinary once he gets a rugby ball in his hands. He's the star player for Wexford Wanderers and dreams of one day wearing the Ireland jersey. A dream like that means hard work, raw talent and never losing sight of your goals.

But Gordon has a wild streak that often lands him in trouble. Mum and Dad think that if he can just channel his energy, all will be well.

Then something utterly mad happens and he gets a chance to live his biggest dream. Can he stay on his game and do everyone proud?

Or will trouble follow him . . . like it usually does?

'A CRACKING READ' *IRISH COUNTRY MAGAZINE*

GORDON'S GAME: BLUE THUNDER

Available in paperback now!

Gordon D'Arcy – the only kid at school with a Six Nations medal hidden under his pillow! Though helping Ireland to win the Grand Slam feels like it was just a dream.

Now, he's been given a brand-new challenge – the chance to play for Leinster.

After learning so many lessons playing for Ireland – including how to make a complete eejit of himself in front of millions of people – fitting in at Leinster should be a breeze. Right?

Unfortunately, not. After his first training session, he sees why the team is mocked for being 'soft' (those stories about players wearing fake tan? All true!). Now he knows why so many people from Leinster support Munster.

But Gordon settles down to work under an inspiring coach named Joe Schmidt. Joe promises that, with hard work, discipline and a bit of self-belief, Leinster can win the European Cup.

Maybe another dream can come true!

He just wanted a decent book to read ...

Not too much to ask, is it? It was in 1935 when Allen Lane, Managing Director of Bodley Head Publishers, stood on a platform at Exeter railway station looking for something good to read on his journey back to London. His choice was limited to popular magazines and poor-quality paperbacks – the same choice faced every day by the vast majority of readers, few of whom could afford hardbacks. Lane's disappointment and subsequent anger at the range of books generally available led him to found a company – and change the world.

'We believed in the existence in this country of a vast reading public for intelligent books at a low price, and staked everything on it'
Sir Allen Lane, 1902–1970, founder of Penguin Books

The quality paperback had arrived – and not just in bookshops. Lane was adamant that his Penguins should appear in chain stores and tobacconists, and should cost no more than a packet of cigarettes.

Reading habits (and cigarette prices) have changed since 1935, but Penguin still believes in publishing the best books for everybody to enjoy. We still believe that good design costs no more than bad design, and we still believe that quality books published passionately and responsibly make the world a better place.

So wherever you see the little bird – whether it's on a piece of prize-winning literary fiction or a celebrity autobiography, political tour de force or historical masterpiece, a serial-killer thriller, reference book, world classic or a piece of pure escapism – you can bet that it represents the very best that the genre has to offer.

Whatever you like to read – trust Penguin.